CODE VIOLATION

RECLAIMED HEARTS
BOOK 4

ELLE KEATON

ONE

Raven - Thursday Morning

Fluttering gracelessly from one precarious mossy limb to the next, Raven followed the Walking Man. Earlier, she'd been on watch when he'd emerged from the hidden lair, much like a bear after awakening from hibernation. After sniffing the air around himself like a predator, he'd nodded, reached back inside to grab a bag, slung it over his shoulder, and began his walk.

Raven's larger wings made flying in the thick stands of trees bothersome. But she was intent on keeping the nasty human in her sights. The time was now. There would be no more hiding. No more secret graves. No more secret deaths. Not in Raven's woods.

A breeze left over by the windstorm gusted through the deep undergrowth, strong enough to make the emerging fronds of the sword and lady ferns nod back and forth as if they too accepted the decision. They were resolute. It had been agreed upon. Things had been set in motion.

Monsters took many forms, too many to imagine them all. Some monsters took no effort to identify and were easy to steer clear of. Others appeared harmless at first, second, even third glances. Those were the most appalling ones.

As if life in the forest here wasn't complicated enough already.

Things couldn't stop now. The actors had been called upon to play their part. Everyone was finally in place. Where they needed to be.

Even so, Raven stayed vigilant, making sure the process didn't grind to a halt. Again. Far too often, humans could not be trusted to stick to the plan, to not be distracted by shiny objects, no matter how important their part was.

This secret was not theirs to keep.

The man continued walking, following a lesser-known trail that had been in use by forest dwellers far longer than Raven's memory. Occasionally, he checked back over his shoulder, but he didn't see Raven over his head. He thought he'd outsmarted everyone, including Raven.

This arrogance would be his downfall.

Eventually the monster came to a man-made trail and began following it. The path was a wide, violent slash of a thing that burrowed through the trees and shrubs with no regard for what had been there before people arrived. It didn't belong. The forest tried to reclaim it but the humans returned year after year, removing barriers and treefall, equally determined to keep it open for their use.

As she flew, Raven heard the sparkling, laughing creek that ran alongside the path. Many winters, it flooded its banks, rising high enough to wash the trail away. But, again, the humans always returned and put it back once the waters subsided.

The Walking Man began to move faster, making his way down the steep mountainside with sure, strong strides. Not as fast and agile as he'd been before Raven was born, but quick enough and still strong. Raven kept him within sight, fluttering and gliding along after him. A flock of witless goldfinches startled—all flapping wings and flashes of color—scared by the man when he rounded a corner. The trees began to thin out, making it much easier to follow him.

He was an arrogant monster of a human, full of his own self-importance. Long ago, he'd stopped paying attention when Raven followed him, assuming the glittering gifts he'd left meant Raven was his beast.

Raven was no one's creature.

Through the cottonwood and birch trees along the edge of the forest, Raven could now see the structure that a great many of the younger, very loud humans spent time in. Sometimes, Raven made friends with these humans. In the past, the man had lurked close by, watching them and waiting, but he was not their friend.

This day he prowled in the opposite direction, still keeping to the shadows. Dressed as he was, he was almost invisible, indistinguishable if the observer didn't know to look for him.

Raven wasn't sure of his intent, not until she saw the lone human girl walk the trail between the school and the neighborhood. Raven had seen this human before; she often had four-legged creatures with her, ones that were loud and nosey. Today she was alone, her head moving to a beat only she could hear.

This was not part of the plan. Alarmed, Raven burst out from the woods, cawing loudly, but the girl did not hear her panicked warnings. Certain the warning was not for him, the monster ignored Raven entirely and kept moving, determined to catch his prey. Within seconds, he was almost close enough to strike.

Someone else did hear Raven's call. Tall and thin, with a beaky nose that Raven appreciated, the Package Man paused to tuck what he was holding into his bag before hastening around the corner to see what the ruckus was about. Raven liked him.

Sometimes he left her sparkly things—gifts that Raven knew were given freely out of friendship, not attempts to buy her favor—and she'd kept them safely tucked away in her nest.

The Walking Man was mere strides away from the girl. Almost close enough to touch. To snatch. To make her disappear forever like the others.

It had to stop.

"You!" the second man called out sharply. "You there, what are you doing?"

The girl kept walking, oblivious to the danger behind her.

The Walking Man had heard though. He turned his head to stare at the other man, who hesitated when he should've run. Before Raven could react, the monster moved in and struck. The kind Package Man had no chance; he fell to the ground in a heap of parcels and envelopes and didn't move again.

Raven hastened back to the protection of the cedar and Douglas fir trees. The girl was gone now, having disappeared into a structure, safe for the moment. From her perch, Raven watched the Walking Man.

Cursing, he dragged the man into the darkest shadow along the street where, Raven supposed, the body wouldn't be found for a time. She would make sure it was found much sooner than the monster planned. Muttering anger at being interrupted, the Walking Man glared at the small, human dwellings in a line before turning back toward The Deep.

Foiled for the time being.

While Raven lingered, gathering her thoughts, a large, black vehicle turned onto the street. It drove slowly as if, perhaps, the driver was lost. When the car pulled to a stop almost directly across from Raven's perch, she made a snap decision.

The driver was looking at something.

Someone needed to find the Package Man.

Acting much faster than the forest would want—perhaps

even impetuously—Raven darted out from the trees and directly into the side of the vehicle.

The resounding thump of her body had the driver glancing out the window. Righting herself, Raven tottered away like a bird drunk on fall blackberries and toward where the kind man lay, then flew up onto a nearby limb. Behind her, she heard the car door open and footsteps on the pavement. She looked down at the Package Man.

Moments later, the driver exclaimed, "Oh my god."

TWO

Nero – Age 14

"CHECK THIS OUT," Donny said, tossing his board down onto the sidewalk. He flipped it back up with his foot and caught it one-handed.

Nero Vik and his cousin—who was also his best friend—had met up at the almost empty park and ride on the north side of town. This one was hardly ever used because most people took the bus to and from the mall a few blocks away.

Their only companions were the crows hanging around patiently to see if they had any snacks to share. Nero liked feeding the birds, especially the albino one. The first time he'd seen it, Nero thought it was covered with flour or something but, no, the crow was actually an odd light gray, not black like the rest of its family.

"Oh man, that's so cool!" Nero held his hand out and Donny slapped it hard, grinning like he always did, making Nero feel like he was really being seen.

Donny was one of those people who navigated life effortlessly, unlike Nero, who was a permanent nerd. It seemed like Donny always knew what to say or do. He had a great smile and perfect hair, not having inherited the mop of curls that was Nero's curse. More often than not, Nero was awkward and flailing. Always the odd person out, last to be picked for the PE teams while his cousin was among the first.

Nerd.

According to Donny, the park and ride had the best practice-skate course around town, and neither of them had the money to bus to the real skate park at the college. Or for knee pads. Who cared about a skinned knee or elbow anyway? Since Donny was the one with the board, Nero was content with hanging out wherever his cousin wanted.

"Who do you have for homeroom?" Donny asked Nero as he caught the board again.

The list had been sent home a couple of days ago. Nero and Donny were close enough in age that they were at the same high school and in the same grade.

"Uh." Nero pretended to think, shrugging to adjust his backpack on his shoulder, as if he hadn't been obsessing about starting high school since school got out in spring. "Ms. Harmon, I think. What about you?"

"Mr. Bernstadt."

His stomach sank. Nero had hoped that Donny would have the same homeroom.

"Dang."

"I'd rather be in Ms. Harmon's with you. Mr. Bernstadt had all my brothers, I'm pretty sure." Donny looked thoughtful. "Maybe not John."

As an only child, Nero was also jealous of his cousin's big family. Five older brothers meant Donny's house was loud and full of laughter twenty-four seven. Nero's apartment was always quiet, and he had to be careful not to walk too loudly and annoy the old man who lived below them. His mom worked nights at the hospital, so he had to be quiet while she slept too.

The constant silence was oppressive, and sometimes Nero could hardly stop himself from running around yelling at the top of his lungs. Stomping too. But he never would because his mom was always telling him how lucky they were to have a place she could afford.

Donny continued dropping, flipping, and catching the skateboard while Nero looked on. The crashing sound echoed across the hot concrete parking lot and the crows on the telephone wire continued to stare down at them. One cawed and fluttered away, tired of the wait. Nero was about to ask if Donny would show him how to toss the board when the sound of tires on the pavement reached his ears.

Looking over his shoulder, he watched a van turn into the lot. It was an entirely unremarkable van. White was all he would remember about it later. It parked away from them, on the other side of the park and ride. Harmless.

"Okay," Donny said, letting the skateboard fall to the ground again. "Let's have some fun!"

This time Donny didn't flip the board back up; instead, he set his right foot on it and pushed off with his left, rolling away from Nero. Just ahead of them was a covered rider waiting area. Beside it were concrete stairs leading up to the street and next to them was a ramp for wheelchair users and other folks—and, of course, skateboards and bikes. There was an old pay phone there too, the receiver hanging down uselessly. They'd checked for forgotten change first thing, but no luck.

Nero jogged after Donny, his pack bouncing against his back. At the stairs, Nero took off his backpack and set it on the ground next to the shirt Donny had taken off.

"It's freaking hot out," Donny explained. "Plus, I gotta get some rays on this bod."

Donny lifted both arms and flexed his biceps like he was Arnold Schwarzenegger or something. Nero laughed so hard he was sure he sounded like a braying donkey, but no way was he taking off his shirt. Again, Donny was the lucky one; Nero was scrawny and pale.

They messed around on the skateboard for a while. A few buses came and went, expelling passengers who ignored them and headed for their cars or took the stairs up to the street. Donny demonstrated how to balance on the board and even let Nero try riding the stairs—which he completely failed at, ending up with a massively skinned knee to show for it.

"Dude, there's no point if there's no blood," Donny pronounced while Nero sat on the ground, holding the edge of his t-shirt against the gash. "Chicks dig scars."

Nero laughed nervously. Did guys *dig* scars as much as girls? He'd never talked to anyone about it. He didn't need another thing setting him apart from "normal people," but he thought he liked both.

"My mom will be pissed if I have to get stitches or something," Nero grumbled. It was even hotter out now, and he was regretting not bringing water or something else to drink along with him. But he hadn't wanted to weigh his backpack down so all he had was a peanut butter sandwich.

"Nah," Donny said, bending to take a look at Nero's shin, "you don't need stitches or anything. But, dude, I don't think Tony Hawk has anything to be nervous about."

Nero snorted and opened his mouth to pretend Donny had hurt his feelings, but he didn't get a chance to say anything.

"Hey!"

Donny and Nero both looked up and over toward the voice.

A man had gotten out of the van that Nero had completely forgotten about and opened the back doors.

"I have a first aid kit if you need it," he called out.

Nero was about to say no, but Donny answered for him.

"Sure, that's awesome. Stay here, I'll be right back."

"Donny..." Nero began.

But his cousin was already jogging across the lot toward the van. Nero struggled to his feet, intending to go after him, try and stop him. Although he wasn't sure what he could do with blood dribbling down his leg onto the new shoes his mom had bought for the start of the school year.

"Donny!" he yelled again, louder this time, as he limped to the curb. "Come back!"

His call was ignored. Donny slowed down as he neared the van. The driver—Nero assumed it was the driver—leaned into the dark interior of the vehicle. Nero saw Donny's lips moving but couldn't hear what was said.

Then it happened.

A terrifying slow-motion video clip that Nero Vik relived for the rest of his life.

He watched as the man grabbed his cousin and tossed him into the back of the vehicle like he weighed nothing. Forcing the back door shut, the man ran around to the driver's side.

The sound of the driver's door slamming had Nero skip-limping even faster toward the van to—what? Stop it? Rescue Donny from someone who was twice his size? Nero wasn't sure, but he kept moving anyway.

The van's engine roared and, with a screech of tires and a cough of exhaust smoke, it raced away, taking Donny with it. Nero outright ran now, but the van disappeared around a far corner and onto another street, a cloud of dust billowing behind it. Panting, bleeding, standing in the middle of the lot for what seemed like forever, Nero caught himself wondering if maybe what had just happened had been an elaborate practical joke.

Donny was well known for his creativity.

Minutes passed. Nero didn't move, and the van didn't

return. Finally, a city bus arrived and he pulled himself together enough to get out of its way. A lone woman disembarked, and the bus left again.

She must have sensed something because she paused on her walk to her car, glancing at his bloody leg. "Are you okay? Do you need help?"

Nero opened his mouth, but the words wouldn't come out. What he needed to say was choking him, making it hard to breathe.

No, he wasn't okay. And he didn't know if he'd ever be okay again.

The police arrived and all Nero had was a discarded t-shirt and precious skateboard as evidence that his cousin had been there and was now gone. He finally broke down and cried.

"It's all right, son," the grim-faced police officer said as she patted his shoulder.

THREE

Nero – March, the Wednesday Before

With a disgruntled sigh, Nero pushed the drawer to the card catalogue closed again. The placard with *Last Update 1998* scrawled on it had been his first clue. He'd hoped to find articles written about the three teens who'd gone missing in the 1980s. One had been found— murdered—but the other two had never been seen again. The distinct scent of the thousands of aging paper author-title-subject cards inside the oak cabinet wafted upward. *Ah, the scent of knowledge,* Nero thought. How many people in Cooper Springs knew how to use the catalogue?

Nero found it aggravating that Cooper Springs Library wasn't fully on the internet; however, that would have made his research too easy. Too modern. The librarian had informed him it was a matter of pride to keep the card catalogue in these days of *computer everything*. But what Nero wanted wasn't there anyway—or had never been catalogued in the first place.

"Frankly, we've never been allocated the money for an update to a full electronic catalogue of our older holdings. Not a large enough library or population in the area. No one seems to mind. The school-aged children use their tablets and phones for everything these days."

R. Fernsby, *Volunteer*, made "these days" sound like their reality was a *Blade Runner*-style dystopian society.

"If they need something for a project, the Timberland cross-county system has OverDrive and some databases," he informed Nero.

OverDrive was just one of many programs that allowed people to check out electronic books with the right library card. "R. Fernsby" also made OverDrive sound like it was kin to Skynet or whatever those robots were attached to in *RoboCop*. Unfortunately, Nero had learned that the building housing the local newspaper had been torn down in the late 1990s. Sometimes progress sucked.

He'd been about to ask "R. Fernsby" what Cooper Springs Library's purpose was if it wasn't serving the needs of the citizens when several young children burst inside, chattering loudly about what each of them was going to pick out for story time. For the last thirty minutes, while he'd been fruitlessly searching the catalogue, Nero'd also been regaled with *1-2-3 Salish Sea*, *The Very Hungry Caterpillar*, and a rousing rendition of *Are You My Mother*.

Obviously, Cooper Springs Library did what all libraries did —provided a safe and fun space for people to read and learn. These little kids were the future of the small town, Nero knew that, but he wasn't interested in the future. Although he enjoyed other people's kids and a quality Eric Carle read-aloud, he was interested in the past right now.

And the past he was hunting didn't appear to be lurking inside the card catalogue.

"Did you find what you were looking for?" Fernsby asked.

Fucking hell, he'd snuck up behind him. Nero about jumped out of his skin but managed not to curse out loud.

"Um, no," he said, turning around to face the older man. "I'm interested in articles and stories about the area from the 1970s and '80s. I know there used to be a newspaper out of Cooper Springs, but I'm not seeing anything listed in the catalogue."

"Oh, you should've said as much. This isn't the original library building," Fernsby explained. "After the Cooper family donated the building to the city, we were moved into the old Cooper Mansion for a while. But in the early '90s, the building had a major leak and we moved here. There are still some documents stored in the mansion's basement, and the catalogue associated with them is there as well. It's possible hard copies of the Sentinel are there. We just don't have the space here and as much as we argued for a larger building..." R. Fernsby shrugged. "It was a dark time in our history."

Nero was amused by Fernsby's attitude. Dark times was akin to the Dark Ages, he figured, when Krakatoa erupted and blocked out the sun for years and years. Crops failed, people starved. Europe plunged into chaos. In Cooper Springs, dark times meant the timber economy had been taken off life support and the town had nothing else. Hard times for everyone.

"Are they accessible? Can I get in there?"

He'd driven by the mansion a couple times, and it didn't seem to be in great shape. If they'd had a leak thirty years ago, what was it like inside there now?

Fernsby pursed his lips thoughtfully at the question. He thought the man—Nero's height and lean to the point of skinny—was somewhere around sixty. He even wore a cardigan a la Mr. Rogers, the ultimate in librarian fashion.

"Unfortunately, you need special permission and a library card. Due to the nature of the collection there and the building's historical importance to the town, we can't just let anyone inside. And to get a library card, you need a local address."

But then Fernsby seemed to come to a decision—maybe that Nero was morally worthy of a library card anyway? Nero had no idea. Brushing past him, Fernsby raised a hinged countertop that kept the hoi polloi from sneaking into Librarian Headquarters. From behind the counter, he plucked a paper from a cubbyhole and slid it across the counter so Nero could read it.

"However, the library always needs donations. Anyone who gives over this amount"—he tapped the paper with his index finger—"is issued a library card regardless of their home address."

Nero scanned the information listed on the library letterhead. Aside from a short history of the facility, there was a plea for money and several checkboxes. The highest listed amount, and the one that Fernsby indicated, was three hundred dollars. Nero looked back up, catching Fernsby's assessing gaze. The man knew he wouldn't back down.

"Of course, a person could always donate more," he said with the hint of a smile.

With a slow shake of his head, Nero reached for his wallet. Might as well put his severance pay toward something worthy.

Twenty minutes later, after filling out the form, he was four hundred dollars poorer—he'd actually had to grab his checkbook out of his car—and in possession of one provisional CSP library card with the promise that the permanent one would be sent to his address at Cooper Springs Resort, Cabin Five.

"Be sure to keep the receipt in a safe place. You can write off the donation," Fernsby reminded him.

Nero nodded, tucking the slim piece of paper into the pages of his battered and barely used checkbook. It was so out-of-date that the address printed on the checks was pre-Austin.

"You're the young man who's doing a story on the missing girls, aren't you? Kaylee Fernsby and the two other girls?"

"News travels fast. But, yes, I am."

"Kaylee was my cousin."

Nero was mildly embarrassed that he hadn't made the connection himself. It seemed everyone was related to everyone in this town one way or another; he supposed this shouldn't have come as a surprise to him.

Fernsby continued to pin Nero with his gaze for several long, uncomfortable moments. Nero automatically straightened his posture, as if that would somehow make him more trustworthy to this guardian to the portal of knowledge. He resisted running his fingers through his hair to flatten it. His hair had a mind of its own.

"What was Kaylee like?" Nero finally asked.

"I babysat her when she was a child. She was a typical teenager for the most part, testing her parents at every turn. My uncle, Bruce"—Fernsby eyed Nero again—"he had traditional ideas about how girls should be. Conservative ideas. Kaylee wanted to experience the world. She was smart, wanted to be an engineer Would have been good at it too."

"Did she have a boyfriend?"

Fernsby glanced down at the counter and back up at Nero. "I don't think she did, but by the time she was in high school, Kaylee didn't want to hang out with me much, even if I wasn't that much older."

Nero cocked his head, trying to figure out what Fernsby wanted to tell him. The tiny rainbow sticker on the corner of his name badge caught his eye again.

"Was Kaylee seeing someone not a boy?" Nero guessed.

Fernsby nodded. "I was the only one who knew. As far as I knew, the only one she ever told."

If Kaylee's conservative father had learned she was gay, would he have been angry enough to resort to violence?

"Do you think—"

"No," Fernsby said emphatically. "I don't. Bruce was devastated, a changed man after Kaylee... was found. I suppose he could have been responsible, maybe in a rage. But he was her *father*."

Nero didn't point out that stranger abduction was very rare. More often than not, women were killed by male family members. Fernsby was probably fully aware of the statistics—he was a librarian, after all.

"Thank you for telling me. I'd like to talk to you again, learn more about Kaylee, so that when I do the show, I can present her three-dimensionally. That is, if you don't mind."

"I'm here two days a week, easy enough to track down." His tone returned to crisp and unemotional. The conversation about his cousin was over for the day.

"UGH," Nero said to the gray clouds.

The weather hadn't changed while Nero'd been inside the library. It was still drizzling heavily. He paused on the steps of the tiny wooden building that had once been someone's home and re-buttoned his peacoat, flipping up the collar so water didn't drip down his neck. The Cooper Mansion was one block down while The Steam Donkey, the town's pub, and a warm lunch were the other direction.

Obviously, he wouldn't be able to get inside the mansion yet, but curiosity tugged at him as it always did. Promising himself a warm meal afterward, he turned toward the historic building.

Wrought iron fencing that surrounded the structure was the first thing Nero noticed as he approached. Nero paused on the sidewalk and took in what had once been a magnificent building. Cooper Mansion was one of those Victorian/Edwardian mashups from the 1880s that looked like the architect hadn't wanted to commit to one style. During his travels, Nero had seen a handful of these spread across the Olympic Peninsula, all built by timber money. The mansion desperately needed a new roof and gutters and every windowpane in the front was cracked. Based on the general air of disrepair, he wasn't sure how anything stored in there was safe from the elements.

Disheartened, Nero decided not to move his truck from where it was parked and turned around on the sidewalk to head toward the pub.

He'd walked a block when he felt his cell phone vibrate in his jeans pocket. Most of the time, the thing served as an expensive paperweight in this town, to the extent that he didn't know why he carried it around with him. The stars and a satellite must have aligned perfectly today because a text from his mother had made its way through.

Mom: I've been thinking about you. I hope you're doing okay.

Nero drew air in through his nose and held it for a minute, along with a healthy dose of well-earned guilt. He should've stopped by for a visit when he sped along I-5 through Olympia on his way to Cooper Springs last month, but he hadn't told her he was coming back to Washington State. He also hadn't told her that he and Austin were finished.

Just another failure on his part.

His mom meant well, and he knew how much she loved him. Which was better than one would probably expect from, say, a devout Christian his mother's age. Nero had been anxious for days and unable to sleep when he'd decided to come out to her. Lili Vik had just smiled and hugged him tightly and then they'd gone and had espresso and croissants together at the French bakery. It was still a favorite memory.

But she didn't understand him.

Visiting with his mom would be stilted, peppered with questions that led to the same answers: *Yes*, he was still actively looking for Cousin Donny. *Yes*, he was aware Donny had been missing for over twenty years. And now he'd added Kaylee and the two missing teens to his list. And the missing girl from last fall, Blair Cruz. He re-pocketed his phone. He'd connect with her later. At some point.

Ten minutes later, thoroughly wet in a way that only drizzling rain could achieve and sporting the frizzy hair to go along with it, Nero stepped inside the Steam Donkey.

"NERO! SIT ANYWHERE YOU LIKE," Magnus called from where he was standing near the taps.

Nero glanced around and almost immediately spotted Forrest Cooper.

He sighed inwardly. Cooper had taken an instant dislike to him, a problem only because Nero was determined to interview the man—along with many other long-time Cooper Springs residents. Plus, his last name was Cooper; chances were high that he was related to the town's founder, even more so than probably half the current denizens. Great for backstory. Hopefully, he'd wear him down.

With Nero's history of making unfortunate choices—Austin the Ex being merely his latest—it was probably a good thing Cooper regarded Nero as if he'd stepped in something particularly stinky. It was a small solace that the first time he and Cooper had crossed paths, he'd looked at Nero quite differently. There'd been heat to his gaze, hot enough to make Nero's dick sit up and take notice.

Nero may have usually made bad choices, but he knew when those bad choices were interested.

Today's glare was Extra-Frosty. Boo.

"Screw it," Nero muttered.

Sitting alone meant he couldn't involve himself in the conversation but sitting at the bar next to Cooper wasn't exactly a hardship. He'd just have to endure the cold shoulder.

Nero walked over to stand by the open spot. "Is this seat taken?" he asked, meeting Forrest's dark gaze in the mirror behind the taps and various bottles of liquor.

"Nope," the guy to Nero's left said. "Feel free to join us. I, at least, don't bite." Chuckling, the guy stuck his hand out. "Tim Dennis, pleased to meet you."

Nero had seen Tim around town with Xavier Stone but hadn't officially met him yet. Tim wasn't on Nero's list of people to talk to—*unfortunately*, Nero thought as he checked out Tim's infectious smile—since he was almost as new to Cooper Springs as Nero was.

"Nice to meet you. Nero Vik," Nero said, shaking the proffered hand.

"I've heard you're a podcaster. Is that right?" Tim asked while Nero made himself comfortable.

"And an ex-journalist." Nero smiled. "Good thing I wasn't keeping it a secret."

"Small town," Tim countered with a mischievous grin and eyebrow waggle.

Dammit, why couldn't Tim be on Nero's list? He was clearly open to conversation—and possibly more. Nero somehow recognized that Tim was trouble, but in a good way. The kind of person who might play harmless but funny practical jokes. Nero thought of one of his favorite words from childhood: rapscallion. It really was too bad Nero didn't have a reason to interview him.

"What can I get for you today?" Magnus asked, stepping over to where Nero sat.

Magnus Ferguson had been pleasant from the first time Nero stepped in the pub. But then, he was obviously a lifelong publican and very good at his chosen profession. He'd even encouraged Martin Purdy to rent the cabin to him, for which Nero was thankful. Car camping on the Pacific Coast in the winter was no picnic.

"I'll have a Tree Hugger, and"—he paused, considering his waistline—"the soup-and-salad combo, with the chef salad." Sitting in front of a computer most of the day was not the healthiest thing, but it happened in epic fashion when he was deep into a story.

"How'd you get into podcasting?" Tim asked as soon as Magnus stepped away again. "Is it a full-time gig for you?" Aside from roguish, Tim was also a curious guy. Why was Nero never interested in the easygoing guys? Why was it always the broody-moody ones? The ones who inevitably broke his heart.

Everybody always asked him that too; podcasting for a living was still something a bit unusual. Maybe he needed a t-shirt: *Get Your Own Podcast* sounded appealing. Much like every time he ended up at the Steam Donkey, Nero knew everyone within hearing distance was listening in. It was like repeatedly auditioning for a part in the school play, only he was less likely to throw up afterward.

"It is now. I was recently laid off from my other job, although there are those who claim journalism isn't a real job either. But podcasting's a natural move for me, so hopefully I can make it work." He grinned and lowered his voice conspiratorially. "Gotta do something to pay for my gaming habit, after all."

Tim laughed at that. "As one does. You have a few shows under your belt already, I heard. How do you decide what cases you look at? I bet everyone asks you this."

"Yes, but it's a great question. There are so many, but I tend to gravitate toward the forgotten ones, the cold cases that got little attention from the very beginning."

Donny's case had gotten attention at first. But when Nero couldn't tell the police anything about kidnapper beyond that he wore a baseball cap and the van was white, they'd started to think he was covering up for Donny running away. Nobody would listen when the whole family kept saying that Donny was happy and had nothing to run away from, so the case had gone cold quickly.

"Like... there just wasn't evidence?" Tim asked.

"That or maybe no one believed the family when a person was reported missing. Or maybe the person wasn't reported because they'd left their family behind, so no one knew something bad happened."

"What you're saying is, it's complicated."

"Exactly that," Nero agreed, warming up to one of his favorite subjects—forensic science. "Identifying human remains is so much more complicated than measuring femurs or looking at hip bones like we see on TV. Dental records are helpful, but only if there is someone to provide them and a match is found." He paused to sip the beer Magnus set in front of him.

"Also, did you know that dentists aren't required to keep records the same way hospitals are? If a dentist stops practicing, their records can be and often are destroyed and lost forever. And if the person never had dental care, then there is nothing to go by."

"Yikes, I had no idea. And there are plenty of folks without dental insurance."

The fact that Tim was still listening to Nero nerd out about cold cases, DNA, and dental records was endearing. Once again, Nero was a bit sad that Tim wasn't on his radar for much of anything. He tried not to wonder if Forrest Cooper was listening as well.

"Right? For sure, dental records are a good place to start, but there is a significant percentage of people who remain unidentified purely because wrong assumptions are made—maybe from the very beginning of the case. Bones don't always tell the full story. Maybe they are misgendered. Maybe the victim was trans. Not every human falls within the bell curve."

Nero would argue that most humans didn't, that everyone was somehow unique. But that was probably more information than Tim wanted to hear right now.

"Wow, that's intense. I had no idea. MBA here, not a science degree." There was that grin again. "So, what brought you here to Cooper Springs in the first place? Pretend I haven't heard any of the rumors flying around."

As Tim had pointed out, Cooper Springs was a small town and the reason Nero was there wasn't a secret.

"I'm doing research for a show surrounding the two teens who went missing in the 1980s. Another girl disappeared too, but she was found later—not alive, unfortunately. Kaylee Fernsby, Morgan Blass, and Sarah Turner. I read that remains were recently discovered, and if any match the girls, maybe we can shed a little light on what happened to them. Just having a show and listeners talking about it online can help solve a case." Nero then added, "I was at the library just now hoping to look at old newspapers, but no dice. Turns out they're stored somewhere else. With any luck, I'll be able to access them soon."

"For fuck's sake, give the man a chance to drink his beer, Tim," Magnus said abruptly, as if he'd only just realized everyone in the bar was listening in. "I think your salad is ready." Swinging around, Magnus headed back into the kitchen.

Tim snickered. He clearly knew Magnus well enough and didn't take the scolding to heart. Nero appreciated Magnus running interference though—it wasn't something he was used to.

Forrest Cooper hadn't moved a muscle since Nero had started talking. But maybe now he'd understand that Nero meant no harm. Maybe, if Forrest would speak to him, Nero could tell him that one of the reasons he'd come to town was because he thought his cousin Donny might be up on that mountain. But he wasn't sharing that now. For one thing, the idea was far-fetched, and for another, Donny was his personal project. Donny had been his cousin but also his friend and Nero was protective of him, even if he'd now been a ghost longer than he'd been Nero's cousin.

Returning with the soup and salad, Magnus set it down in front of Nero with a thump, then grabbed a set of flatware from somewhere underneath the countertop.

"Here you go," the publican said before looking around again at the people lining the bar. "I'm not running a damn zoo here. Let the man eat his meal."

Nero's stomach rumbled. He picked up the fork and shoved a bite of lettuce in his mouth.

Was it bugging him that he and Cooper were sitting next to each other, but the man hadn't done more than growl his direction? Hadn't even bothered to acknowledge the message Nero'd left on his answering machine earlier in the week? Yes, it did. Nero accidentally caught Forrest's gaze in the mirror again and thought he saw that flash of heat. His dick thought so too.

Those mixed signals were killing him.

Nero wasn't exactly everyone's cup of tea. Flaky. Unwilling to commit. Elusive. Entirely too attached to his computer, always researching and recording *Grave Secrets* or gaming. Once again, Austin the Ex and his grumbling popped into his head. Maybe it was best to ignore the now familiar simmering spark of attraction that popped up whenever he was in Forrest's proximity. It wasn't as if he planned on staying in Cooper Springs forever.

"He says he's not running a zoo, and yet he lets the likes of us in here almost every day," the woman sitting on the other side of Tim said. She'd introduced herself to Nero as "the better half of the Critter and Mags team." Mags wore her usual forest service uniform, and her curly dark hair was tied back in a long, neat braid protecting it from the damp. Maybe he should try something like that too. "Speaking of zoos, have you all seen that Reptile Man is back?"

Rufus Ferguson, who must've been in the kitchen or just come inside, spoke up from near the end of the bar. "Reptile Man? I thought they were out of business. Didn't that Bernie guy finally die? Wasn't he strangled by one of his own boa constrictors? Fitting death, I say."

Speculation erupted around Nero as the other folks at the bar ignored him to discuss whether or not the business in question had gone bankrupt or been put out of business by Fish and Game for trafficking in endangered species. And whether Bernie was really dead or if he'd faked it by putting out the story of the boa constrictor.

"Nope," a man also wearing the forest service uniform insisted. Nero thought he was called Critter. "They got busted but paid the fine. And Bernie's definitely still alive."

"Critter, pull your head out. They'd never pay the fine," Magnus countered, confirming Nero's memory. "I bet they waited a while and just opened up again, hoping the state isn't paying any attention."

"I always thought that place was cool. I used to beg my dad to take me there when I was a kid," said a woman Nero didn't know. He'd seen her around a couple times though and thought he'd heard she was competing in the upcoming chainsaw festival. "I must have spent three or four birthdays petting crocodiles and holding snakes."

"Personally," Rufus interjected, "that place always gave me the creeps. I didn't like it back in the seventies when— what's his name?" He snapped his fingers. "Harry Dixon first opened it up. Harry was creepy and so were the animals he had caged up. And his creepy son owns it now?"

"Yeah, I think it's still in the family, Pops. And as far as I know, Harry Dixon is still alive and kicking," Magnus said. "I can't believe you took me there if you hated it so much."

"Maybe hate is a strong word. And anyway, you know I'm not a fan of snakes. They should be left alone, far away from human settlements. It was typical of him that Magnus was weirdly fascinated by them as a boy."

"Did I ever tell you about the time I brought a garter snake into the house?" Magnus said to everyone sitting near him.

Rufus groaned and shook his head but suffered listening to his son tell the story.

Magnus pointed a hand at his dad. "Here is a man who has spent the majority of his life outdoors hiking and camping in the wilderness with no backup. He's canoed in the Yukon Territory. Been held captive by a moose and later the same day had a badger charge him. Climbed glaciers and mountain peaks before we had satellite phones. We all know about the Bigfoot thing. And he is frightened of snakes."

"Snakes are creepy," Rufus insisted, dragging a stool around to sit at the opposite end of the bar from Nero. "And I'm sticking to it."

"So anyway," Magnus continued, "when I was around twelve, before Mom got sick, I found this sweet, innocent little garter snake in our front yard and brought it inside to show them." He threw his head back and guffawed loudly at the memory. "I am not kidding you guys, Pops shrieked and fainted dead away. We had to take him to the ER for stitches because he banged his head on the doorjamb. The snake slithered somewhere and disappeared. We never found it. I was devastated."

"Yes, and your mother never let me forget it, either. I ended up with three damn stitches." He glowered at his son. "And the incident did nothing to change my opinion on snakes."

Everyone was laughing, including Forrest Cooper. Even Rufus Ferguson, who was probably tired of having that story retold, started chuckling. Nero caught Forrest Cooper's reluctantly amused expression in the bar mirror. Smiling himself, Nero scooped up the last bite of salad and jammed it into his mouth. For the first time in ages, he felt like he belonged.

Cooper Springs was a town of weirdos, and he suspected he might fit in if he let himself.

FOUR

Forrest – Wednesday

"I don't trust him," Forrest repeated. Another word rolled around in his mouth before he spit it out like a sour grape. "*Podcaster.*"

Nero Vik had finally departed after drinking his beer and eating his damn salad. Thank fuck. Vik made Forrest feel too many conflicting emotions at once. He'd accidentally caught a glimpse of him in the backbar mirror and had been snagged by his smile—which irritated him.

"He's very pleasant and well-mannered," Magnus said, ignoring Forrest's derision and continuing to wipe down the surface of the bar where Nero had been sitting. "Stops in every few days and has a beer and a burger. Doesn't strike me as a mass murderer. I had a listen to one of his shows, and he seems to know what he's doing. It's not as if he's hiding or lurking around corners and jumping out at people with a microphone. You should give him a break."

Wonderful. Now Magnus the Great was championing Nero Vik. And was also an expert on what mass murderers looked like. *Pleasant and well-mannered*. What did that even mean? Didn't everyone say that about their serial killer neighbors? Forrest glanced at his old friend again, and Magnus caught the look and smirked.

Smirked.

Wait, was Magnus giving him the side-eye? Was *give him a break* a euphemism? One never knew with Magnus. Or with Rufus, for that matter.

Could Magnus suspect that Forrest was both repelled and drawn to the hack podcaster? No. Just no. Wasn't going to happen. Forrest had some standards.

He suppressed a growl and focused on his drink, positive now that the look Magnus shot him had been loaded with innuendo. Good fucking god, the man was a damn busybody. The first person to spark Forrest's interest in months was exactly the wrong person, and Forrest wasn't giving in. He'd leave town soon, and Forrest could go back to being happy enough alone.

Vik would go away, disappear, leave Cooper Springs forever. Forrest didn't want him getting comfortable in town, making people—Magnus and Rufus, for instance—like him.

Making Forrest *want* him.

The Fucking Scales of Desire and Loathing were swinging so wildly one direction and then the other that Forrest didn't know what he wanted, really. Up from down, what the fuck?

Therefore, there was going to be nothing. This was good.

However, Forrest for sure *didn't* want Vik roaming around town and asking people questions, even if those questions had nothing to do with him. Because they easily could.

"He's an... ambulance chaser, a *podcaster*," Forrest repeated as if Vik was Satan himself. "He feeds on other's misfortune. Fucking bottom-feeder."

Some people's biggest fears were heights, spiders, or the monsters under the bed. They were the lucky ones. Forrest was afraid the monster living in the forest still lurked out there. Especially after Levi Cruz's sister disappeared last November.

No one had seen Forrest's parents, or anyone from their group, since they'd gone into the woods before Forrest was born. Well, except for Forrest and Lani, and Forrest truly wished they hadn't seen them. As far as he knew, no one had looked for the group either. Grandpa had said they'd made their wishes very clear. Surely if they were still alive, someone would have reported spotting them. He reminded himself about that one guy in Maine who'd lived in the woods for about the same amount of time, and no one had known he was out there, either.

It was possible.

The mere thought of Witt and Dina Cooper made his heart race and the palms of his hands get clammy, almost as if he might accidentally summon them from wherever they were now just by thinking about them. With any luck, it was hell for Dina. Forrest didn't know about Witt.

"Now, how do you know that?" Magnus asked calmly, bringing Forrest back to the present. Magnus still dragged the pristine bar rag back and forth. "As far as I know, you haven't given the man the time of day." He cleared his throat and the next words came out softer than the usual Magnus bellow. "Give him a chance, Forrest. I can tell you want him. I worry about you, and so does Pops. Grab the golden ring while you can because who knows when you'll meet someone like him again."

Forrest ignored the emphasis on *day* and the throat-clearing and sipped his lemonade before replying. "Nick did a little research for me. I don't trust him and I'm not giving him a break or a chance or anything else."

His old friend was right; Forrest hadn't given Vik the time of day. And he didn't plan on changing his mind.

Magnus's eyebrows rose an inch. "Oh, and our Nico is a glowing example of seeing things clearly and judging fairly?"

Magnus's teasing tone pissed Forrest off even more, counteracting the calming effect of his lavender lemonade. Maybe Nick Waugh was a bit of a hothead, but Nick cared. He cared about Cooper Springs and the people who lived there.

Forrest squinted at his lemonade again. Okay, maybe Nick caring about more than Martin Purdy was a bit of an exaggeration. He did care about the town itself, but not many of the residents made Nick's list. It was an attitude Forrest understood.

"And so what if he is a podcaster?" Magnus added. "He's providing a valuable service. From what I gather, he's helped solve a few cold cases already, and families were finally able to bury their loved ones. They have closure now. I think it's time you got over yourself and dealt with the past head on."

"He's only here for the gory details," Forrest insisted hotly, his ire rising again. He was pissed off that Magnus thought he could *get over* his past. Closure be damned. "The past can stay where it belongs. Forgotten and *in the past*. Don't forget he was also an investigative journalist."

Fuck, even he knew he sounded ridiculous and petulant.

And maybe scared. Not that he would ever admit that one out loud. Mostly because he knew as well as Rufus, Magnus, and anyone else who'd lived in Cooper Springs forever did that the chances of his parents being still alive and living in The Deep were almost zero.

Almost zero, but not quite. Dammit, these remains and Blair Cruz missing had him all tied up in knots.

Magnus paused his aimless wiping of the sparkling bartop to give Forrest another hard glance. "I think he will ask good questions. Questions that should've been asked years ago. What about the stuff up on the mountain? If the bones have family left alive, don't they deserve to know what happened? It's not all about you, Forrest. Have you ever considered that the past is overdue for a good rummage?"

Forrest felt his jaw slacken and his mouth gape. He wasn't sure which pissed him off more: the *not all about you* comment or the idea that a good rummage was needed. Both. Both pissed him the fuck off. Pissed him off more.

"A good rummage?" Forrest hissed back. He'd lost his tenuous grip on his temper. He leaned across the bar to get as close to Magnus as he could. To his credit, Magnus didn't step to the side or react at all. But then, Magnus had known Forrest most of his life. "You of all people—more than most people living here anyway—know what needs talking about and what can be left dead and buried."

Dead and buried. Fingers fucking crossed.

Frowning, Magnus shrugged. "Well then, you need to do something to control the narrative if you're so worried about the past. Me? I'm happy to have some fresh eyes in town. A neutral party, taking a look-see and maybe stumbling across something we've all been missing when it comes to these bones."

Magnus tapped the gleaming mahogany countertop with one fingertip while Forrest pressed his lips tightly together, stemming the angry tide of words that threatened to escape past them. Magnus was not his enemy. Nero Vik was the enemy. A sexy-as-fuck enemy—but still, the enemy.

Magnus had a point though. He wouldn't have any idea what Vik was up to if he shut him out. He hated that Magnus might possibly be right.

"If it makes you feel better, you can call it sleeping with the enemy," Magus added. "Get to know him, find out what he's looking for, be ready for it."

"I'm not sleeping with anybody," Forrest growled, distracted again when an image of Nero Vik popped into his head. All that long, wild, dark hair and those soulful eyes. "Especially not for information."

Magnus's eyebrows rose higher. "I didn't mean literally

sleeping with, Forrest, but whatever floats your boat. Which, like I said before, maybe that's exactly what you need—a roll in the hay."

"Can you just quit with the sexual innuendos?"

Tossing the bleach rag aside, Magus shook his shaggy head. "Oh, for fuck's sake, Forrest, it's not innuendo." He snorted. "I just meant if you *cooperate*—admittedly, an issue even when you aren't worked up. Which suggests maybe you do need to work off a little sexual frustration. Vik just wants to talk to people. Maybe he won't want to talk to you at all. Maybe you aren't important to what he's doing." Magus shot him an annoying grin. "That would be hilarious."

"Ah, fuck you."

FIVE

Nero – That Wednesday Night

The sharp shrill of sirens dragged Nero from an already restless sleep. Glow from the red lights of a fire engine cut through the darkness in the cabin, splashing the walls with an eerie light. Blinking, Nero hoisted himself out of bed and stumbled the few steps it took to get to the window that looked out over Cooper Springs.

"What the hell? Is that what I think it is?"

Half-awake, he hurriedly pulled on his jeans, a t-shirt, and a thick wool sweater. Shoving his feet into his boots, Nero shrugged into his peacoat and headed out the door. At the last minute, he remembered to lock up and then tucked his keys into his coat pocket.

Hurrying down the footpath to the parking lot, he decided not to drive to the scene; the Explorer would just be in the way. Hands shoved deep into his pockets, Nero crossed the highway and walked quickly toward the flashing lights. Selfishly, he hoped it wasn't the historic Cooper Mansion, but he was very afraid he was wrong.

Within blocks, he knew he was wrong.

For once, it wasn't drizzling, showering, or otherwise raining. But with all the storms they'd had recently, maybe the general damp would save the old building. He quickened his pace, as if his arrival would stop the hungry flames from devouring the town's history.

A water truck blocked the street and a second engine was parked on the sidewalk. Nero wasn't the only one who'd come out to watch the firefighters do their jobs. He recognized the rumpled form of Rufus Ferguson and walked over to stand by his side.

"Hi, Rufus. What happened?"

"Hey, Nero." Rufus shook his head. "No idea yet. Looks like someone called the fire station in time, but who knows."

Several people were milling around but staying behind the yellow tape that had been stretched across the street. Rufus, who seemed to know everyone and probably did, raised his hand in greeting toward the group.

"I was hoping to get access to the archives stored there," Nero said morosely. "I'm guessing they no longer exist."

Even with the responders' lights and the streetlamps, it was dark. Nero peered around at the rest of the crowd. If a fire had been purposefully set, an arsonist often would stick close by to watch their work. Unsurprisingly, Nero didn't recognize anyone. He did see police chief Andre Dear and the two brand-new officers directing traffic. But no one was looking particularly guilty while also holding a lighter and something inflammable.

"Doesn't look good, that's for sure," Rufus said. "If it makes you feel any better, whatever was stored there was probably destroyed long ago. There was a flood or something, I remember."

"I heard there'd been a leak. The librarian told me about it. But he seemed to think the old newspapers might still be okay."

Rufus glanced up at him. "The Cooper Sentinel? Magnus claims I'm a hoarder, but I have a few years' worth."

Nero eyed the older man. "A few years?"

"In my defense, it was a weekly, not a daily. But my Da always saved them and after he passed, I guess I just kept it up."

As horrified as Nero was by the loss of the historic Cooper Springs home, a thrill shot through him at the thought that he might be able to look through copies anyway.

"Do you think I might be able to take a look at them sometime? I promise to be careful."

Someone from the growing crowd bumped into Nero's back, sending him stumbling toward the yellow tape. Rufus grabbed Nero's sleeve to keep him from falling. He turned to frown but whoever it had been, they were already gone.

"I'm happy to have you look. Stop in at the pub tomorrow and we can set up a time. Looks like they're wrapping up. Good thing it didn't spread to other houses." Rufus turned away from the ruined mansion. "I might be able to set you up with Robert Butler too. He was the last publisher, ran the Sentinel until the end."

Nero followed Rufus's lead, heading back toward the highway and the relative comfort of his tiny rental cabin.

"Robert lives in some kind of bougie assisted-living place south of Aberdeen. He loves to get visitors, especially folks interested in the past."

Nero smiled at Rufus's use of the word bougie.

"I'll find you tomorrow," Nero promised as he continued back across the highway and up the path to Cabin Five. As he drew close, he thought he saw a human-shaped shadow dart along the side. Maybe he needed to get his eyes checked or learn to leave the outdoor light on because when he looked again, there was obviously nothing and no one there. Just a figment of his imagination.

Who would be hanging around the resort this time of night anyway? As far as Nero knew, he was the only resident until Martin opened a couple of cabins for the upcoming test run during the first annual Cooper Springs Chainsaw Art Festival.

When he got to his small front porch, Nero realized his door was slightly ajar.

"Motherfucker."

He obviously hadn't secured it as well as he'd thought. If something happened to his equipment, he'd be in trouble. Without thinking, Nero pushed inside to the dark of the cabin, flipping up the light switch by the door as he did so.

"Mother fucking hell."

The cabin was a mess. His bedding was strewn around, the mini fridge's door hung open, and the few books he'd brought with him were flung to the floor. Nero stood stock-still, trying to take it all in.

The plastic bins packed with his recording equipment had been pawed through but at first glance, nothing seemed to be missing. He heaved a huge sigh of relief. Even his laptop was still propped against the wall underneath the table where he'd left it. Had the intruder just missed it, had they been after something else, or had it just been kids looking for booze? Nero didn't have much; they had to have been disappointed.

The shadow he'd seen must not have been his imagination, after all.

If his laptop had been stolen, it would have been inconvenient but not the end of the world. Everything was backed up to several external hard drives as well as the cloud because Nero was that paranoid and had learned his lesson the hard way years ago.

The recording equipment would have been much harder for

him to replace seeing as how he had no job and no verifiable income to parlay into a loan.

He flung the door open again, looking around but not seeing anyone or anything. There didn't appear to be any footprints that weren't his.

The half hour he'd been away had been just long enough for someone to break in. Had it been Forrest Cooper? Nero shook his head. No, he just didn't see Mr. Cranky being behind this, and he wasn't sure what his reason would have been besides a general hatred toward Nero.

But who could it have been? He was new to town, new enough that not many people even knew him yet. So far, Forrest Cooper was the only one of those who did who also appeared to actively dislike him. Even Nick Waugh was starting to come around.

He briefly considered calling Cooper Springs' finest but—he glanced back out the window toward the mansion—they were all still at the scene of the fire. Morning would be soon enough.

Had the fire been set purposely, Nero wondered, to get him out of the cabin? That seemed ridiculous. Someone had just taken advantage of him being gone when the rest of the town's attention was elsewhere. It was only a short walk to the mansion and back; if the fire had been planned, the thieves couldn't have known how long Nero would stay away.

"Dammit."

The open mini fridge suggested it was kids, maybe looking for alcohol and something easy to carry away and sell, but they'd left the computer. Maybe they didn't know that the equipment the bins held was worth a great deal of money. Maybe it had been deemed too hard to carry? He hoped they'd been disappointed by what they'd found.

Tomorrow he'd talk to the police and, he reminded himself, to Rufus about the newspapers. Nero wanted to read any original news reports that had never been scanned and put online. He also still planned on trying to speak with Amy Blass, the mother of one of the girls who disappeared.

After cleaning up the best he could, Nero tossed the clothing into a pile and changed the sheets before crawling back under the covers.

Sleep didn't come easily.

SIX

Forrest – Thursday Morning

Huddled deep in the prickly brambles, Forrest squeezed his eyes shut, trying to make himself as invisible as possible. Whoever—or whatever—was out there, he didn't want to see it. Or it to see him. He wrapped his arms tighter around Lani's little body. She was shaking so hard. They were both shaking.

The only reason he wanted to hear it was so he knew where it was. So they could run if they had to.

Thankfully, his sister was quiet for once. She'd only just started speaking in full sentences, and some days Forrest wished she would go back to the babbling and pointing. But right now she must have sensed something was very wrong. The same way Forrest did.

He'd been playing outside, building a house for the fairies that lived in the trees. Not that Forrest had ever seen a real castle, but he'd read about them and it seemed to him that fairies might like a castle just for them, one made of bark, moss, twigs, and other things he found in the woods.

Dina, their mother, told them that the forest was full of fairies and he and Lani needed to be nice to them because they were magical. "If you do something bad, the fairies will take you in the middle of the night, and we'll never see you again." Her lips curved into a cold smile that Forrest had learned not to trust.

Maybe building them the castle would keep both Forrest and Lani safe from the fairies. Dina'd tried to scare him with Native American stories about Raven, Coyote, and Beaver, too. But those stories didn't scare Forrest, not that he told Dina. He liked how clever they were at outwitting their enemies.

There was more than one voice out in the dark tonight, he thought. Forrest couldn't tell who was talking. Was their mother out there too? Where had Papa gone? Why had Papa made Forrest come to this spot with Lani? Why had Papa told him to keep Lani quiet, to stay until someone came for him?

Then the screaming started and it wouldn't stop. He needed it to stop. In desperation, he put his hands over his ears. Lani wrapped her thin arms around his neck, pressing against him. Forrest was going to be strong for Lani. Whatever was out there would have to come through him first.

Forrest was just about to shatter into a million pieces when the screams abruptly stopped. It seemed like hours passed, although Forrest had no idea of the time. Even when the sun began to rise, he stayed because Papa had told him to. Then, somewhere off in the distance, he heard the sound of footsteps. They were coming closer.

FORREST BOLTED UPRIGHT, the blanket slipping down and pooling around his waist. That had been the worst dream in a while.

"Jesus fucking Christ," he whispered into the early-morning gloom of his bedroom. He glanced around, noting the antique dresser that had been his grandfather's, the closed closet doors, the cheap lamp on his bedside table. They were all where they belonged, reassuring him that he was a forty-three-year-old man, not the seven-year-old who lurked in his dreams. Nightmares.

It's fine, he told himself, *just a dream. Go back to sleep.*

For years, the dreams had been less and less frequent, less disturbing. But ever since Nick and Martin had discovered more fucking bones up on the mountainside in January, the dreams had returned with a vengeance.

He always woke up when the screaming ceased— for which he was thankful. After all the time that had passed, he was still never certain who was doing the screaming. Him? Dina? Lani? Witt? Or had it been someone else, someone Forrest hadn't known about? The shrill sound echoed in his memory, chased him across the decades.

Terrified him.

Maybe it *had* been his father screaming, he didn't know. But he also didn't remember Witt Cooper much at all. Witt was a shadow to Forrest, a ghost. His father had almost always been away, outside, working on something. Forrest couldn't even be sure when the last time was that he'd seen Witt.

And he'd tried his best to remember.

Forrest's next memory was of waking up in a warm, sunlit, unfamiliar room, curled up under heavy blankets with his sister. A man who sounded like Papa sat near the bed reading a story aloud. When Forrest finally risked opening his eyes, the man, who also looked a lot like Papa, had explained that he was their grandfather and they would be living with him from now on. When Forrest asked him if Papa would come too, Grandpa had shaken his head, sadly saying, "I don't think so, son."

What Forrest knew about his father came from his grandfather's stories, the ones he told Forrest and Lani about Witt as a boy, as well as the few photographs that had been saved over the years. If Forrest had been unsure whether Witt was actually his father, the photos proved it beyond a doubt. Both he and Lani took after him and their grandfather.

Rolling on to his side, he pounded a fist into the down pillow to make it more comfortable, more sleep-able. But it was too little too late; he was fully awake and there was nothing to do but get his ass out of bed.

"Motherfucker."

The only time Forrest was a morning person was if he stayed up all night. He flopped back down, wondering if maybe just this one time he'd be able to fall back asleep. Minutes later, watery daylight slipped through the gap in the bedroom curtains and crept across his face, directly into his eyes.

"Give me a break. Fucking sunshine now?"

Why couldn't he ease into consciousness, have a nice espresso waiting for him on his bedside table, and just start the day? Instead of feeling like he'd gone nine rounds with a boxing champion in his sleep.

"Because you can't, that's why. Get over it."

Stumbling into his kitchen, Forrest started the coffee pot, then stood at the counter and stared outside while it gurgled and hissed. The floor was chilly—he probably should have put socks on. But he hated the feeling of socks against his skin and generally waited until his feet were blocks of ice before giving in.

His cell phone vibrated from its spot on the kitchen table. Forrest glared at it before shuffling that direction. The screen declared *Unknown Caller*.

"Fuck that."

He wasn't going to answer the call at first, but then changed his mind.

Snatching up the phone, he pressed Accept.

"What?" he demanded.

There was no reply.

"Is this a prank call?"

Was there no one on the other end of the line? Forrest thought he heard an intake of breath.

"Well? Hurry up, I haven't got all fucking day."

He did have all day since he was self-employed. And it was, the stove clock informed him, almost nine in the morning now. And not yet late March. He had another month before he'd be out mucking in the fields.

"Er—"

Forrest's thumb jammed against the red telephone icon. There was something satisfying about hanging up on a cold call first thing in the morning. If it was important, they'd call back.

He lingered in the kitchen another few minutes, waiting for the coffee machine to finish, then poured himself an extra-large cup—black like his redheaded soul. As much as he wanted to sink onto his couch and stare at the ceiling, he did have work to catch up on, vendors to call, and general shit he tended to ignore over the winter months. The pile of mail on his desk was getting out of hand.

But after stepping through his office doorway, his mug gripped in one hand, Forrest halted so quickly that a splash of hot coffee sloshed over the rim and landed on his fingers.

"Fuck." Changing hands, he wiped the hot coffee off on his jeans.

The light on his ancient answering machine was blinking red-red-red in a foreboding rhythm. A deep sense of unease flooded through him, and his heart thumped loudly. No one ever called the landline.

It was a joke between his sister and him that he still had the damn thing, inherited from their long-dead grandfather. The fact that it still functioned had been in question—that was how long it had been since someone had left a message on it.

All of his friends—and Lani, of course—knew to call or

preferably text his cell number. Even with the crappy cell service in the area, he'd get a message eventually.

The mix of dread and irritation flooding his system peaked. He should be immune to the feeling by now. Maybe that was just the caffeine taking effect. Had something happened to Lani? He couldn't bear it.

No, he told himself. Chief Dear wouldn't just leave a message. But of course Forrest's brain jumped to the worst possible scenario.

Moving closer to the desk, his hand shaking slightly, he reached out and pressed his finger against the Play button. After a series of clicks and raspy squeaks, a monotone voice informed Forrest the message had been left a few days earlier. An unfamiliar, but not entirely unknown, voice began to speak.

"Hello, this is Nero Vik leaving a message for Forrest Cooper. I hope so, anyway. I hope this is Forrest Cooper's number and not some random other Forrest Cooper."

"Oh, for fuck's sake," Forrest groaned. This would explain why Vik gave him the side-eye at the pub yesterday. He thought Forrest was ignoring his call. He was, just not until now.

He had no intention of talking to Vik about anything and contemplated just deleting the message. On the other hand, Nero Vik had a nice voice. Forrest just didn't plan on talking to him. It wouldn't be weird if he played this over and over, right?

"Anyway, I think you know I'm an investigative reporter—well, ex-reporter—but you don't care about that. I'm working on a podcast about Cooper Springs. It's a long story but while I'm in town, I'm hoping to interview people regarding some teenagers who went missing in the late 1980s."

Vik cleared his throat before starting up again.

"Not that you had anything to do with missing girls. But when I research these, I like to talk to as many people as possible. The story's not only about the missing young women, but about Cooper Springs as well."

Vik paused again, or maybe Forrest couldn't hear him speaking over the pounding of his heart.

"I'm very interested in talking with you, hearing your take on Cooper Springs as a kid, and nowadays too. I'm setting up interviews with Rufus and Magnus Ferguson, Mayor Moore, and a few other folks who've been living in Cooper Springs for years to get a feel for things, fill in some blanks. Please give me a call back so we can set up a time."

He rattled off a phone number that Forrest again didn't bother writing down. If he wanted to talk to Vik, he knew where to find him. As soon as the message ended, his finger smashed against the Delete button.

Forrest absolutely would not be granting an interview. Without thinking about it—or rather, without thinking it through—Forrest pulled his cell phone out of his back pocket. His fingers still shook as he punched in a message to his sister.

F: Did Nero Vik call you about an interview?

Lani didn't immediately answer. Which, fine, wasn't worrisome; she was a deputy with the Cooper Springs Police Department. Lani was also still recovering from a gunshot wound and since the department was short-staffed, she was busy as hell even though she was supposed to be deskbound.

F: I don't want you talking to him. Call me before you do.

... ...

When Lani's response came, Forrest realized he'd miscalculated and groaned out loud.

L: I have better things to do than argue with you about who you think I should talk to. If he wants to ask me questions, I'll do my best to answer them.

Telling his sister what to do always worked out so well for

him. Especially when she was overworked and generally stressed out.

Instead of dealing with the paperwork waiting for him, Forrest finished getting dressed—including socks—and headed out to his truck. He needed to get out of the house and away from the cobwebs of his dream and put some food in his stomach.

THE PUB WASN'T QUITE open yet, but Magnus lived in the apartment above the bar and Rufus could almost always be found there too. Forrest wasn't above barging in so he could have some company. Rufus was the closest thing he had to a father these days, and Magnus relished the part of Irritating Older Brother. He banged on the door several times, shivering as a particularly strong gust of wind blew.

Several *just a damn minutes*, thumps, bumps, and rattles later, the door opened to reveal a disheveled but awake Magnus Ferguson.

"Ah," Magnus said, eyeing Forrest, "had a nightmare, did ya?"

That Magnus knew about Forrest's nightmares was both good—he didn't have to explain anything—and bad. Magnus thought Forrest should talk to a professional, as in a therapist. That wasn't happening. Forrest talked to as few people in town as possible and he'd known them for most of his life. He wasn't about to spill his guts to some stranger.

"Yes, and I don't want to talk about it. Can I talk you into something to eat?"

Magnus rolled his eyes but opened the door wide so Forrest could slip inside.

"Of course, you're always welcome in our house."

Forrest was unsurprised to find Rufus sitting at the end of the bar. Since selling the Steam Donkey to Magnus, Rufus had bought his own small house and was currently "stepping out" with Wanda Stone, but he still could be found in the pub on a regular basis. Especially when it was too rainy or cold to be up in the woods.

"Morning, Rufus," Forrest said as he crossed to the bar and claimed the spot next to older man. "How's it going?"

"It's closer to noon, but whatever floats your boat, Forrest."

Rufus knew about his nightmares too. By the time he'd died, Ernst Cooper hadn't had a lot of friends, but Rufus Ferguson had been one of them. Ned Barker and his ex-brother-in-law, Oliver Cox, had been the others. Rufus, Ned, and Oliver had often come over to shoot the shit, and they'd eventually let Forrest hang around with them too.

"Brain's working overtime, I guess. Same dream, just a few tweaks. Woke me right up." Sweating and ready to crawl into a closet. "I got a message from Vik. How did he get the landline number?" Forrest suspected Magnus was the culprit, thinking he knew what was best for Forrest. "Like I told you, I don't trust him and I'm not going to talk to him."

"Methinks the man doth protest too much," Magnus intoned in a hideous, supposedly English accent. However, it wasn't an admission that he was the one who gave Forrest's home number out.

"Protest what?" Forrest demanded, knowing full well what he was protesting.

"I'm no expert on affairs of the heart, Forrest, but he's had his eye on you almost as much as you've had yours on him. Not in a creepy way." Magnus waggled his head back and forth. "More of an *interested* way. No harm in him having a way to get a hold of you."

"He has not had his eye on me." Forrest scoffed. "And

anyway, do I need to repeat that I don't trust him? Why would I want him to have my number?"

Rufus snorted. "We both saw *you* watching him the other day when you thought no one was paying attention. Forrest Ernst Cooper," Rufus said with the slightest smirk, "I've never known you to back down from a dare in your life. Now"—he jabbed a thick finger Forrest's direction—"I dare you to face down your past and acknowledge whatever the hell is sparking off the two of you. Let yourself live a little and find out—something good might happen."

"Something bad might happen."

Dammit. Fucking Rufus Ferguson had fucking *dared* him. Being dared was like catnip. He and Xavier had dared each other so many times as kids that they'd spent more time in the principal's office than out of it. Forrest always had to prove he wasn't afraid of anything. And Rufus knew it.

"I'm not responding to that."

The thing was, doing the scary thing didn't mean he wasn't afraid of it.

Rufus snorted—again.

"You're both assholes," Forrest said without heat. "I came in here for some food and advice, and you're taunting me about fucking Vik instead."

"This is advice, Grasshopper. Exactly about *fucking* Vik. Whatever it takes, I say. I remember your grandpa used to dare you to do stuff all the time," Rufus said, chuckling while he did so. "Sometimes it was the only way he could get you to listen to him or do something he wanted you to do. Oliver always said you were worse than Ned."

"Seriously?" Forrest let himself think about his grandpa for a minute. "On second thought, that doesn't surprise me. I still miss the old man, but he could be sneaky. I wonder what he'd make of the mansion burning down now, too. Can almost hear him." Forrest dropped his voice even lower, to the register he always remembered as distinctly Ernst Cooper's sound. "Fuckin' A, Rufus. What the hell is this town coming to?"

The last was mostly rhetorical. Mostly. Something funky had been set in motion and Forrest thought it stemmed from the discovery of the remains. He'd sensed something in the past four months, a growing menace he couldn't explain.

"We all miss your grandpa." Rufus turned in his seat to face Forrest fully, his expression serious. "So, grab the bull by the horns, boy, and don't let something that could be good pass you by."

"Did Wanda give you one of those inspirational calendars or some shit?" Forrest faked a shudder. "Maybe I'm just better off single."

"So, you're afraid of taking a chance? Is that it?" Rufus shook his head again. "I expect better of you, Forrest Cooper. You need to live, not hole up in Ernst's old house talking to ghosts."

Rufus was fucking daring him *again*? Forrest resisted the urge to argue. Arguing would only make Rufus feel he was right about both Vik and talking to ghosts. Rufus wasn't right.

And Forrest would prove it.

SEVEN

Nero – Thursday

"Hi, what're you drinking today?" the dark-haired young woman asked him. Nero thought her name was Tilly but didn't want to freak her out by asking. No one liked strange old white men—ancient at nearly forty—asking their names. Today, possibly-Tilly was bundled up in a thick sweatshirt and knit cap and only opened the order window about halfway to keep out the chill.

"A triple cappuccino, extra foamy." He peered at the menu posted on the side of the wood-shingled building. "And one of those veggie burritos."

"Coming right up." She turned from the window to the gleaming espresso machine that Nero could see from the driver's seat.

When he'd first arrived, the tiny town of Cooper Springs had appeared to Nero to be tired and run-down. But he knew better now. More than a few residents drove newer model cars, which meant decent jobs were within driving distance.

Martin Purdy continued to upgrade the rest of the cabins at

Cooper Springs Resort —a much-needed remodel that would give visitors a place to stay in town for at least a few days. And he'd heard from a guy at the Steam Donkey that there were more plans in the works for new businesses, a new winter festival—something beyond the Cooper Springs Chainsaw Art Festival—and reviving something called Shakespeare on the Beach in August.

But most importantly on this late morning, this drive-through espresso stand had recently opened up on one end of town. It was within walking distance of his cabin, but he'd chosen to take his SUV over instead, planning to drive by the Blass home afterward and then to the station to report the weird break-in.

He crossed his fingers. Hopefully, Amy Blass would be home and willing to speak with him. Of those related to the teens who'd gone missing in the 1980s, she was the only parent who still lived in town as far as Nero knew. The third teen, Kaylee Fernsby, had been found eventually, yes, and all three young women deserved justice, but he had to start somewhere.

Nero normally dealt with older cold cases, but he'd wondered if there was a chance that Blair Cruz's case could somehow be connected to those earlier ones. She was around the same age as Morgan and Sarah had been when they vanished. Stranger things had happened.

"That was some fire last night," he commented just to say something while she ground the coffee beans and poured milk into a stainless steel pitcher.

"Yeah, it was. I've always thought that place was creepy," possibly-Tilly said with the sangfroid of a longtime resident. "When I was a kid, we pretended it was haunted."

A kid. Nero managed not to laugh. Tilly couldn't be much more than twenty. While waiting for his coffee drink, he listened to the raspy buzz of several power tools starting up at once, like they were warming up for a concerto.

The sound of chainsaws was something else he'd found himself getting used to since he'd arrived. From the many yard signs, posters, and banners around town, the chainsaw art festival was a lot bigger than he had first thought and was set to happen in just a couple of weekends. Nero had to give the town credit; all the signage had sparked his curiosity from the moment he'd arrived.

Nero debated how to best approach Amy Blass. He hadn't wanted to leave a phone message that might be misunderstood and give false hope that there were new leads about Morgan's case, so he'd decided approaching her in person was for the best. Finding her address had been easy, but the rest was making Nero edgy. He did not want to get this wrong.

While he idled at the order window, a battered postal vehicle drove past the stand, heading north along the main road, probably ready to deliver the day's mail. It turned in at the backside of Cooper Springs, where the town came up against the timberland.

The forest was doing its best to take back the land Cooper Springs occupied. The battle was between man and nature, and he didn't think it would take much for nature to win.

"Here you go." Tilly interrupted his thoughts by holding out first his burrito and then his coffee. "Have a great day."

Leaving the coffee stand, Nero crossed the highway and drove slowly down the smaller residential streets that led toward where Morgan Blass had grown up, left from one day for school or possibly work, and then never returned to.

Because of last night's wind, the roads and sidewalks were covered with branches and pine needles. A bundled-up blond man walking toward his car waved to Nero. Nero realized that the man had been the source of at least some of the power-tool rumbling he'd heard over the past few days, so he slowed down and pulled over to the curb. He wasn't on that much of a schedule, so maybe checking out the chainsaw art that populated the man's front yard would help him see what the big deal was about the art form. Nick Waugh's penis forests hadn't shown him much.

There was a lot of it. Mixed in with the obligatory bears, eagles, and Bigfoot renderings were an owl in flight, a merman, and several intricate sea monsters, including a huge kraken. The artist was obviously very talented. Nero felt a pang of regret that he didn't have space for one of the gorgeous carvings.

Irritated with himself—he was, after all, the one who put himself in the position of not having a permanent home—he waved back to the stranger, stepped on the gas, and pulled back into the street, continuing toward the address he'd jotted down.

Absentmindedly, Nero lifted his to-go cup out of the cup holder and took a big sip of his espresso. It was a close thing, but he didn't spew it all over the car.

"Oh my god," he gasped after swallowing the molten liquid. "Because I want to cold-knock on someone's door while covered with coffee. Good job there, Nero."

The drive took him to the oldest residential part of town. What was left of the Cooper Mansion was just two blocks away, along with several other historic homes. The miniscule town library was the next block over too. All of them were luckily undamaged. The smell of smoke and ash was strong, still hanging in the air and reminding everyone of the tragedy. Nero wondered how Fernsby and the rest of the library staff were dealing with the loss of historic documents.

Nero grumbled to himself as he tried to navigate the tangle of roads that curved around the forest, many of them ending in dead ends. He spent at least ten minutes driving up and down the various streets, trying to figure out addresses.

"Where the hell is this place?"

The house numbers seemed to make no sense, with even and odd addresses sometimes on the same side of the street. There were a couple of addresses only differentiated by an A or B. He saw the same postal van parked along the road, but the mail person was not inside. If he ran across him, he'd ask for help. Surely the postal carrier would know where Nero wanted to be.

"The town founders must have been smoking some funny stuff when they planned this out. More likely not planning at all."

Turning yet another corner, he discovered another dead end. By his reasoning, the house should have been down that way, but it wasn't. He'd already come across one place where he'd seen numbers painted on the curb but no discernable entrance. It turned out the front of that house was on an alley, which made no sense at all.

"Come on 1109 Yew, where are you? Ha, ha."

He picked up the scrap of paper again, checking for the fifth time that he had the address right. Maybe he had it written down wrong. He pulled over to check on his phone even though the chances of having a cell connection in this spot was somewhere between zero and nothing.

Nothing.

Frustrated, he stared out the windshield at nothing and sipped at his espresso while the burrito grew cold beside him.

Thump. A bang on the driver's side window startled the fuck out of him. He flinched so hard he spilled the remainder of his coffee on his lap *and* hit his head on the roof of the car.

Because when disaster struck, Nero always managed to go full bar. It was always the worst outcome.

Twisting around, he looked out the window—banging his forehead on the glass as he did—to see what had hit it. Nero was even more shocked to see a stunned raven on the concrete a few feet away. Ignoring his damp jeans, he hastily opened the door and climbed out.

"Shit, do you need help?" he asked the bird. "What the fuck am I doing asking a bird if it needs help?"

Was there a vet around that would take a raven?

He carefully approached the bird, not wanting to scare it. After a moment, it seemed to gather its wits and then struggled to its feet. Shooting him an almost haughty glance, the big bird tottered off toward the looming stand of trees before testing its wings and flying up to a branch over Nero's head.

"Are you okay?" he asked the bird again. Why was he still talking to the bird? Maybe he needed to go home and take a nap before trying to talk to Amy Blass.

Surprisingly, the bird seemed to answer him with a loud, raspy *caw*.

"Are you being chased? Why did you bang into my car?" Again, stupid question, as the bird still wasn't going to answer him. At least not in a language Nero understood.

Moving closer, Nero peered up at the raven. It seemed unhurt and it had been able to fly up to the tree. It cocked its head, its intelligent black gaze downward, and Nero instinctively did the same.

That was when he saw the boot.

The boot with a foot still in it. A foot attached to a leg and a body. A man's body lay half obscured by brambles, and he didn't appear to be breathing.

"Oh my god."

EIGHT

Nero – Thursday

Nero didn't end up trying to speak to Amy Blass, not after finding the mail carrier's body. By the time the CSPD finished interviewing him, he wasn't prepared to talk to a stranger about the loss of their child. Instead, he retreated to the relative safety of Cabin Five. He'd also forgotten to mention the break-in, which seemed small compared to finding a dead man.

"Make sure you're available," Chief Dear had said before letting Nero go home—well, commanded. "We may have more questions for you. Don't talk to reporters."

He'd stifled a laugh at that, figuring that Dear maybe wasn't aware of his past career. Still, Nero had no intention of writing publicly about what had happened. The postal officer deserved justice, not Nero's rambling account of discovering a murder victim.

And where would he go anyway? His mother's house? Not that Chief Dear or anyone else in town knew that Nero was one four-hundred-square-foot cabin away from being homeless.

The officer who'd responded to his call had told him the

victim's name was Ned Barker. Probably he wasn't supposed to share that kind of information but he, the cop, was new to the job, Nero figured, and obviously a bit queasy about the dead man.

Nero figured he wasn't considered a suspect—he'd never met the man before finding him dead. But he had discovered the body—so maybe he was? Dear had seemed more harried than suspicious though. And it was obvious the shorthanded police force was still struggling to regain its footing after the weird stuff that went down in January. Nero for sure wasn't a cop, but he was a damn good investigator. Why not put his skills to use and see if he could help out CSPD?

"Because every cop in the world loves it so much when *amateurs* interfere with active investigations," Nero muttered as he attempted to pace from one side of the cabin to the other. His voice sounded loud in the too quiet space.

He was antsy and needed something to distract himself. Dead bodies weren't new to him; Nero had seen them before. But this time he'd been the first person on the scene. He'd been the one to call 9-1-1—and thank god he'd gotten a signal at that moment. He'd been the one to place his index and middle fingers against the man's throat to see if there was a chance he had a pulse.

The turtleneck Nero had pushed aside had still been warm, and so had the carrier's skin. But there'd been no pulse, and Nero hadn't really expected one. Not with the victim's head at that angle.

The traitorous raven had flown off almost immediately, leaving Nero alone with the body. He—Nero, not the dead man—thought he heard something in the woods. But after peering into the dense brush and the trees grown too close together with no results, Nero had convinced himself it was nothing more than the clumsy bird and his own overactive imagination—

although his imagination had never been quite this overactive before.

Still, while waiting for the police to arrive, Nero hadn't been able to rid himself of the feeling of being watched. Spied on. Even now, several hours later, he felt oddly exposed and twitchy, like a very large target had been painted on his back. He'd found himself staring into the woods at odd times over the course of the day. They'd simply stared back, offering him nothing.

The officer who'd responded to his call had looked around the scene, but he hadn't found anything and, not wanting to disturb possible evidence, he hadn't gone very far. Once other officers had shown up, focus had been on the scene at hand, not the looming trees around them.

On the short trip back to the cabin, Nero had driven past the Steam Donkey. The parking lot seemed suspiciously full, and Nero hadn't stopped. The last thing he wanted was to be interrogated by the citizens of Cooper Springs. It would happen eventually, but it didn't have to happen right now.

When he'd caught himself looking for Forrest Cooper's purple vintage farm truck in the lot, Nero stepped on the gas pedal. He was far too intrigued by the lanky, bad-humored man as it was. Notably, Cooper still had not returned his call, and Nero suspected the message had been deleted—which was fine. He had no idea why Forrest Cooper had taken such an instant dislike to him that the man wouldn't even return a simple phone call.

Now, Nero's not-quite-pacing picked up a bit.

"*Too intrigued*, Nero. Note to self: you are the unemployed drifter. He is the descendant of the founding Coopers and obviously emotionally unavailable if his snarky comments are anything to go by," Nero said to himself as he turned at his double bed and tried not to think about how much the situation sounded like a Hallmark movie.

"It's for the best," he told himself about his decision to end the relationship that hadn't even started. "I'm not staying in town. I don't need to add to my own baggage." He paused at the small window with quirky curtains. "And I probably need to stop talking to myself out loud too."

NERO FINALLY SAT down at the cabin's miniscule table and opened his precious laptop, intending first to work on the podcast about his search for Donny. But instead, his fingers typed in "Ned Barker" + "Cooper Springs" + "Murder" and hit Enter.

He knew what he was doing was a coping mechanism. He couldn't bring the mail carrier back to life, but he could learn as much as possible about him. The same way that, after twenty-four years, he still wanted to solve the disappearance of his cousin. Did he know the likelihood of solving either mystery was small? Yes, but he wasn't giving up.

The first result was a Facebook page that apparently substituted as the main news source for the town. The sting of being laid off flared. This wasn't news and these weren't facts.

"Chief Dear must just love this," he muttered as he scrolled further down the page. There were tons of posts and comments about Barker's death. After only a few hours, there was already speculation about what might have happened. Was it a cover-up? Was Bigfoot involved? Barker's ex-brother-in-law and also head of the Cooper Springs postal service, one Oliver Cox, had apparently been VP of the local Bigfoot Society. A commenter brought up this fact as a possible-conspiracy angle. Nero frowned. Did they think Bigfoot committed the murder? Someone else chimed in that maybe aliens were responsible.

"Okaaay," Nero said to the screen. "Moving right along."

"Anonymous" claimed to have seen "someone weird" creeping around a few days earlier and speculated that was the killer. A moderator then piped up—one Robert Butler, Nero noted—asking that people please be respectful as someone important to the town had died.

Nero continued scrolling in the hope that he'd find worthwhile information. Mostly, folks were expressing their sadness that Barker had been murdered and wondering what was happening in their town. Some blamed it on newcomers. Nero winced at that; he definitely fell into the new-to-town category.

Then, buried deep in the comments, another anonymous commenter said, *Maybe someone should look into other deaths. Didn't Ernst Cooper die the same way?*

Heart pounding and fingers fumbling over the keys, Nero typed in "Ernst Cooper" + "Death" and hit Enter once again.

The Daily World—the Aberdeen online newspaper—began to load. Slowly. Nero was about to give up when it finally finished. He clicked on the old headline, *Death in Local Pioneer Family*.

Ernst Cooper, grandson of the founder of Cooper Springs, died on October 20, 2004, due to a fall. Cooper was found outside his home by his grandson, Forrest Cooper, and could not be revived.

The article went on to talk about Ernst Cooper's life and how he'd become reclusive as he'd aged. As a young man, he'd been a part of the business community but as the area's economy shrank and the last of the mills closed, Cooper turned his back on the town his father and grandfather had built in order to care for his grandchildren.

"Judgey much? He took care of his grandchildren, for fuck's sake."

His death had been ruled an accident, but, like Ned Barker, Cooper's neck had been broken and he'd had a head injury. Nero wished he could get his hands on the original case file.

Sitting back, he stared at the screen. "What are the chances they both die in a similar way but in vastly different circumstances? Was it a coincidence? Barker's death certainly couldn't be confused as an accident, that's for sure."

Sitting forward again, Nero continued down the rabbit hole he'd entered. He was about to take a stretch break when a general article about Cooper Springs popped up. It appeared to be one of those town history link sites, and while he knew it wouldn't have anything about Barker's death, he wondered what other information it may provide.

He clicked on it.

The page was old and appeared to not be maintained. There were a few gritty scanned-in photos of Cooper Springs in the 1880s and early 1900s scattered along the webpage's edges. Sitka spruces, large enough that ten logging men couldn't wrap themselves around their bases. Logging trucks caravanning down the main street, all loaded down with a piece of a tree trunk so huge that one truck wasn't enough to haul it. Many of the links inside the site were broken, but not the one leading to a four-line *On This Day* article.

On This Day: Forrest and Lani Cooper, brother and sister, came to live with their grandfather, Ernst Cooper. Ernst is quoted as saying he is pleased to have his grandchildren living in his home. After spending their early lives in a pioneer encampment somewhere in the Olympic forest, the children seem happy and healthy. Ernst Cooper declined to be interviewed for this story.

Curious and curiouser.

The author was Robert Butler, one of the moderators for the

Cooper Springs Facebook page—and the man Rufus had mentioned at the fire scene, the one who used to run the Sentinel. Nero noted his name, intending to look this Robert person up at some point.

The search continued. Nero used a variety of keywords and techniques from his days as a reporter, but he couldn't find more information about the Coopers as children. Which was fine. He was interested in Ned Barker, not Forrest Cooper. But it didn't hurt to write down what he had learned. He turned to a fresh page in his notebook.

Forrest Cooper – owns a lavender farm outside of town, Purple Phaze.

Nero rolled his eyes; Cooper probably found the name amusing and it explained the color of his truck.

Forrest's younger sister, Lani Cooper – one of the officers who'd shown up at Ned Barker's crime scene. After being shot in the thigh last month, Officer Cooper was still using one crutch and Nero very much got the feeling Chief Dear hadn't been able to convince her to stay back at the station.

Their grandfather, Ernst Cooper – died from a fall and a broken neck like Ned Barker.

Nero wasn't sure what kind of fall ended up with a broken neck but from the meager accounts of his death, Ernst Cooper seemed to have been healthy before the accident. There was no mention of stairs or horseback riding. Ned Barker had been a healthy-looking mail carrier. Surely he'd been in good physical shape as well.

Call Cooper again.

He looked at the last line on the list. "I'm a sucker for punishment."

But who better to tell him about Ned Barker than the grandson of one of his friends? The grandson who'd likely known Ned Barker fairly well. The *hot* grandson with smoldering eyes and an ass that Nero very much wouldn't mind squeezing.

He snorted. "I am fucking ridiculous."

Before Nero could set his fingers on the keyboard again, there was a banging on his door.

"Um, hello?" he called out over the thumping of his heart. He pressed the lid to his laptop closed. "Who is it?"

While he'd been online, night had fallen. The sky was dark and overcast, the only light coming from the streetlamps and businesses across the roadway. Nero hadn't thought to turn on the outside light.

There was no one in town who would come to his door except for Martin Purdy and Nick Waugh, and they weren't the type to surprise him without good reason. He appreciated that in his de facto landlords.

"Martin? Nick? Is that you?"

No answer.

A healthy dose of self-preservation had him stepping to the side of the window and peeking out through the curtain, to try and see who—or what—was out there.

No one stood on the tiny area at the top of the front steps as far as he could tell. There were no shadows, no silhouette of a person waiting for him to answer. Not even the pizza delivery he craved but had yet to call in.

Maybe it had been a wrong address. Someone playing a prank on him. Or just the wind.

Cautiously, Nero moved to the door and slowly turned the handle. He felt like a bit player in a horror movie, but he'd rather feel stupid than dead. It wasn't a basement door, and he wasn't a virgin. He'd be fine. Unfortunately, the image of Ned Barker's lifeless body, his neck crooked all wrong, popped into his head.

He pulled the door open with a jerk, revealing nothing but

rain coming down in sheets. No one was there. His pulse raced, his body readying for flight.

Nero called out another cautious, "Hello?"

Again, there was no answer, but by then he didn't expect one.

As he started to shut the door, Nero glanced down. Maybe someone had been making the rounds and stuck a flyer under the welcome mat or something. He didn't see a brochure but on top of the weatherworn rubberized mat lay a wrist-sized loop made from some kind of grass.

Tentatively, he bent down and picked it up, then studied the strange thing as he held it between his thumb and index finger. It hadn't been there when he'd come home, had it? Had he been so oblivious when he'd returned to the cabin that he hadn't seen it? Or had someone left it more recently?

Nero couldn't shake the feeling that he hadn't missed it, but he also couldn't be sure. Had persons unknown crept to his front door, knocked, then left the weird bracelet for him to find?

If so, why? What could it mean? After the break-in last night, this... offering seemed odd. Was it related to everything else going on, or was Nero just paranoid? He was going to go with paranoid.

Glancing around and still not seeing anything that seemed off—the town looked just like it always did, fairly quiet at this time of night—Nero was tempted to toss the loop back to the ground. Instead, he brought it inside, setting it on the kitchenette counter next to his cell phone while he contemplated his next steps.

He wasn't leaving town but he wanted to get away from the four walls of the cabin; the small house felt claustrophobic and the strange knocking had thrown him off more than he wanted to admit. He decided to take himself for a drive, maybe grab a bite to eat in Aberdeen.

When he arrived at his car, Nero saw Cooper's truck pass by on the highway. As he watched, it slowed down and turned into the resort's parking lot. Assuming Cooper was there for Nick or Martin, Nero climbed behind the steering wheel of his beat-up SUV.

Right when Nero pulled his door shut, the asshole blared his horn and indicated with a jam of his finger that Nero should stay put.

Nero was easygoing, but he wasn't a damn dog to be ordered to sit and stay.

Yes, he wanted to talk to Cooper, but not when the guy was obviously feeling the need to be an asshole. Ignoring the gesture, Nero started the engine and put his car in reverse.

He could be an asshole too.

Except fucking Forrest Cooper blocked him in.

"What the fuck?" After weeks of pretending Nero either didn't exist or giving him the cold shoulder, Cooper was going to stop him from driving away? He'd had a shit day, as one does after discovering a dead body, and an unhinged Forrest Cooper was the last person he wanted to deal with. And, he realized, he was *hangry*.

NINE

Forrest - Thursday

"Ned Barker is dead, murdered," Nick stated baldly.

"Ned Barker?" Forrest repeated his friend's words, wondering if he'd heard right. His voice rose in shock, but Nick made a shushing sound at him as if there was someone close by who might hear them. "What the hell?"

This was not what he'd expected after Nick called and asked if he could come by because there was something Forrest needed to know sooner rather than later. Since Forrest had been doing nothing but staring at paperwork, he'd agreed.

After learning that the mansion had burned the night before, he'd expected it to be something like a mummified body had been discovered in the basement. That wouldn't have surprised him. Ned Barker being murdered did.

"I didn't want you to hear it from some rando. I know you guys were close."

His arms crossed over his chest, Nick nodded and shook his head at the same time, as if he also couldn't believe what he was saying, and his lips were pressed into a grim line. They were in

Forrest's living room, Forrest sitting on the red velvet couch that was his favorite piece of furniture and Nick standing next to a wing chair covered in a flowery upholstery.

"Should you be telling me this?" Forrest asked. "Aren't there rules about police investigations?"

Nick had only recently inherited the office manager job at Cooper Spring PD. There were lots of things he likely shouldn't have been talking about to regular citizens, including active murder investigations. Unfortunately, neither Nick nor Forrest were very good rule-followers. Breaking rules was like falling off a log, easy and sometimes fun.

"Would you sit the fuck down so you're not looming?"

He could not process with Nick being all twitchy.

Nick conceded by perching on the arm of the chair. "I can't stay long. I'm not telling you anything that isn't already confirmed. Besides, you know as well as I do that the entire town already has a pretty good idea what happened. And what people don't know for sure, they're speculating about. You, my friend, are late to the party. Since he was found near the high school, the whole county probably knows already. Those kids have some kind of underground information highway. You should check out what's on the Facebook page." Nick shook his head in disgust.

The last thing Forrest was going to do was check various social media sites. He didn't even have a personal account, just a page for the farm. And that was only because Lani insisted he needed one if he planned on ever turning a profit.

"Do the police know anything yet?"

Forrest still couldn't wrap his head around the news that Ned Barker was dead. As in, not alive any longer. Barker had been a part of Cooper Springs' two-man postal team for years. Although Ned was more fun-loving and less responsible than Oliver Cox, his former brother-in-law and the nominal head of the town post office, Ned was—*had been*—dedicated to his job. He was a weird but friendly guy who loved to hike—often with Rufus and Oliver—on his days off.

Like the other two men, Ned had been a good friend of his grandfather's. He'd been around the house a lot when Forrest and Lani were growing up, a fixture of Forrest's childhood. The four men would sit around the patio at night drinking whisky and swapping tall tales about, well, pretty much everything. Ned was the one who would take a break to show the two young kids the joys of card games and playing catch. When Forrest had been deemed old enough to join them on the patio, he'd lorded it over Lani for months.

Fuck.

Another thought occurred to him. The Cooper Springs PD was stretched to the limit as it was—how was Chief Dear going to investigate this too? Lani was still recovering from being shot (so was Forrest, frankly) and the new officers were still in training.

"Yeah. Believe it or not, Nero Vik was the one who discovered him," Nick informed him. "Other than that, there's not much to know for certain. He was found off Yew street," Nick added. "Chief might be calling in some favors. Apparently, the murder of federal employees is a big deal. But who knows if they'll respond."

"For sure, murder?" Forrest asked. What the fuck? Ned was really gone?

"Old Ned didn't break his own neck and crawl into the bushes by himself. His mailbag had been tossed into the blackberry bushes too. I think we're lucky it was Vik who found him and not some high-school kid cutting through to town."

Nero Vik. Again. Popping up like fairy circles after a good rain. Vik was everywhere, making it very difficult to ignore him the way Forrest wanted to. The want that flared when he saw him in the pub or walking down the sidewalks of Cooper Springs. Or sat next to him at the pub.

"*That* guy," Forrest said with a half-hearted sneer.

Many, many times, Lani had told him he needed to pull his head out of his ass, that he needed to trust that most people weren't creeps or grifters. The vote was still out on Vik though.

"He seemed pretty shaken up about it when I talked to him at the station," Nick said.

Ned Barker dead—murdered. Discovered by fucking Nero Vik. What were the odds of that anyway? And what was Vik doing in that part of town? It was a good country mile from the resort.

"Is Vik a suspect?" Forrest demanded. "He discovered the body, after all." He had to do something to distract himself from the well of sadness that threatened to overwhelm him. Ned, along with Rufus and Oliver, had been there for Forrest after his grandfather died. They'd helped him navigate the funeral, sort out the will, and find his balance again in the months afterward.

"Nah." Nick shook his head, almost apologetically, which Forrest appreciated. "He was seen getting coffee at the Gull and Sandpiper. Tilly Sanders and Vik both reported seeing Ned driving by before Tilly finished making his coffee. Then Liam saw Vik drive past his house too; he even stopped and checked out the yard art. It would've been a tight timeline. Too tight."

"Huh, but still a possibility," Forrest said, secretly wishing it really was that simple. Mostly, he wished Ned wasn't dead. "Who would want Ned dead? He was harmless. And for crying out loud, who's going to deliver the mail? Ollie can't take that on, not with his back issues. Oh god, Ollie's going to be devastated by this. Ned told me he was out of town on vacation with his grandkids. And," he added, "what was Vik doing over that way?"

"No idea why Vik was over there. That's probably something Chief or your sister know. As for the mail, do you have a pen pal you're sending letters to? Don't worry too much. Chief says there will be a temporary delivery person to help Ollie out, so you'll get your damn love letters." Nick made googly eyes at Forrest. Forrest resisted resorting to violence.

"Fuck you."

"Aw, I love you too, Forrest."

Forrest rolled his eyes.

"I need to go," Nick announced, standing from the chair. "Stuff to do and Martin wants to head to Aberdeen later tonight. But I thought you'd want to know. I know you and Ned were friends."

"Thanks, I guess."

"Sucks, for sure. I'll catch you later."

With that, Nick was gone and Forrest's house was quiet and empty again. For a few minutes, Forrest stayed on the couch and stared out the front window. It was just starting to get dark and the outdoor light hadn't flicked on yet, but there wasn't anything to see outside anyway.

What he needed was to see the scene of the crime.

FORREST TOLD himself that he was just going to talk to his sister, make sure she was doing okay with the news. Lani had been close to Ned as well. He got behind the wheel of the Ford and headed to Lani's house first. He could have tried calling and saved himself a trip to town, but he figured that Lani might still be holding down the fort at the station—or pushing her luck by insisting on helping with the new investigation. Nick had come by around early afternoon, and it was now barely evening, so it was a possibility. However, he decided to drive past her place first and see if she was home.

All the lights were off in her little bungalow, so Forrest didn't bother stopping. Like some kind of rubbernecking ghoul, he headed toward where Nick said Ned had been discovered. He figured it wouldn't be hard to find.

Crime scene tape hung haphazardly between a tree and a bush, marking the spot. No police car was around to guard it, but a jumble of cheap bouquets and stuffed animals already marked where Ned's life had ended. As Nick had said, the spot was very close to the cut-through to and from the high school.

What had Nero Vik been doing out here?

Nick claimed Vik was in the clear, but Forrest wasn't going to be quite so quick to accept his innocence. Surely, he could be the murderer. The question, Forrest supposed, would be why? What motivation might Nero Vik have to kill Ned Barker, someone he'd probably never known?

Maybe he had met him? Vik had been living at the resort for a month or so now, Forrest thought, and Ned delivered to most of the town.

For now, he would tentatively accept that Chief Dear was right, and someone else had offed the grizzled mail carrier. But he wasn't letting his guard down around Vik, no matter how hot and bothered he made Forrest feel.

It had to have been someone strong, Forrest thought as he took in the murder scene. He'd been in his late sixties, but Ned had been healthy, strong, and in good shape. Maybe it had been someone he was familiar with. Weren't most victims murdered by someone they knew? Of course, that would make most of the residents of Cooper Springs suspect; Ned Barker had always been friendly to everyone.

As he sat in his truck and mulled things over, a cop car pulled up behind him, its headlights illuminating the interior of the truck's cab. Without having to check, Forrest knew the officer was his sister. As she got out and limped to the driver's side of the Ford, Forrest rolled down his window. Lani had only recently been cleared to drive, and Forrest knew she wasn't following doctor's orders to take it easy.

Hands on her hips, Lani asked, "What the hell are you doing out here, Forrest? You're as bad as everyone else in this town. I'm disgusted with every last one of you."

"Busted. I was curious, I guess."

"Well, take your curiosity elsewhere. I've had enough of everyone."

Forrest would never say anything out loud, but Lani looked tired. When were the new hires going to be deemed fully ready?

"What happened, Lani?"

"You know I can't tell you much."

"What *can* you tell me?" He wasn't admitting what Nick had already told him.

With a put-upon sigh, Lani crossed her arms over her chest and leaned one hip against the door of the truck.

"We don't know, Forrest. He was discovered around noon. He had a head wound and his neck was broken. The coroner who came out said he probably died quickly, at least. It appears he was killed in the street and dragged into the bushes in an attempt to hide him, but there were no witnesses. At least, no one who has come forward to tell us anything. People were at work or wherever they go during the day." She waved a hand. "I imagine some were over snooping around the fire scene instead of at home. That's about all I can tell you—and it's about all we know. Hopefully, something will come back from the autopsy or from what was collected around the scene. And don't get huffy with Officer Cavanaugh, he did the best he could until the Chief and I arrived."

Forrest wasn't sure if he was glad or not that he'd been right about Lani not taking it easy.

"It's hard to believe he's gone," Forrest said instead of scolding his sister.

Meeting his gaze, Lani released a soft sigh. "I'm having a hard time wrapping my head around it. I guess I kind of thought Ned would always be around. Our world has always had those old coots in it, hasn't it? I'm going to miss him."

Straightening up away from his truck, Lani banged the door with the flat of her hand. "Now, get your ass out of here and go home. Seeing you out in the wild is disturbing. And leave Vik alone. I know you, Forrest, and as far as we're concerned, he had nothing to do with Ned's death."

Forrest watched his sister slowly walk back to her cruiser before turning his vehicle around and heading back home. The rain that had been threatening all day began to pour down. Huge, fat drops that seemed to defy physics plummeted from the sky, spattering against his windshield.

FORREST HADN'T PLANNED on stopping in town before he got home, especially not anywhere Nero Vik might have been—he was too worked up At least that was what he told himself. But when he ended up at the stop sign across the highway from the resort, a hundred feet or so in front of Nick's penis glade, he noticed the lights in Cabin Five were blazing.

Sleep with the enemy.

The thump of his windshield wipers echoed the beat of his heart. Thump. Want. Thump. Want.

Rufus had literally dared him, so it's not like Forrest had to take responsibility.

He could just drive over and knock on the door. Take the bull by the fucking horns. See if Vik could tell him anything about what had happened. *Make* Vik tell him. See if Vik smelled as good up close as he did from a few feet away.

Forrest veered into the lot, but just as he did so, Vik came outside and headed to his car. Where was that fucker going? Forrest gestured for him to wait, but the asshole got into his car and the white reverse lights flashed on.

Oh, hell to the no.

Forrest jerked his truck to a stop behind the Explorer so he was blocking Vik in. Who drove boring black cars like that anyway? People with no imagination, that's who. People like Nero Vik, who stuck their noses where they didn't belong. Who had wild hair and smelled good. People who had Forrest all twisted up even though they hadn't exchanged much more than a few words over the last weeks.

Now what are you going to do, a little voice wanted to know.

His cock twitched, definitely on board for fucking. And that pissed him off even more. Why did it have to be this guy to start everything running again? Forrest sucked a lungful of oxygen in through his nose. It did nothing to calm him down.

Groaning, he slammed his palm against the hard plastic of the truck's steering wheel. Why was his brain like this?

Lani would tell him it was oppositional behavior disorder. Damn that psychology minor of hers. She insisted Forrest always did the opposite of whatever was the smartest choice. But he'd agreed to stay away, right? No, the jury was out; he didn't remember saying yes.

His body sure didn't want to ignore Vik. His body wanted to know what made Nero Vik tick. His body's pull toward Vik was irritating as hell, like an itch in the middle of his back that he couldn't quite reach.

"I'm a fucking mess."

He could smile and say it was a mistake, pretend that he needed to talk to Nick. Or Martin. Except their car wasn't around. They'd probably headed for Aberdeen as soon as Nick's shift was over. And Forrest was a terrible liar.

The only person he was good at lying to was himself.

And right now he was failing even at that. He wanted Nero Vik, and he was fairly sure Vik wanted him too. At least, Rufus and Magnus seemed to think he could trust that. Gritting his teeth, Forrest backed the truck into a spot across from the Explorer and got out.

"What the actual fuck are you up to?" Vik demanded as he got back out of his car.

They stared at each other across the gravel lot for what felt like eons. Forrest tried to still his racing thoughts, but it was difficult with Vik staring him down. He couldn't tell if Vik was pissed off or turned on, and his cock did not care.

This was good, he told himself. They'd talk. Forrest would calm down and prove to himself that he wasn't just a raging ball of hormones. He'd find out what Vik had seen, if anything, and they'd go their merry ways.

Right.

Ignoring the voice of snark, Forrest made his way through the pouring rain, skipping past the puddles that dotted the parking lot.

"We need to talk."

Was his voice rough? Fuck.

Nero stared at him for a moment, one eyebrow raised. "About what? And why would I want to talk to you now or ever? You've done nothing but talk shit and ignore my messages for days. I've given you plenty of chances to talk with me."

The rain increased in intensity as if Mother Nature had also been listening to Forrest's bullshit and agreed with Vik. They were both getting soaked; Forrest felt the chill of the damp seeping through his jeans and Chuck Taylors.

He *had* talked shit about Vik. In his defense, it was his knee-jerk reaction to anyone new to town. Which may not have been a defense after all. But, fucking fuck, he probably owed him an apology.

Not probably. He did. Dammit.

"Can we do this inside?"

"Why?" Vik was scowling at him now and fuck, it was hot. "Why should I invite you inside? Maybe I have somewhere to be? I truly don't understand why I should bother rearranging my evening for you. Talk about fucking presumptuous. It's been a shit day for me already, so why would I want to spend time with someone who only wants to rip me a new asshole?"

Because he was a selfish tool, it hadn't even occurred to Forrest that Vik would be upset from finding a murder victim. He was an idiot, and an insensitive one at that.

"Please?" The word popped out in spite of himself. Fuck. Lani would never let him hear the end of it if she found out.

Vik seemed shocked into silence by his plea, staring at him a few seconds before coming to a conclusion.

"Sure, I guess we can talk." Vik started back toward Cabin Five and Forrest followed behind.

"Don't sound so excited."

"Should I be? Should I bow down to your assholery?"

"Look, I'm sorry for acting like an asshole. I'm actually not one."

Vik cocked his head and raised a skeptical eyebrow.

"You are so an asshole. You just fucking blocked me in."

"Fine," Forrest huffed. "I am often an asshole, but not always. I have good points that offset the asshole part."

Rolling his eyes, Vik let out an exasperated sigh to rival Lani's best, opened his front door, and said, "Just... I'm cold. Get inside already."

Inside, Forrest was at a loss for words. The place was smaller than he remembered, or maybe he was older, larger. The last time he'd been in one of the resort cabins was years ago with Xavier, and, like usual, they'd been up to no good. Also, he didn't want to talk. Not with words anyway.

This is a Very Bad Idea. He cock throbbed, proving that at least one part of his body thought this was a Great Idea.

"Can I take your coat?" Vik asked with a politeness that Forrest was certain he didn't feel.

Forrest didn't deserve politeness, and he wasn't sure where his coat would go in the cramped room anyway. Vik pointed to three hooks fixed on the back of the door. Silently, Forrest shrugged out of his waterproof duster, hung it up, and turned to face his de facto host.

Vik's dark eyes still revealed nothing. "Want something to drink? No beer, just whisky. I also don't have anything to eat. I was planning on going out."

Forrest noted that behind Vik was a micro-size kitchen and on the counter sat a bottle of Angel's Envy.

"Whisky's good. Thanks."

"You can sit on the bed or stand, whichever you want."

Vik left Forrest where he was and moved into the kitchen. Forrest ogled his ass for a brief second before reminding himself not to be a creep. Opening up a cupboard, Vik lifted out two small glasses and set them on the counter, then proceeded to fill them halfway with the golden liquid.

The single small table was holding up a laptop and several stacks of spiral-bound notebooks. It looked cramped and Forrest's back gave a sympathetic twinge.

"Here," Vik said, holding out one of the tumblers.

Their fingertips brushed against each other when Forrest accepted his drink and sparks of pure lightning-fed lust shot up his arm. Forrest glanced at Vik again and was rewarded by the flare of heat in Vik's gaze.

This *bad* idea was getting worse by the second. Or better if his dick had anything to say about it.

And yet here he was anyway. Alone with Nero Vik. Rufus's words from earlier played in his head. Was he too chicken to start something? Yes.

But also no. Vik was safe; he wouldn't be sticking around, so Forrest wouldn't have to deal with any stupid emotional ties and expectations. Forrest sipped the whisky, savoring the taste of it on his tongue and its heat as it flowed down his throat.

"For godsakes, sit down. You can take the bed. I promise I don't bite."

What if I want you to bite?

"I shouldn't have come," Forrest managed to say over the twitching of his cock. "But Ned Barker was a friend of mine."

"Oh." Remorse and pity filled Vik's gaze. "I'm sorry for your loss. Finding him—that's not something I would wish on anyone."

"And yet you talk about brutal murders all the time."

"Well, yeah, but usually long after the fact." Vik pressed his lips together. "Look, if you're not sitting, I am. After the day I've had, I deserve some whisky." He proceeded to sit down, leaving plenty of space on the bed for Forrest. "See, I *am* a nice guy." He patted the covers.

With a sense of inevitability, Forrest lowered himself down next to Vik. The quivery feeling of anticipation he'd always gotten when accepting a dare ran up his spine. He took another sip of the drink, then awkwardly held the glass in his lap with both hands wrapped around it.

Smooth, Forrest, smooth.

"This place is really small."

Vik acted like he hadn't just pointed out the obvious.

"It is. But at least my stuff is safe from the elements.

Although I think someone broke in last night. I don't suppose it was you?"

Forrest decided not to take offense. "Nope, I was at home. You're not sure you shut your door?"

""I locked it, but the knob is old, so maybe I didn't pull it shut tight enough and the wind blew it open? Not sure. But I suppose the fact that someone rummaged through my things means there really was a break-in. I was just kind of hoping otherwise. And, no, I didn't report it."

"You should. It could've been kids, but I haven't heard Lani complaining about anything like that recently."

"I suppose. It just seems silly since nothing was taken."

They fell into silence. He didn't know what Vik was thinking about, but Forrest was imagining Vik spread out underneath him. Or over him. Forrest wasn't terribly picky. His stupid cock enjoyed those images.

"Was your stuff not safe before?" he asked, trying to stop himself from just jumping Vik now.

Vik waggled his head, and Forrest was distracted with wondering what those curls would feel like against his skin. "I was living out of my car for a bit after I arrived here. Poor planning on my part, really. I tend to make spur-of-the-moment decisions."

"Where'd you drive from?" Forrest asked, instead of *just how spur of the moment*? His cock did not like the question Forrest ended up choosing.

"Indiana. Left the ex-boyfriend and haven't looked back."

Forrest's damn cock twitched again. Ex-boyfriend meant that Vik might be open to some commitment-free sex. He tossed back the rest of his whisky like it was water. He could work with this.

"Another?" Vik's eyes glittered.

"Yeah, sure. Thanks."

His reluctant host finished his drink, rose to his feet, and sauntered into the kitchen. Forrest couldn't take his eyes off Vik's butt, the worn denim leaving little to his imagination. The only thing better would be his *naked* ass.

Glancing up, Forrest caught Vik looking over his shoulder at him. *Busted.*

"Here you go," he said, handing Forrest his second drink and sitting back down. "Nothing like good whisky on a dark and rainy night." His voice sounded a bit raspy, and irritatingly sexy.

Forrest nodded, wondering what the hell he thought he was doing. Vik was The Enemy. The one who could destroy him. Except he didn't look or feel like the enemy at the moment. And somehow, it was Vik controlling the narrative now. How had that happened?

Reaching up, Vik set his whisky on the kitchen counter— that's how small the cabin was. Then he proceeded to take Forrest's glass from his suddenly weak fingers and set it next to his.

Forrest felt like he was dreaming, having an out-of-body experience. He was normally the one in charge, the one pushing everything to the next level. Right now, he felt a bit lightheaded and slightly discombobulated, and he wasn't sure what to do with that.

He'd been the one to come to Vik's door though, hadn't he? He had no one to blame but himself.

"Is this all right?" Vik asked. His voice was rough.

Forrest nodded and managed to force out an equally rough, "Yeah."

Vik curved a hand around the back of Forrest's neck and pulled him close, close enough that Forrest could smell the drink on his breath in the seconds before their lips met.

Without letting himself think too hard about what they were doing—*what did they think they were doing?*—Forrest parted his lips to better taste Vik, who closed the gap between them so there was no space between their bodies. The heat of Nero Vik made Forrest dizzy. It made him want.

His groan was matched by Vik's, who brought both hands around to cup Forrest's face without breaking the kiss. Forrest didn't know what to do with his own hands. Of their own accord, they tucked under the hem of Vik's t-shirt and, as they used to say, his fingers did the walking. Or was it talking?

"Shit, those are cold. And that tickles."

"Fuck, sorry." He started to pull away.

"No, put them back. They'll warm up," Vik whispered against his lips.

There was no chance in hell Forrest was stopping now. He ran his hands across Vik's abdomen and up his ribs. His fingers brushed against Nero's taut nipples, frustrating Forrest because he wanted more skin.

"Shirts off," Vik murmured.

God, yes. Good idea.

Pulling back and reaching over his head, Forrest grabbed his own shirt and tugged it off his body, then threw it toward the small table. Vik did the same, revealing the chest Forrest had just been caressing. Forrest took a millisecond to admire what he saw before placing his hands on Vik's shoulders and pushing him back onto the bed.

The mattress was small, just a double, but they somewhat managed to fit.

"Spread your legs," Forrest whispered. As it was, one of them was going to fall off.

Vik obeyed and Forrest settled himself on top of him. They both wore jeans that were damp from arguing in the rain, but that didn't stop their erections from brushing against each other. Pulses of need shot through Forrest, making him moan.

"Not enough," Vik said. "Naked. All the way naked."

Forrest didn't argue. He craved skin on skin too much to put up a fight. They struggled to divest themselves of soggy jeans and boxers but were finally naked moments later.

Vik lay back and Forrest covered him with his body again. Closing his eyes, he found Vik's lips with his. The lips parted and Forrest delved inside. The taste of drink still lingered. Forrest pushed his tongue as far inside Vik's mouth as he could, swirling across his palate, feeling the pattern of his gums, enjoying the lingering flavor of the whisky. They sparred briefly, tongues fighting for dominance.

Arching his back and thrusting into Forrest, Vik captured Forrest's tongue and began sucking on it. Forrest's body seized and he had to hold his breath, forcing himself not to immediately release all over Vik.

Vik pulled back. "You okay?" he asked.

"Fine," Forrest managed. "It's just, it's been a while."

"Well, then, let's not make you wait any longer." Vik grinned.

Spreading his legs even further apart, he slid a hand between their hips. Forrest lifted up slightly to make whatever the man planned happen a little easier.

"I don't have any condoms and haven't had a well check since the ex. Didn't expect to find someone like you in Cooper Springs," he told Forrest as he wrapped his fingers around Forrest's aching cock. "I think we can make do though."

Forrest wanted to protest that they both needed to come. But he didn't want Vik to stop what he was doing; he'd take care of Vik after.

"Raise your ass and fuck into my fist."

A burst of precome forced itself out his tip.

"Ah, you like that idea. Come on."

Locking eyes with Vik, Forrest lifted his hips into the air.

For the first time in a very long while, he wanted to bottom. He wanted to feel Vik's cock in his ass, burrowing inside of him.

"What are you thinking about?"

"Your cock. My ass."

Vik's eyes widened. "Fuck, that sounds good."

With that, Vik began to stoke Forrest with a furious intensity that had his already tight ball sac rock hard and ready to blow.

"Jesus."

"No, just little old Nero Vik."

Forrest didn't have time to respond or the wherewithal to even roll his eyes. Vik did one last fancy move—down, back up, a twist at the top—and Forrest couldn't hold back any longer. With a shout, he came, long ropes of come pulsing from his very core and landing on Vik's chest and stomach. Vik kept his hand moving but slowed until he was simply caressing Forrest's softening cock. At last, Forrest sat back on his haunches and gently moved Vik's hand away.

"My turn. You look good wearing nothing but my come."

Vik smiled, shifting on the bed so his thick cock bounced. "That's what all the boys say."

Forrest wanted to be irritated by his comment, but he was too blissed out by endorphins and a happy cock. Instead, he shot Vik a glance with one raised brow, scooted backward, and sucked Vik's cock down his throat.

"Oh my god!" Vik shouted, arching upward. "Warn a guy."

Smiling, spit dribbling from his lips, Forrest did not stop. He kept sucking, taking Vik in as far as he could—no gag reflex made it easy. Vik writhed underneath him, begging for release. Maybe just begging, Forrest couldn't be sure.

"Cooper," Vik said in warning. "Gonna come."

Forrest ignored him and instead sucking harder. Seconds

later, he was rewarded with a flood of come across his tongue and down his throat. He swallowed, of course.

Letting Vik's spent cock slip from his lips, Forrest rolled to the wall side of the bed.

"That was..."

"Great?" Forrest prompted.

"Great," Nero repeated with a laugh. "Unexpected and yeah, great."

A fierce gust of wind blew up. The windows rattled and the door vibrated in its frame. Raindrops smacked against the panes, leaving streaks behind as the water ran downward like tears.

Forrest caught Vik's eye. "We still need to talk."

Nero stilled.

"About what happened today. About Ned Barker."

TEN

Nero – Late Thursday Night

"What kind of things about Ned Barker?" Nero asked reluctantly, relaxed from an intense orgasm and also exhausted by the long-ass day. "There's not much to tell you, really. In case you don't know, I left a polite message on your answering machine a while back—with my cell number. We could've talked on the phone instead of you ambushing me." Nero stopped for a second. "Not that I'm complaining about the surprise sex."

A sex ambush by Forrest Cooper was now Nero's weakness.

"I didn't get the message until this morning."

Nero suspected he'd deleted the message and was low-key tempted to call him on it.

"And what does that have to do with me?"

He didn't want to be mad after mind-blowing sex but there he was, already getting vaguely pissed off. On the other hand, perhaps being pissed off by Forrest Cooper was just an expected state of mind. He was going to have to ask Magnus.

"Well?" he prompted when Cooper didn't immediately answer.

Forrest nibbled at his bottom lip before appearing to come to a decision. What Nero would give to know what the man was *really* thinking. What he was really worried about, more like it.

"I want to know what happened earlier today and the real reason you're in town." Forrest looked up at the ceiling before continuing. "Ned Barker was someone I considered a friend. He and my grandfather were friends too. I want to know what happened to him and if the reason you're in town has anything to do with his death."

"How would I know if the reason I'm here has something to do with Barker's death? I didn't know him; I'd never met him or seen him except when he was driving the mail van. And then I can only assume it was him. It's not like I saw the driver."

Besides, if Forrest had been listening in at the pub, he already knew the "real" reason Nero was in Cooper Springs. But if it made him feel better to rehash it all, he would.

Forrest nodded and his eyes narrowed. "Keep talking."

Over the years, Nero had learned that sharing what had happened to Donny often made the witnesses he interviewed less hesitant to talk to him. They were victims together. Nero may not have been abducted that day, but his childhood had been brutally stolen. In this case, Nero had no idea if his story would make Forrest more or less willing to trust that what Nero told him was the truth, but it was worth a try.

Blowing out a big breath, Nero began. "A long time ago, my cousin disappeared. I was fourteen. He was abducted and I was the only witness."

A look of horror crossed Forrest's face. "Oh, shit, that's awful."

"It was. The event basically split my life into two parts. Before and After." Before, when Nero had been just a boy on the cusp of adulthood. After, when he'd learned just how evil humankind was. And how frail hope was.

"So, let's fast forward." Nero rolled onto his side to be more comfortable, pulling the cover over them both. This was perhaps the oddest post-sex conversation he'd ever had. And he'd had some weird ones. The major exception was Austin and frankly, Nero should have seen that as a sign.

"In college, I took a class in forensic anthropology—it wasn't the big field it is now—and things kind of went from there. My degree isn't in forensics but journalism. I am the king of lost causes. But, because of Donny, I always read up on missing persons and, by extension, Doe cases here in the US. Stranger kidnappings like Donny's are rare, but there are lots of unidentified remains. Which is how the podcast came about. It was just a side gig up until I was laid off this past fall."

Forrest nodded. "Okay, so you were laid off and just randomly decided to move to Cooper Springs?"

"Why does it matter?"

Forrest shrugged. "It doesn't, I guess. But I want to hear the whole story."

"Okay. A few years ago, a forensic anthropologist friend of mine, Lindsay Horton, and I helped out on a Doe case in Florida. It was our first success. That's the one Tim Dennis was talking about the other day at the pub. All the police had was a femur that had been stored in a freezer since 1988 and where it had been found by some schoolgirls. It took over a year and an incredible amount of legwork, interviews, and eventually DNA testing that led to a positive family match. But we were finally able to give their siblings closure. In the back of my head, I'm hoping someday to find my cousin. But even if I don't, I get to help other families lay their relatives to rest. I ran across a news story about the bones recently found around here. I want to know if they could be Donny's and if they aren't, I'd like to find out who they belong to."

Cooper frowned. "But seriously, why a podcast? Seems grim."

"I get that question a lot," Nero responded, smiling. "I think you'd be surprised how many people are fascinated by true crime. Crime podcasting isn't without issues, of course. Poorly done, it can be exploitative, sensationalist and—most disgusting of all—create celebrities out of killers. But on the whole, I think the good outweighs the bad, especially when justice is served. And who knows? Maybe I can make a living at it."

So many families kept their lives on hold while they waited for a loved one to walk through the door. Nero's aunt had been waiting for her baby boy to come home for almost twenty-five years.

"I guess that's not really surprising if what's on TV is anything to go by." Forrest's tone was trending back toward thoughtful instead of belligerent.

Suddenly it felt very important for Nero to convince Forrest Cooper that what he did was important. One victim, one Doe, at a time, he was making a difference. This was his chance to make his case.

"That's true. But what we see on TV is the tiniest fraction of cases involving missing persons. And don't get me started on all the fictional bullshit. The most recent estimates conclude that there are around eighty thousand missing persons on record and forty thousand Doe files in the US. Those numbers are since data began being collected, of course."

Watching Forrest's profile, Nero saw the other man purse his lips and let himself remember how they'd felt on his cock.

"Of course," Forrest repeated. "And probably some of the missing are the unidentified, right? So there's overlap. But there are tons of people who are never reported missing because they're estranged from their family, ran away, or"—he waved a hand—"whatever. You said you're a reporter too."

"Investigative reporter, yeah. Well, I was an investigative journalist. Got laid off in the last round of budget cuts." Nero tried not to sound bitter about it, but he was. He'd loved his job, even when his bosses had driven him crazy. "I didn't come up with this, but some folks call the unreported the *un-missing*. It kind of gives me the creeps to think about."

Forrest didn't respond right away and Nero wanted to know what he was contemplating. The man seemed like the kind of person who took their time deciding things—when they were important anyway. Otherwise, Forrest was most likely the King of Shooting His Mouth Off.

"You help figure out what happened to Ned," Forrest finally said, "and I'll give you that interview you want. You can ask me anything you can think of."

"I'm a reporter, not a trained investigator. I've helped identify people, but I've never been involved in something current."

"Tomato, Tomahtoe. You have experience investigating things. I want Ned's murder solved. Seems to reason."

"Seems to reason?" Nero's voice rose. "What about the police? Don't you think they'll be mad if I butt in?"

He'd already been planning on poking around, but there was no reason to tell Forrest that.

"If *we* butt in, as in you and me together, because I'm going to be in your pocket. I can get you in to talk to people who might not want to otherwise. And this way I can keep my eye on you. Ned Barker doesn't need his personal life dissected on a podcast. Besides, Cooper Springs PD is shorthanded at the moment. Dear may not approve of us asking around, but he and Lani aren't superheroes."

"I don't think you'd fit in my pocket," Nero snarked. He decided to ignore the part about Forrest keeping his eye on

Nero. Trust was still clearly going to be an issue, and he wanted to learn Forrest's story; from what little he knew, Nero had a feeling it would be interesting. But he'd do this side quest first if that was what needed to happen.

"Is that a yes, a no, or a maybe?" Forrest asked. "Should we try and see what'll fit in your pocket?" He waggled his hips, drawing Nero's attention to his cock and making him snort.

Was Nero horny and hoping for more, or was he out of his mind to even consider agreeing to this proposition? Eyeing Forrest, Nero couldn't decide which it was. Forrest eyed him back and very deliberately ran his tongue across the lips that Nero had stolen a glance at earlier.

Both. Absolutely both.

The temperature in the cabin was suddenly stifling. Again. It was stifling again.

"I need to use the bathroom," Cooper announced.

Nero rolled over and sat up. "Right there. Not hard to find."

He rose to his feet, stretched—giving Nero a nice view—and glanced around the cabin again. Then he froze with his arms over his head.

"Where did you get that?" Forrest asked.

It took Nero's brain a couple of seconds to get back online. "Get what?"

Leaning across Nero, Forrest plucked the grass hoop that he'd left on the breakfast bar.

"This."

ELEVEN

Forrest – Thursday Evening

Forrest stared down at the grass circlet. He was lightheaded and needed to sit down. His heart crashed against his ribs—or maybe it was trying to claw its way out through his esophagus—but Nero was watching him closely, so he tried to school his expression.

"Where did you get this?" he repeated, sitting back down on the bed next to Nero. His voice shook no matter how hard he tried to stop it.

"Are you alright?" Nero asked. "I found it on my steps just before you showed up tonight. Do you know what it is?"

Forrest looked up from the bits of dried grass shaped into a crude circle that he held in his hand. Another wave of dizziness washed over him. Déjà vu.

What the fuck was this? How come Nero Vik had this in his cabin?

"Cooper?" Nero said his name quietly as if he was afraid of startling him.

"You found this? Just now?" He did his best to sound perfectly normal and figured he'd failed.

Vik nodded. "I was working and heard a noise—well, I thought someone knocked—but when I opened the door, there was no one there. Just that bracelet thingy. Are you sure you're alright? You look pale."

Forrest shook off the uncomfortable feeling that he'd somehow traveled back in time. "I'm fine. Low blood sugar. Just hungry," he replied. "It looks like something a kid would make, doesn't it?" Looking over at Nero again, he added, "Call me Forrest, alright? You say Cooper and I keep waiting to hear Springs afterward."

"Sure, okay. Forrest. Call me Nero."

From the skeptical tone and matching expression on Nero's face, Forrest hadn't been very convincing with his excuse.

"So," he said, wanting to get as far away from the artifact as possible. If the cabin had had a fireplace, he would have burned the thing. "How should we get started on our investigation?" He nonchalantly set the band of weeds back where he'd found it. As if it wasn't the most terrifying thing he'd laid eyes on in decades.

Since coming down from The Deep.

He earned himself another look from Nero, who was obviously aware that Forrest didn't want to talk about the bracelet.

"There are rules." Nero tapped the tip of one index finger with the other. "First of all, we are not the Hardy Boys. Or Starsky and Hutch. Or Cagney and Lacey. Or any other buddy detective pairing that I can think of." He tapped his middle finger this time. "Second, I'm in charge. Think Magnum or Sherlock. And, third, that makes you the sidekick. Understood?"

Forrest opened his mouth to protest but Nero held up his hand, stopping what Forrest had been about to say, which was, *In your fucking dreams.* Something else occurred to him, something that wasn't pertinent, but that he was now insanely curious about.

"I need to learn everything there is to know about Ned Barker," Nero continued. "Since he was friends with your family, you get to tell me everything you can think of."

"Wait a sec."

"Wait a sec, why?"

"My grandpa loved dime-store detective novels. He collected them. Wanda used to set aside any that came into the shop."

Forrest pictured the bookshelves Ernst had built into the living room walls. They were still packed with old-school paperbacks that his grandfather had loved. Their covers mostly depicted scantily clad women and fierce-looking manly men with guns, and one series had featured an extremely rotund man who was almost as smart as Sherlock Holmes.

Forrest had devoured them all in just a few months when he'd first come to live with Ernst because there'd been nothing else to read in the house.

Nero's expression was resigned, like he knew where the conversation was going. "Why is this important, Forrest?"

"Just wondering. Are you by chance named after the great Nero Wolfe?"

Nero visibly deflated. "Do you know how many people have ever asked me that? Maybe three." Now he was scowling at Forrest. It was very sexy.

"Well?" Forrest prodded, trying not to grin.

"Fine. Yes. Are you happy now? I was named for a fictional character who had a sidekick named Archie. Shall I call you Archie?" He raised his eyebrows.

"Hell, no. And hey, at least you're not named after a stand of trees."

Nero perked up. "'True. What about your sister? Where did her name come from?"

"No idea. Our mother's twisted imagination?" He did not want to talk about his mother. "Maybe she let Witt name her."

"And Witt was your father?"

Forrest was pretty sure Nero knew the answer to that, but he'd play along, sort of. He wanted to trust Nero Vik now, but years of ingrained suspicion of humanity at large was hard to fight.

"Yes, but remember the deal. You help get to the bottom of Ned's murder first."

Forrest could tell Nero wanted to ask more questions, but if they went down this road, it might be hard to get back to their true purpose.

Nero rolled his eyes and sighed. "So, Archie, what's the plan?"

Forrest tried not to grin. "You're the hotshot investigator."

"Then sorry, but we start with you. Tell me about that bracelet. Why would someone leave it on my doorstep? Also, I need to get dressed. It's hard for me to take myself seriously while naked."

Nero rolled off the bed and beelined for a three-drawer dresser against the wall. Forrest did not avert his eyes. Nero Vik was incredibly sexy. While the other man dug out fresh clothing, Forrest snatched his jeans up off the floor and forced his legs back into the damp denim, then pulled his long-sleeved t-shirt back over his head.

"Ready?" Nero asked. "Sorry, I don't have a clothes dryer here."

"Meh, they'll warm up in a minute." He sat back down on the messy covers and leaned back on his hands.

"Spit it out, Cooper. What's with the bracelet?"

Nero came over to stand next to the bed. The expression on

his face told Forrest he wasn't letting him bluff his way out of answering.

He tried anyway. "Why start with that?"

Nero already thought Forrest was weird; if he shared his suspicions, Nero was going to think he'd been watching too many reruns of X-Files or Twilight Zone. Forrest didn't watch TV though. He could just replay the crazy shit in his head.

"Because if we're doing this, I need to know everything. That"—Nero pointed at the seemingly innocuous hoop—"freaked you out. Investigative reporter, remember? So what is it?"

Forrest glanced at the grass circlet again, hating its existence. "It can't be important." He didn't want it to be important. He needed it to be a fluke.

"You don't get to decide what is important and what isn't," Nero said with more than a tinge of exasperation. "If you want to try and bring Ned Barker justice, we need to look at everything. Every angle. All the facts. No stone unturned."

"I get the point, no need to pummel me with it."

Nero ignored his attempt at humor. "Who were Ned's other friends? What were his hobbies? In my opinion, it's unlikely that some random stranger attacked him."

Forrest let out a groan and flopped all the way down onto the mattress.

"Start by explaining that bracelet."

"Ugh, fine. It's something Dina used to do. She'd make grass things like that and leave them for us to find. She said they were secret messages. Dina was odd, to put it lightly, and not in an endearing way. But honestly, Vi—Nero, it's something a kid would make."

Nero narrowed his eyes, clearly mulling over what Forrest had shared. "If that's the case, why does it scare you?"

Sitting up again, Forrest raked one hand through his hair

and tried not to shout in the confines of the tiny cabin. "Because I have a ridiculous fear that my crazy-ass mother is still alive and living in the woods, okay? And I'm not okay with that."

Forrest tried to take a deep breath but failed. Instead, he was covered with sweat and it felt like his heart was trying to fight its way out of his chest.

"I have recurring nightmares that she's still out there. My dreams are memories, I think, things that I can't remember when I'm awake. They scare the crap out of me. I have to keep telling myself that she can't be out there any longer. It's been decades, for godsakes."

Fuck. His hand was shaking slightly, so he clenched it into a fist.

Nero grabbed it, holding the fist in a tight grip. "Sorry for pushing—it's a bad habit. We'll set the *whatever it is* aside for now."

The vise around Forrest's lungs loosened ever so slightly.

TWELVE

Forrest – Friday Afternoon

"What?" Forrest snapped into the receiver.

"Get your ass into town. Chief Dear is making an announcement in half an hour," Magnus said. "He says it will be quick, which is good because he's messing up my afternoon rush."

What afternoon rush? Forrest almost asked. But for once in his life, he held his tongue. Then recalled what Nero had done with *his* tongue last night. He wanted more, which could be a problem. He'd let future Forrest solve it; right now he needed to get to the Steam Donkey.

"They found Ned's killer already?" he asked, tossing the book he'd been staring at—but not reading—to the floor. Instead, he'd been rehashing what had happened last night with Nero. *Over My Dead Body* landed face down, the block letters NERO WOLFE staring back at him. Yeah, he was a sucker.

It was a damn good thing he'd switched his truck to biodiesel. He'd be bankrupt driving to and from town every time he turned around. Fuck anyone who didn't like the smell of french fries.

"No. The DNA results are back from the bones Jayden Harlow found back in the fall and the ones Nick and Martin found up on Crook's Trail in January, so Dear's calling a town meeting. I guess he's doing his best to make sure that us common folk have the correct information."

Magnus liked Chief Dear, so something else must have been bothering him. Maybe he and Rufus had argued.

"I'll be there in fifteen minutes." He probably needed to find clean clothes to put on.

Fuck that. This was Cooper Springs, not New York city.

Racing to his bedroom, he glanced around and then pulled a pair of jeans out of the clothes hamper. He rummaged in his top dresser drawer and came up with a clean t-shirt decorated with an illustration of a T-Rex with grabby arms declaring *Now I am Unstoppable* across the front. After slipping his bare feet into a pair of ratty Vans, Forrest searched around the living room for the keys to his truck, only to find them right where he'd left them—hidden between the cushions of the couch.

It took a record twelve minutes for him to drive to the pub. When he arrived, Forrest swore loudly and colorfully. The parking lot was full.

Since everyone who could make it was already parked and heading inside, the closest spot he could see was at the resort. Impatiently huffing, Forrest gunned the truck further down the highway and pulled into the resort's lot, pretending he didn't see the Residents and Overnight Guests Only sign. Martin and Nick would know why he'd parked there.

After he locked up his vehicle, Forrest shivered and jammed his hands into his pockets while he waited for a couple of cars and an RV to drive by. As he started to cross, he thought he heard someone call out his name, but he didn't stop. He didn't want to miss what Chief Dear had to say. Besides, he told himself, it also could have been his imagination.

The Steam Donkey was packed with Cooper Springs citizens. After looking around, Forrest contented himself with sliding into an open spot against the back wall.

"Cooper," Dante Castone greeted him as they crowded in elbow to elbow.

"Castone. I suppose you know what Chief Dear is going to say?"

"Actually, Andre's pretty careful about what he shares with me. He just told me I might want to be here. I knew something was going on, though, because he got an early phone call and left right afterward. At first, I thought it was about what happened yesterday, but he assured me this is totally separate."

Fuck, Ned had been dead over twenty-four hours already.

"Ah," was the only thing Forrest could think of to say. He hadn't forgotten, of course. In fact, he'd been awake most of the night thinking about it and what he probably needed to share with Nero.

Nero, who he'd very nearly almost practically fucked. For the first time in his adult life, he hadn't felt an immediate need to leave. The mattress had pushed him out. The bed was too small for the both of them, and Nero had claimed he needed to get some sleep if they were going to be sleuthing today.

Across the room, Chief Dear stepped up onto the low dais where, very occasionally, the Steam Donkey hosted open mic nights and, even more rarely, talented musicians. Knowing Xavier, he was probably already working on bringing actual bands to Cooper Springs too. Critter and Mags, the two permanent staff forest service officers, stood off to one side. They'd helped to retrieve the remains last fall and in January. Forrest knew they felt a certain responsibility toward them.

Dear tapped the microphone. "Is this thing working?"

"Yes," Dante said, smirking while a few other people also chimed in.

The mic squealed. Forrest made a note to tell Xavier he needed to upgrade the sound system if he was serious about bringing music in. The crowd hushed and Forrest snickered at Mags smacking Critter when he didn't immediately stop talking to someone Forrest couldn't see.

"Good." Dear nodded. "I'm sure there will be questions, but if you could hold them until I finish, that would be much appreciated. And even then, I will only answer what I can, which isn't a lot."

The door near Forrest opened to admit a few more people, one of whom was Nero. Nero caught Forrest's glance and winked but turned the other direction, squeezing in next to Tim Dennis and Xavier, who'd stationed themselves by the window. Forrest hadn't seen them when he'd arrived. Xavier waggled his fingers in Forrest's direction.

Winked at him?

The PA system crackled again and Forrest turned his attention back to the Cooper Springs police chief.

"Alright, I'm going to make this as quick as possible. Otherwise, we'll have to shut the pub down for being over capacity and we don't want that."

There were a few titters and throat clearings before absolute silence fell again as everyone in the building waited to hear what Dear had to say.

"I'm standing before you today with good news and bad news. First off, please know that the parties concerned have already been notified, so there's no reason for any of you to call or text them. Be polite. Give them time to process and grieve." Dear glared around at his audience, daring them to disobey him. "With great sorrow, I'm here to tell you that the remains found in January and last fall have been officially identified. Using DNA sampling and the hard work of genealogy volunteers, we now know their names, and Morgan Blass and Sarah Turner will be returned to their loved ones."

The crowd murmured but Dear kept talking, speaking over the rule-breakers.

"Sarah was barely seventeen when she left her home in the summer of 1988 and never returned. In the spring of 1989, Morgan Blass, aged nineteen, also disappeared, never to be seen or heard from again."

The rumble of the crowd increased. Dear raised his hand, asking for quiet. Forrest realized he was quietly grinding his teeth and tried to relax his jaw. He didn't know what other kind of evidence, if any, had been found. Would there be something that would definitively tell Forrest he wasn't wrong to think the girls could have been killed by one of his parents? Sometimes when he dreamed, there was a girl's voice, but he could never make out what she was saying.

"As I said, the relatives have been notified. Please give them —especially those who continue to reside in Cooper Springs— time to process these developments."

"Who did it, Chief? Did you figure that out?"

Forrest couldn't see who'd asked that ridiculous question, but there was always one. Dante caught Forrest's glare, grunted, and rolled his eyes in agreement.

"At this point, there are no leads," the chief responded with a great deal more calm than Forrest would've been able to muster. Maybe it was a good thing he'd decided against working in the public sector. Lavender didn't talk back, and it was known for its calming qualities. "A great deal has changed when it comes to policing and forensic science, but I like to think that every effort was made at the time of their disappearances to find out what happened. That is all the information I have for you today."

When the audience realized that Dear wasn't going to say

anything further, people began filing out of the pub, heading back to their normally scheduled lives. As they passed by, Forrest heard snatches of conversations that included ideas about what might have happened to the girls, questions on whether there would be a public memorial, and the occasional and obligatory *I always knew something bad had happened.* Forrest headed to the bar. He needed a cup of coffee and while the stuff they served to the public was generally terrible, Magnus usually had a pot of it on the warmer.

Forrest noticed Rufus still sitting at his spot near the end of the bar, a shocked expression on his face.

"What's up? Are you okay?" Forrest asked, a little worried.

Was it possible that Rufus had known the girls and their families? Forrest wondered. He probably had. Forrest glanced around; Magnus was over talking to the chief by the stage, probably trying to see if that was really all he had to tell them.

"You look a little pale. Should I call Magnus over?"

"No thanks. I just..." The older man didn't continue, just shook his head.

"What's up? Rufus, you have me worried. I'm gonna be calling someone anyway." Finally, Rufus directed his gaze at Forrest. His hazel eyes were watery, as if he was about to cry.

"Did you know the girls?" Forrest asked. He hadn't; he and Lani had been living with their parents in The Deep around that time.

"No, no, I didn't." Rufus shook his head. "Not really, not more than a passing hello. But I always thought they'd run away to find a better life than what Cooper Springs had to offer them. Thought maybe they'd met a sailor or soldier, traveled off to distant lands." His voice broke on the last word and he stared at Forrest, his expression shattered.

"How could you have known?" Forrest asked. "How could anyone have known who the remains belonged to?"

"We could've listened to Amy Blass, who insisted her Morgan would never just leave. Same with Sarah—I think she wanted to be a veterinarian, was planning to apply at WSU if I remember right."

"Rufus, you couldn't have known it was them," Forrest insisted. His heart pinched at the devastated expression in Rufus's eyes.

"And now Ned's gone too, the same way as Ernst. Forrest, I should have known."

Forrest eyed the older man, wondering if the identity of the girls was all he was worrying over. He opened his mouth, intending to ask if Rufus thought Witt or Dina could still be alive and living in the woods. But he chickened out; it was too ridiculous. Rufus would just tell him he was overthinking, that Forrest's nightmares were thirty-five years old and had little basis in reality.

"You couldn't have known anything," Forrest repeated instead, swiveling to look over his shoulder, intent on getting Magnus's attention. The publican was nowhere in sight, probably out chatting with folks still milling around in the parking area.

When Forrest turned back, Rufus's seat was empty, and Forrest spotted him making his way out the front door. Damn, the old man could move quickly. It was easy to forget Rufus still hiked the woods on a regular basis, something he'd done since he was a young boy.

The comment about Ernst bothered Forrest; he didn't want there to be a connection between the two deaths, even if Nero had suggested it last night. He didn't want Ned dead at all.

If his grandpa's death hadn't been an accident, had the same person killed them both? If so, why? And why wait almost twenty years between the two?

Forrest was tempted to chase after Rufus but decided

against it. He'd stop by his or Wanda's place later and check in on him. Maybe Rufus just needed time to process the news. In the meantime, Nero Vik was lingering by the door and talking with Tim and Xavier.

Forrest scowled. He suspected Tim Dennis was a player—he was friends with Xavier, after all. Maybe he and Nero weren't a thing, but he didn't want Tim Dennis looking at him, either.

"Seriously, Forrest, maybe you should haul him off somewhere private and take care of that itch." Magnus's voice made Forrest jump.

Forrest hadn't noticed that the asshole had returned to his post behind the bar. No way was he going to publicly admit that he and Nero already been there, done that, and that, even worse, he wanted more. Wanting more wasn't what Forrest *did*. And Nero probably wasn't sticking around anyway.

Forrest wondered if he wanted him to.

Crap. Did he *want* Nero to stick around? Had Magnus seen his truck over there last night? Probably, but it was too late to fix that now.

"Fuck you. What's up with Rufus?"

"What do you mean, what's up with Rufus?" Magnus looked around. "And where is he?"

"He left." Forrest gestured the direction most everyone, including Rufus, had headed. "Seemed a bit off. Definitely shaken up by the news."

"I think we all are, aren't you? Those poor girls, up there all this time. I was in high school the same time as they were." Magnus frowned, something Forrest wasn't used to.

"Yeah, but... *more* shook up. I can't explain it."

Magnus stared at him for an extra beat, seemed to realize Forrest was serious, and came to a conclusion.

"Keep an eye on the bar for a minute. I'll find out what's going on."

"Me?" He looked around to see if there was someone else Magnus might be talking to. But no, it was just him. Most of the townies who'd stopped in to hear the announcement were already gone.

Magnus rolled his eyes. "Yes, you."

After untying the half apron he wore, Magnus tossed it on the bar as he came around to the seating area and headed to the exit.

"Hurry up. Can't just sit there and twiddle your thumbs."

Bemused, Forrest slipped off the stool and moved to stand behind the bar until Magnus returned.

He stood there and watched the stragglers depart, not sure what to do with himself. Now he knew why Magnus was wiping the bar down all the time; it gave him something to do with his hands.

Forrest noticed Xavier and his suspect college friend had left already, but Nero wandered over to stand at the end of the counter.

Forrest blinked.

He wanted to kiss him. In public. The realization rattled him. He'd hated him at first sight, he'd avoided him as much as possible, and now he wanted to kiss him? In *public*?

"What are you doing?" Forrest asked instead of performing unnecessary mouth-to-mouth resuscitation. He was curious if, in the hours since Forrest had slunk back to the farm, Nero had discovered anything. Maybe he had needed to sleep; it had been well after midnight by the time Forrest had left. Nero needed to be investigating, not lingering at the pub.

Nero overtly glanced around. "The same as you, I think."

He also looked like he was trying not to smile, which both irritated and turned Forrest on. Maybe he was starting to understand why Xavier had been so fucking *weird* last fall when he'd opened his eyes and really seen Vincent Barone.

"Have you found anything out yet?"

"You have a remarkable trust in my skills considering you were bad-mouthing me as recently as yesterday morning."

Forrest leaned across the bar. "I'll bad-mouth you more if you want me to," he murmured.

Nero's cheeks turned red—but so did Forrest's. This kind of talk was not like him.

Finally, Nero broke the only slightly awkward silence between them. "You know, Magnus is much better at this bartender thing than you are. He at least would've asked what I wanted to drink by now."

"Fine. What do you fucking want to drink? Happy?"

Nero stared at him for a minute and then began to laugh. Actually laugh. Nero had a deep chuckle that seemed to reach into the darker part of Forrest's brain and turn it off. His entire body was reacting like he was abruptly tuned into a frequency he'd never experienced before. Forrest gaped at the chuckling, snorting man a few seconds before he also started to snicker. He couldn't stop himself.

"It's not funny." Forrest struggled to get control of himself, but the more he tried the less he could stop himself. When was the last time he'd just laughed? "I make an awful bartender."

"It is funny, and you are terrible," Nero agreed while he wheezed and brayed at the same time, making Forrest laugh harder. "I thought *I* didn't have good people skills. I, at least, come up with good excuses before running out on guys, not, 'This mattress is awfully small, see ya, later.'"

He paused to try and get a breath, which looked to be unsuccessful, but he kept going.

"At least I use excuses like 'Oh, I left my game on pause, and I need to get back to the quest.' Or 'There's a murder from 1965 that I need to help solve.' Guys love it when I use that one. Like I'm a Jessica Fletcher superhero." He mimed peering around and smashing his fingers against the keys of an imaginary typewriter.

"That mattress is too damn small!" Forrest protested quietly. "I'm not a tiny guy. I stay over there and I'm gonna need a chiropractor. You haven't really used getting back to a game as an excuse, have you?"

Those dark eyebrows waggled again. It wasn't charming. It couldn't be.

"I guess that's for me to know and you to find out."

Damn it, it was fucking adorable. Forrest didn't know what to do with himself. He never bantered with hookups, and he *still* wanted to hop over the bar and kiss him. Huffing, he grabbed a pint glass off the shelf, stared at the taps for a second, and then, remembering that he'd ordered it the other day, poured Nero a Tree Hugger IPA. As one does for someone one finds compelling, frustrating, and sexy as hell.

And scary too, a little voice murmured. Because Forrest could see himself breaking his own code with Nero.

"Seriously, have you really used a role-playing game as an excuse?" he asked over his shoulder.

"It was a particularly bad date," Nero said dryly. "And even a bad D&D campaign was more fun than that guy."

The laughter started again. It had been several months—god, maybe even a year, not counting last night—since Forrest had been with anyone. At over an hour's drive away, trips to Olympia may have been hard to fit into his life, but they were much safer. Less chance of running post-hookup into a stranger that he had no intention of ever fucking again. This bantering shit was going to break him.

But maybe this would be okay. Forrest reminded himself

that Nero wouldn't be sticking around once they figured out who'd murdered Ned.

He stopped snickering.

By the time Forrest turned back around, Nero had gotten control of himself too. Somewhat. His laughter having subsided, his shoulders still shook as Nero swiped at his eyes with the cuff of his sweatshirt. Setting the glass down in front of the other man, Forrest turned back and poured a second pint for himself, then set it at the spot next to Nero's.

Fuck it. Fuck that. Fuck finding out that some poor girls had been murdered and buried up on the mountain where his crazy-ass mother had lived and—while he fucking hoped not—she still might.

He'd just sat down when Magnus returned.

"You're fired, and Rufus seems all right," he informed Forrest. "Just shaken up by the news, I think." Plucking his apron from the bartop, he rewrapped it around his hips and secured it. "I'll check on him again once Garth gets here."

After finishing his beer, Forrest considered inviting Nero out to his house—for research only, of course. But he ultimately decided that was too much change too quickly. He didn't invite strangers into his sanctuary.

But he was considering it. Probably would do it at some point. Fuck.

For his part, Nero promised to call Forrest if he discovered anything.

Forrest scowled at this and narrowed his eyes, hoping Nero got the message that he better damn check in.

"Dude, I pinky-promise I will call you first if I learn anything. No need to try and laser me with your eyes."

FORREST HARDLY NOTICED his drive back home, distracted by both the news Chief Dear had shared about the remains and images of fucking Nero Vik. Almost fucking. He had a very good imagination.

Passing by Levi Cruz's place, Forrest pressed on the brakes. Two cars were parked in front of Levi's house. Forrest recognized Levi's beat-up Ford but not the late model SUV. Did Levi buy a new car? He should have known, but they hadn't talked in a while.

Tattered and faded ribbons of all colors had been tied along the fence that ran along the road. They fluttered pathetically in the constant breeze, a testament to Levi's missing younger sister, Blair. Forrest was sure Levi suspected the worst. He tried to imagine what his life would be like without Lani in it and his breath caught. He couldn't do it.

It looked to Forrest like the lights in Levi's house were off. Maybe Levi wasn't home at all. Maybe he was huddled inside, grieving and yelling at the world. That's what Forrest would be doing. Had he heard the news already? Dear or Lani had probably alerted him before the announcement. Forrest hoped so.

What did you say to someone whose family member was missing and had been for months? Whose little sister just disappeared off the face of the earth? There was no Hallmark card for that. Deciding against turning into the drive, Forrest continued up the highway another mile.

Veering right onto the long driveway that ended at his house, Forrest passed by fields of Lavandula angustifolia, Lavandula latifolia, and Lavandula officinalis. Currently, they were just gray mounds but in a few months, they would be a million different shades of lavender, white, and purple.

Purple Phaze Farm was Forrest's pride and joy. He knew he was lucky; there wasn't much similar acreage this far down the peninsula. Sequim, one hundred miles to the north and often referred to as the Palm Springs of the region, was where most of Western Washington's lavender crops grew.

When Ernst Cooper died, he left the house and land to both Forrest and Lani, to which Lani'd reacted with, "Have at it. I'm not interested in dirt." They'd found her a cute cottage in town with very little dirt around it.

Neither of them cared about the small house their mother had been raised in. After all these years, it still sat empty. If any structure could be malevolent, Forrest swore that building was. Maybe it was time to tear it down and build something new in its place.

AS HE APPROACHED HIS RAMBLER, Forrest's phone lit up. But he continued driving past the pay-as-you-go flower kiosk and parked next to the detached garage before checking to see who'd messaged him. He doubted it was Nero, not so soon.

Yes, the bus is still available.

The small frisson of excitement at the text made him feel guilty. Ned was dead, Blair Cruz still missing, and her brother Levi was losing himself to grief.

But a few weeks ago, Forrest had been driving back from his monthly browse at his favorite store in Elma. The owner called it a used bookstore, but he collected and sold everything from vinyl records and guitars to small pieces of furniture and eclectic clothing. Forrest had picked up an AC/DC t-shirt to add to his collection.

On his way back home, he'd taken a different route, one that passed by an old farmstead, and what he hadn't known he'd needed in his life had been parked right there, in front of the barn. Even better, a big For Sale sign was stuck on the side.

A custom-painted 1963 Greyhound bus.

It was love at first sight. Someone with a great deal more

talent than he ever had shown had painted a luscious pink and lavender mermaid along the side and surrounded her with sea stars, octopuses, a few colorful fish, seaweed, and kelp.

The owner hadn't been home but Forrest had dared to trespass, taking a peek through the windows into the interior, which was fully restored and also gorgeous. Before leaving, he'd taken about fifty pictures of it with his phone.

On the way home, he'd come up with a bunch of scenarios to fit the bus in with the farm. He'd keep the mermaid art but have someone transform the seaweed and kelp into strands of lavender, a sea of purple flowers. Maybe Liam could do that kind of work—a true renaissance man, he seemed to be able to do almost anything.

Once they figured out what fucker had murdered Ned Barker.

Ned had seen the photos and immediately loved the bus too.

"Go for it." The mischievous sparkle in his eyes had been bright. Forrest's breath caught at the memory.

Once he was parked, Forrest texted back, offering a lower price but cash up front. Yes, he still felt guilty about being excited when Blair was missing and Ned was lying on a slab somewhere.

But then he thought of Ned's attitude and Blair's smile. If a person wanted to own a custom 1963 Greyhound bus, why not? Life was too short. A person could wake up dead one day.

Five minutes later, Forrest was the proud owner of yet another vintage vehicle. Lani would hate it, for sure. He imagined her scolding him about wasting his money, his safety, and whatever else she could think of.

It wasn't until he automatically stopped at the mailbox only to find it empty that grief turned to anger again.

"Fucking fuck you, whoever is responsible for this."

Ned Barker, Cooper Springs' happiest letter carrier, was

dead, murdered. The man wouldn't be stopping in for lavender iced tea, bitching to Forrest about mailboxes being vandalized by high schoolers or sharing pictures of his grandchildren.

Forrest didn't like small kids that much, but he appreciated that something happened to previously normal adults after children or grandchildren were born. He'd enjoyed teasing Ned about how unfortunate it was that his grandkids had managed to take after him.

Angrily, Forrest slammed the front door shut behind him, hard enough that it rattled in the frame.

Someone was going to pay for this.

Without thinking too deeply about it, he punched the cell number Nero had given him into his landline. With luck, the other man would have service today.

THIRTEEN

Forrest – Saturday Morning

"Thanks for coming."

Nero smirked at him. "It didn't sound like I really had a choice."

"Don't they say the first forty-eight hours are the most important? We're just about in day three. I want answers."

Forrest led the way inside. He hadn't bothered to straighten up the house. Nero was just going to have to deal with Forrest's bachelor mess. Stacks of unread books next to the couch, several empty coffee cups—he spotted one on the bookshelf in the corner—plants that needed watering. He was better at keeping them alive outside, but Lani was always giving them to him anyway.

"It's the first seventy-two hours and it's only been forty-eight, but I understand what you are saying. I'm pretty sure that Hollywood came up with twenty-four hours to justify their shitty plots."

"Where do you want to set up, the kitchen or my office? The kitchen is probably better. I can sit at the table too."

Nero raised one dark eyebrow. "So you can watch my every move? Make sure I don't take too many coffee breaks? I'll work wherever you want me to, but you can't hang over my shoulder. If you do, I'm packing up and heading back to town."

"I won't hang over your shoulder," Forrest said without meaning it. Nero shot him a glance that told him he wasn't fooled, either.

"Alright, so. This is my living room, obviously." He didn't mention the mess. It wasn't going anywhere. "The kitchen is through there." Forrest pointed the other direction. "Bathroom's that way if you need it."

"So, it's *sit my ass down and get to work, Nero* time?"

"Duh."

Forrest led the way into the kitchen and pointed at the table. He liked working there as it was near the sliding door and got a lot of natural light.

"If you sit here, the light won't glare off your laptop screen."

Nero huffed and set his backpack on the table.

"Maybe you can get started on the aforementioned coffee? I don't work well without it. And you can tell me about Ned Barker before I get started. What you tell me could help us find a direction. But remember, this could've just been something random, and those are harder to solve. I'll need your Wi-Fi password."

"WinstonSmithLives."

"What? Is that a reference to *1984*?" Nero looked impressed.

"Yes. Most people don't get that."

Not that he had guests over all the time who needed his password. Well, and Lani got it just fine. She claimed it was another moment of Forrest being ridiculous.

"Most people aren't me."

No, Forrest had to admit that Nero Vik was one of a kind.

As shitty as Forrest had been since he'd come to town—and after Forrest had left abruptly Thursday night—Nero was here, in Forrest's house, ignoring how much of an asshole Forrest could be.

The other man set up his laptop on the table and turned it on, then fished a notebook and a pen out of his bag to put next to the computer while it powered up. He watched Nero's fingers fly over the keys as he typed in the password.

Forrest returned to the subject of Ned's killer. "If this were Seattle or someplace big, I'd consider that maybe some random person is responsible for Ned's death. But Cooper Springs is a small community. And maybe I'd feel different if it was July or August, when people start coming around for vacation, but there aren't many strangers here at this time of year."

"Except for me," Nero pointed out.

"Lani told me they cleared you." Nick had also, but Forrest wasn't going to throw him under the bus. Lani could take care of herself.

"I didn't kill your friend." Nero sounded a tad pissed off that Forrest had even hinted at the possibility.

"I know that *now*," Forrest huffed back. "Look, I'm not the most trusting person in the world. And you put me off-balance."

There. That was the most he was going to admit about how Nero Vik had sent his insides reeling since the moment he'd turned up in Cooper Springs. How close he was to violating his own rules about men.

Nero paused his typing and assessed Forrest from over the laptop screen. Forrest felt the slightest bit uncomfortable but also as if maybe he'd passed a test of some kind.

"Coffee?" Nero finally asked. "Seriously, I'm not typing another letter without a huge cup of hot, steaming coffee within my reach."

"One huge, steaming cup of coffee coming right up." Forrest

turned his attention to the assigned task, thankful the moment had broken. "Do you want anything else?"

FORREST SET THE *BELIEVE—CSBFS* coffee mug where Nero could reach it and took the chair next to him. His cup matched Nero's, both decorated with a silhouette of a Sasquatch set against a simple map of the region with red map pins where there'd been supposed sightings.

Nero stared at the cup, his lips moving as he silently figured out what the letters stood for.

"Ah, yes, Cooper Springs Bigfoot Society. But Bigfoot is one word. Are you a member?" he asked.

"Yeah, but Rufus didn't think BS worked very well for the merch. And of course I am." Forrest scoffed. "Rufus wouldn't let me into the pub if I wasn't a member and in good standing. For most of us, it's a joke, but Rufus is a believer. He doesn't think all the sightings are valid, of course, but he had an experience when he was a boy, and he firmly believes the big guy saved his life."

"That's cool."

"Are you serious?"

"Well, yeah? Why wouldn't I be?"

"A lot of people make fun of the Bigfoot Society and Rufus."

"In case you hadn't noticed, I am not like a lot of other people."

"Oliver Cox is also a member, and Ned was too. My grandpa gave them all endless amounts of shit about it, and they kept trying to convert him."

"So Rufus and Ned were good friends? Maybe I should talk to Rufus about him. I was going to talk to him anyway."

"Sure." Forrest shrugged. "Might be a good idea."

Nero turned in his seat. "So, tell me about the Ned Barker you knew." He picked up the pen, turned to a fresh page in the spiral notebook, and waited for Forrest to begin.

Where did he want to start? It was hard to talk about Ned without bringing in his own early childhood, but maybe Nero had heard something already. Maybe that was why he'd wanted an interview? That seemed far-fetched even for Forrest and his tendency toward conspiracy-theory thinking.

Nero raised his eyebrows when Forrest didn't start speaking right away.

"I'm sorry. I know this is hard for you. You said he was a friend of yours. How about you start with how you met and go from there?"

"It's complicated."

"Most things are."

"I first met Ned—and Rufus—when I was seven. Which was also the first time I met my grandfather."

"Keep talking..."

"There's a lot I don't know because Grandpa never talked about what happened up there. I think he wanted Lani and me to grow up as normal as possible for the most part and thought leaving the past behind was the best way to do that."

If Forrest's nightmares were any indication, Grandpa had been right.

"What I do know, from things he said and what Rufus has told me since he died, is that our dad got involved in a survivalist movement way back when. An end-of-the-world sort of homesteading pioneer movement. His wife—girlfriend, whatever she ended up being—Dina Paulson was a big part of it too. Dina may have been a leader. They left town and moved into the woods. These days we'd call it living off the grid."

Forrest's memory was sketchy, but he remembered practicing

his reading before bed so they must have had some kind of power for light, possibly a generator or a camp light. It could even have been solar power. Expensive, but maybe Dina'd had money.

"I know this doesn't seem to have much to do with Ned, but this is how I know him. He, Rufus, and Oliver Cox were Grandpa's best friends. When I wasn't raising hell in school, I hung out here with them, listening to their stories about, well, Bigfoot and anything else they came up with. Ned was the one that remembered we were kids. He convinced Grandpa that a Happy Meal wouldn't kill us. And he got me my first Halloween costume. It was a clown mask."

Nero shook his head. "How did that go over?"

"That's a story for another time. When Grandpa, uh, died" —Forrest guessed the jury was clearly out now on whether it had really been an accident—"Rufus and Ned stepped in to help us. I was an adult, of course, but they kept me from going completely off the rails. Xavier's mom, Wanda, stepped up too. She invited Lani to live with her. Lani was a senior in high school, so living with me was torture anyway."

"Was Ned married?"

"He was once. They split up a while back, but it was friendly. I know, everyone says that and then it's not. But it was. They kept in touch, and both doted on their grandkids. Ned always said they were better friends than lovers. I imagine Kit— she's Oliver's sister—will help Oliver arrange the funeral or celebration of life."

"So, he was happily divorced, had grandkids, was healthy, had a good job. No enemies that you are aware of?"

Forrest thought. "Not really. He started working the mail route when Oliver's back got fucked up and he couldn't deal with big packages and stuff anymore. Ned would complain about people leaving their dogs out or having attack geese. Stuff like that. People thought he was odd—like they think I'm odd—but no enemies that I know of."

"Would Rufus know more?" Nero asked.

"Probably."

"So, after you and Lani—er, after your grandfather—how did he come to have custody of you anyway? I mean, did he know where his son and grandchildren were living the whole time?"

Forrest blew a puff of air out. He'd never really learned this part of the story.

"You don't have to talk about it. It probably doesn't matter. I just don't like coincidences. I've done a little research and found some information about your grandfather already, but I'd like to hear it from you."

"Yeah, alright." Forrest stood up and ran a hand through his already unruly hair.

"You were the one who found your grandfather, right?"

"I did. Worst fucking day of my life. I'd gone to visit Xav where he'd ended up moving after high school. I can't even remember what we were doing anymore, probably been entirely too stupid. Street racing or sneaking into abandoned buildings somewhere. Being assholes for sure. Neither of us were in good head spaces. Anyway, I dragged my ass home around four in the morning and found him outside."

Forrest remembered it like it had been only yesterday. Parking his car and walking toward the house, confused at first by the odd shape in the semidarkness. When he'd realized it was his grandpa, he'd collapsed to his knees in the gravel, thinking Ernst had fallen, but when Forrest had touched his skin, it had been cold. Too cold.

"Stupid me, thinking he'd live forever. That someday he'd have time to tell me all the stories I wanted to hear. But you asked about custody. To be honest, I don't know if he officially had it. You don't know what a pain it was to just get birth certificates. But Grandpa was a Cooper, so no one in town questioned him. And no one in town liked Dina. What I remember is that—look, this is a crazy-ass story."

"I need to hear everything," Nero said, his eyes practically boring into Forrest.

"Okay. So we lived up there with some other people. Maybe six or seven adults besides Dina and Witt? Honestly, I don't know. Deep Dwellers, that's what Rufus always called them anyway. My folks were self-sufficient and lived off the land. Like I said, survivalists."

"Were you both born up there?"

Forrest nodded. "As far as I know."

"Jesus. I mean, I know women have been giving birth for millions of years, but modern medical care is pretty cool."

They were both quiet for a moment, imagining what it was like to give birth in the middle of the woods.

"I think I was around five when Lani was born," Forrest continued. "My memories are fractured, but I do remember that night. Talk about terrifying. Learned some new curse words too." He smiled. "Don't ever tell her or she'll get a big head, but I loved Lani from the minute I got to hold her. Which is funny because kids really aren't my thing. I don't think they were Dina's either," he added thoughtfully.

"It wasn't like we starved, or that she actually hit us. There were threats though. The first time I met Wanda Stone, I didn't know how to react to a woman who wanted to actually hug me. My dad hugged us all the time, wrestled with me, carried Lani around. But Dina." He twitched.

Talking about Dina made Forrest anxious.

"I wonder why she had kids, then?" Nero asked. "Not that I'm sad you're here."

"No, I've wondered that myself. Maybe it was Witt who

wanted kids? Maybe it was a lack of birth control? Although she was rumored to be a witch, but not the nice kind. I've heard that people used to go to her mother and her for potions and shit like that. I'd be surprised if Dina hadn't known about some natural herb to remedy an accidental pregnancy."

"That's not creepy at all." Forrest caught the slight shiver that went through Nero. "I'm assuming you don't mean love potions?"

"Nope. Anyway, I think the homestead must have been falling apart? Like I said, I was around seven when we came to live with Grandpa. I remember a lot of fighting, loud voices. On one particularly bad night, Witt took us for a walk. We went to a special place, a cave, and he told me it was my job to keep Lani safe. If I heard anything, I was to stay put and keep quiet, that someone was going to come for us. He kissed me on the forehead and that was the last time I remember seeing him."

"And your grandpa came."

Forrest nodded.

"So just to be clear—no sign of your parents since then? Or anyone else from up there?"

"Not that I know of. Look, I've never told anyone this before but—" Forrest paused, not sure what words to use that wouldn't make it sound like he'd completely lost touch with reality. "Sometimes I dream they're still alive, living up there in The Deep. Which can't be true. What I think, for real, is that something very bad happened back then."

"Do you know how Ernst found you? I know there are hundreds of square miles of forest that've basically never been touched."

"Some lost hikers is what I've been told. They had to have veered way off course, but I remember strange voices that I'd never heard before. Like I said, everything is scrambled. I don't even know if I'm remembering stuff in the right order."

"Okay." Nero nodded. "So, Ned Barker. Was he a good enough friend that he might have helped your grandpa find you?"

"Maybe? He had to at least have been aware of any hikers reporting children living in the woods like Hansel and Gretel or something. Only creepier."

Nero picked up the pen again and jotted down what Forrest had told him. Forrest supposed that's what he was doing anyway; his handwriting was a messy scrawl that easily could have been a code.

"I wouldn't consider linking Ned's death with your grandfather's except that everything I've read makes it impossible to ignore."

"But it's been twenty years," Forrest protested. "And almost thirty-five since Lani and I came to live with him."

"Bear with me while I think here."

Forrest watched Nero make his list. Ned Barker, Ernst Cooper, Witt and Dina, Morgan Blass, Kaylee Fernsby, Sarah Turner.

"What about Blair Cruz? Or Lizzy Harlow?" he asked.

Nero added the two names to the bottom of his list, then looked at Forrest with a thoughtful expression.

"Say you were around seven. Your dad was what?"

"Early thirties by then. Dina same, I think."

"Your grandpa was likely in his fifties when he, uh"—Nero was obviously trying to come up with the right word—"brought you here. We can use public records to figure that out. So, maybe midsixties when he died. I know Ned was seventy, not much younger. Twenty years ago he was maybe around fifty, so when you came, he was fortyish?"

"I think Rufus and Ned are close to the same age. Were close."

Forrest pinched the bridge of his nose, hating having to use the past tense.

"My point is that Ned was in great health. He had no issue with his mail route, right? Wasn't going to retire until they forced him out?"

"No matter what Ollie always said, he was never forcing Ned out. Where are you going with this?"

"I don't know, thinking out loud. I just know that Ned Barker didn't kill himself and it wasn't an accident. Let's assume he's a good guy and not connected to the girls' deaths. Ned was also good friends with a man who died years ago in a similar manner, which is weird. He was close to your family. Remains were found up on that mountain that have been identified as young women who went missing during the time a survivalist group was known to be up there. Could be connected. I'd like to find out the other names in the survivalist group, if possible. Have they turned up anywhere else? Are they even still alive? It's a long shot, but what if someone from the group is living in Cooper Springs under an assumed name or something, and Ned recognized them?"

"After all this time? Why? How is this list going to help find who killed Ned? He didn't kill those girls."

"I know it's hard, but we don't know that with certainty. I do tend to think that he didn't."

Forrest released a huff of frustration. "Nothing makes sense." He laughed, adding, "You show up in town and all hell breaks loose."

"Remember the conversation I had with Tim Dennis earlier in the week? Jeez, that seems forever ago. I came to do a story on the remains, on the missing girls of Cooper Springs. I've been here for a while, just kind of settling in and finishing up my most recent podcast. When I finally get around to doing some more in-depth research, there's a fire at Cooper Mansion, which means any records that might have been there are lost now. Any idea yet if it was arson? Maybe you can talk to your sister?"

Forrest nodded.

"Then my place is rifled through, don't know by whom. Ned Barker is found dead—by me. And I have to repeat, I never want to go through something like that again. Oh, and a handmade bracelet thingy that freaks you out shows up on my doorstep."

Forrest groaned; he'd managed to forget about the bracelet.

"I'm not egotistical," Nero continued, "but it feels to me that, due to the timing around my investigation, these incidences are about the remains. We finally learned who they belong to just this morning. Will something else happen? Maybe I'm making connections where there are none, but that's why we want to gather as many facts as possible."

"There's still a chance Ned was killed randomly."

"Do you really believe that?" Nero scoffed. "When his death is so similar to your grandfather's? I don't. If Ned wasn't killed by a stranger, he was killed by someone he knew—duh, I know. Maybe your grandfather was killed by someone he knew, as well? But everyone seems to have liked Ned. Which again leads me to something in the past."

"Yeah, Ned was quirky, but he was kind. He made friends with a raven. Left it treats and sparkly things. The darn bird would wait for him to come around. He told me it would almost be mad at him if he didn't have anything."

"Oh, yeah? That's pretty dang cool. Anyway." Tapping his list, Nero asked, "Are you willing to talk to Ned's ex and ask if he had any enemies?"

"I can do that. I should give her my condolences anyway," Forrest said, even though the last thing he wanted to do was call Kit Blinker nee Barker nee Cox. She lived on Vargas Island in British Columbia, population around thirty unless the uber-exclusive retreat had guests.

"Let's find what she has to say. Maybe we can add to what you know. We should also reach out to Ollie Cox if you think he'll be up for it. It's possible the two groups, dead teens and folks living in the woods, could have nothing to do with each other. But the remains were found fairly far along Crook's Trail. Do you happen to know how close to where you had lived?" He tapped the paper with his pen. "Not that I want to just paint a reclusive group of people with the murder brush."

"I stay the fuck away from those woods if at all possible. But from what Critter and Mags have said, both sets of remains were found off known trails. I don't recall trails other than the ones we made where we lived."

Nero stared at Forrest, but he wasn't seeing him.

"Could any of them still be up there? Or, alternatively, is it possible that one or more of the group returned to town at some point? Would anyone have necessarily recognized them? Logically, they're all dead or have moved out of the area, but maybe not." He shrugged. "If we can cross any of them off the list, it will help. We need to find out all the names of those involved."

Forrest was having trouble breathing. Nero had just jammed his finger into the source of Forrest's greatest fear. Ever since the first remains had been found and Blair Cruz had gone missing, he'd become terrified that Witt and Dina were up there. Still alive. He hated that his memories were incomplete. Worried that the reason he had nightmares was because he'd witnessed something no young boy should.

"How much of all this does your sister know? Does she have similar suspicions?"

"I don't think so," Forrest said after thinking for a second. "She was so small and, surprise to you, I'm sure, I don't like to talk about it."

Nero smirked and rolled his eyes. "You brew us some coffee and call Kit Blinker. I'll get on my murder map."

FOURTEEN

Nero – Saturday

MUMBLING QUIETLY ABOUT caffeine addicts but working quickly, Forrest got the coffee machine going before disappearing into the other room for a few minutes. Nero heard the murmur of Forrest's voice but couldn't make out if he was on the phone or talking to himself. It was kind of cute that he talked to himself, but Nero wasn't going to comment. He mumbled too.

Forrest was worried about what they might find; that much was clear.

"I had to leave a message for Kit to call me back," Forrest said when he returned to the kitchen. "I told her it was important. Hopefully, Chief Dear or someone from the police already talked to her."

Forrest poured them both coffee and then tried to pretend he wasn't lurking around trying to see what Nero was doing. Nero wasn't fooled at all. While Forrest had been on the phone, Nero had hopped onto his laptop, planning to see if there was more information online about the Coopers or the off-the-grid group. He wondered if Witt and Dina had been preppers too. If so, that gave even more credence to the possibility of them still being alive up there.

"If you keep hovering over my shoulder, I'm going back to my cabin. Track Rufus down. Maybe he knows the other names," Nero ordered.

"Maybe my grandpa did," Forrest remarked, moving away to lean in a distractingly sexy way against the counter. "He always kept a diary. I read a couple after he passed away, but most of the entries were centered around 'I don't know if Forrest will live to be twenty-five' kind of stuff. I never read the older ones."

Nero spun around in his chair, pressing his lips together in a vain attempt not to express his extreme frustration by growling —loudly.

"Your grandfather. Kept a diary. And, not only that, but you still have it?"

His mind boggled. A fucking *diary*, and Forrest just forgot? He lasered him with a look that he hoped Forrest translated as *What. The. Actual. Fuck.*

"Diaries. And yes. I just don't think about them much."

"Your job now is to read through them, and the book report is due by the end of the day." He made a shooing motion, encouraging him to get a move on already.

"Fine." Forrest huffed, stomping out of the kitchen. "I never have been good at homework!" he said over his shoulder.

Nero snickered as he listened to Forrest move around in the living room and mutter to himself while he searched for the diaries. When he returned for the second time, he held a stack of Moleskine journals in his hands. He plopped down across the table from Nero.

"Shh, no talking or we'll get in trouble."

"Pffft, I bet you never got in trouble," Forrest shot back.

"You think not?"

He hadn't, but how did Forrest know that?

Forrest's narrow gaze pinned Nero to his seat, assessing him, causing a shot of lust to spark up his spine. Now was not the time, he told himself.

Finally, Forrest said, "I think you could've been the mastermind behind the trouble but as an expert in raising hell, I don't see you doing it. I bet you never had study hall or were made to stay after school and clean up trash around the grounds."

"You're right," Nero admitted. "I even graduated early. Mostly so I could get away from the assholes I went to school with. Now, get to work."

HIS COFFEE HAD CHILLED by the time Nero shifted and straightened, then settled back in his chair to stare at the screen. Much of what he'd come across he'd already known. Some facts he hadn't. Now there was even more to speculate about.

"What?" Forrest asked impatiently. "Did you find something?"

Nero quickly scanned through his notes again.

"First and foremost, I want to know what kind of people would choose to live in the deepest, darkest part of a forest, far away from any humans. No running water. No easy way to communicate if something went wrong. How the hell did they survive for eight years or longer?" He looked over at Forrest. "I'm using eight years only because you say you were around seven when you came to live here."

Dina Paulsen had even given birth to both children out there, far from any medical help. Another mind-boggling fact.

"I can relate to the need to escape the rat race, but what your parents chose to do was extreme."

"Yeah, I know. They had to take the sovereign citizen movement to eleven."

"Did they consider themselves sovereign citizens?"

Sovereign citizens—if they were serious—could be scary, unyielding people. The family involved in the FBI standoff in Oregon ten or so years past were sovereigns.

"I don't know if it was official, but they sure didn't believe that laws applied to them. They didn't pay taxes, they lived where they wanted—this is hearsay, obviously, because no one talked to me about this kind of stuff. Why?"

"I covered a couple of sovereign stories in my career as a journalist. It doesn't really change much of anything except that, if the group was made up of people who believed in the anti-government survivalist aspect of the movement and those people are still alive, we'll need to be very careful. I'm not saying all SCs are dangerous, but one of their creeds is to always be prepared. They stock food, guns, and fuel in preparation for the failure of society. Not to be fucked with."

"From what I remember, it wasn't a huge compound," Forrest said thoughtfully. "I think they used the natural area as much as possible, caves and protected places that already existed. Could they have gotten all that stuff up there? My memories are so weird that I really can't judge."

"Yes, it's possible. But okay, we'll put that idea in our back pockets for now and keep going. I've found one more article about your 'rescue' but nothing else. Just basic information. Thinking about it, your grandfather must still have had a lot of clout in the region at the time. He was a Cooper, after all—only, what, two generations away from the town's founder? Still powerful enough to block a lot of publicity about children raised in the woods with wolves."

"I don't remember wolves, thank fuck."

There was no mention of the children's parents, Witt and

Dina, in the piece. The article was written almost as if the Cooper siblings had merely been missing for a few days before being rescued by their worried grandfather. Unfortunately, since it'd been pre-internet and had happened in a relatively isolated small town, the story hadn't been picked up by other news sources.

Nero growled his frustration at the lack of information and clicked further into the search results.

"Oh, check this out." Nero pointed at the screen and Forrest came to stand next to him. "The World did a human-interest series on modern pioneers in 1979. Like the ones in the 1800s who traveled by wagon train, lived in log houses, and died of dysentery. Did you ever play that game? No? Moving right along. One of the stories mentions that Witt Cooper handfasted with his beloved, Dina Paulsen, and they planned to homestead, joining a growing movement of people who wanted to go back to the land. So, possibly SCs, but maybe just their own brand of antisocial. I still want to know the names of the rest of the group."

"Handfasted?" Forrest repeated. "That's so eighteenth century. What the hell."

"I think that was the point. Okay, so." Nero clicked over to another tab. "Back in that era. See there? There were acres of what's now the Olympic National Forest that existed only nebulously officially. These woods weren't actually part of the national forest. Not yet anyway. They weren't protected from timber companies or anyone else—for example, wannabe pioneers. I bet Witt and Dina weren't the only ones who'd had the idea to live off that land."

Nero stood up to stretch his legs and spotted the two stacks of diaries sitting on the table. Forrest had set the ones he'd scanned through off to one side.

"Have you learned anything from those?"

"Nothing. No names so far. Could be they had a pact of silence or something. Wouldn't surprise me."

Nero's cellphone vibrated, and he grudgingly tugged it out of his jeans pocket. **Mom** stared back at him from the screen.

"I should answer this. It's my mom."

"Be my guest." Forrest nodded.

Nero stepped to the patio door and looked outside where Forrest's dormant lavender fields lay.

"Hi, Mom. How's it going?" He infused his voice with extra cheer.

"Oh, hi," she said after a weird pause. "I didn't expect you to answer."

He hated talking on the phone, something his mother did not understand, but he refused to apologize for it. Answering phones was not a requirement for modern life—that's why texting was invented. He shuddered, starting to feel a bit sympathetic toward Witt and Dina for wanting to get away from it all.

"Well, here I am." Was he being too hearty? "What's up?"

"I don't have too much to tell you, really. Just checking in."

Nero pulled his phone away from his ear and glared at it. See? That right there was why he hated phone calls. Always so awkward.

"Any plans for spring?" he asked. "Are you going on a cruise or anything?"

A few years ago, his mom had discovered she loved the cruise life. Nero sometimes wondered if they were related—but all he had to do was look in a mirror, and yes, they were. Nero, however, was not a cruise person. The idea of being trapped on a ship on the open sea with a whole bunch of people he didn't know sounded terrifying. But hey, the trips seemed to make his mom happy.

He wandered away from the window and back into the kitchen where Forrest was flipping through another Moleskine.

An email pinged Nero's inbox. He leaned in to see who it was from: R. Fernsby from Cooper Springs Library. Nero really wanted to know what the R stood for.

"—so you might not be able to get a hold of me for a few weeks. I've heard the internet isn't reliable," his mom said.

He'd totally missed hearing where she was heading. Hopefully, it was on a cruise and not a road trip.

"Okay, Mom, no worries," he assured her. "I'll try to get out there when you get back." Did he feel bad insinuating he was somewhere other than Washington? Yes. When he did finally see her, Nero would come clean with his mom. And maybe he'd have news to share.

"Love you, honey."

"Love you too," he said quickly, eager to get off the phone and back to his laptop.

"Sorry," he said to Forrest. "That was my mom. I haven't talked to her recently."

"You get along?"

"Yeah, she's great. Honest. I'm just the loser son who's been laid off and broke up with his boyfriend."

He clicked open the email. Fernsby was merely notifying Nero that his library card had been sent out. Nice of him. The library card that he'd paid four hundred dollars for and now couldn't use for the purpose he'd wanted it for in the first place. The fire had likely destroyed any documents stored in the mansion. If it was possible that some of the documents and old newspapers would end up salvaged, it would be months before Nero *might* be able to see them.

At the tail end of the email, Fernsby had added, *"Regarding our conversation, I may have some information for you, but it could be nothing. I'm at the library today—Saturday—until five."*

Huh. But okay. They could use all the help they could get.

Maybe R. Fernsby had remembered something after the two of them talked earlier in the week.

"Why loser?" Forrest asked. "Not the laid-off part. I get that, the economy is shit."

"Oh, Austin," Nero groused, taking his seat again and pondering how best to describe his ex. "Now that I look back, Austin was a mistake. Hindsight and all that. We are very different people. In the beginning, I enjoyed his utter *solidness*. Reliable. Safe. I should have known better since I've always been attracted to bad boys before. I thought it was a sign of personal growth or some nonsense. But I've come to realize I don't actually care for his brand of reliability or safety." Nero glanced across the table at Forrest. "And I'm still drawn to broody types. Austin didn't like change, didn't enjoy adventure. He hated that I wanted to hop in my car and just drive somewhere. He didn't even like to go out to eat without picking the place before we left the house."

"What about the podcast stuff?"

"Oh, you mean my 'obsession' with dead people? Supposedly that was the last straw for him, but in reality it was over already. What about you? Any skeletons in your closet?"

He was curious to know if Forrest had had a boyfriend or long-term partner at some point. He was so utterly single that Nero doubted it. Definitely just the wrong kind of person for him to be drawn to. Moth to flame and all that.

"Skeletons?" Forrest grimaced, probably wishing now that he hadn't raised the subject. "I'm not good at relationships, so I don't really do them." He waved his hand vaguely. "In the past, I just hooked up with guys who have no connection with Cooper Springs. I've never been ashamed of my sexuality and anyway, most people around here seem to not care. It's a *me* thing. A Forrest thing."

"My mom would say you haven't met the right person yet,"

Nero said. "She's a huge fan of romance books as well as the old detective novels. I haven't told her about me and Austin yet."

"Surely your mom wouldn't want you to stay with someone who doesn't make you happy?"

"No, of course not. She wants me to be happy. It's a Nero thing, feeling like a failure."

A half smile played on Forrest's lips. "If it's any help, I don't think you're a failure. I think you're brave. You just picked up your life and moved forward."

The compliment felt good but made Nero squirm a bit. "Enough about me. What do you think about going into town and seeing what Rufus might know? Looks like there's not much in the diaries, so I don't know if finishing them is worth it."

"Sure, let's do that. I'll drive."

"I'd like to stop by the library too. It closes at five."

FIFTEEN

Forrest – Saturday afternoon

Forrest liked having Nero in the passenger seat. It felt right. He was almost as proud of the truck as he was the farm.

Painted a dark purple, the truck even had wooden slats along the bed. *Purple Phaze Farm* was painted in a funky font across the doors. As a final touch, the tops of the L and the H were lavender fronds in different stages of bloom.

"This is damn cool," Nero commented, running his hand across the dashboard. "Original radio too, wow."

"Thanks." Forrest grinned over at him. "It's my pride and joy." He patted the steering wheel. "But I did just buy a 1963 GMC Greyhound bus. It has an incredible custom paint job, almost magical. Sea creatures, mermaids, all this underwater shit. Blues, pinks, and purples. It even runs. I can't wait to get it over here."

With everything that had happened, Forrest hadn't had a chance to make plans to pick it up yet.

"What are you going to do with a bus?" Nero asked. "Your farm isn't big enough for a driving tour, is it?"

"Nah." Forrest turned left onto the highway and began heading south back into town. "I might turn it into a shop though. The kiosk is great and I'll keep it, but I want to sell other stuff too. Might put an espresso machine in it, maybe have some seating for customers. It's a behemoth."

"I'd love to see it."

For a mile or so, they were both quiet, Forrest feeling guilty as they passed Levi's place. He didn't know what Nero was thinking about.

"It's a shame about Cooper Mansion," Nero said, breaking the silence. "Have you ever been inside it? I know it was donated to the city in the 1980s."

"Yeah, that's a no fucking thank you very much. Gramps forbade it."

"And I can tell you always listened to what he had to say. Why didn't he want you inside there?"

Forrest didn't have an answer. Ernst Cooper had never lived there himself, his father having moved out before he was born.

"You've got me there. But the mansion was one place I at least stayed away from. Maybe other kids, the ones who had baby teeth before being told scary stories, checked it out."

"Oh, yeah?"

"Yeah. Dina believed in scaring the shit out of me."

"Can I ask you something?" Nero asked.

"You just did."

"Ha, ha."

"Go ahead."

"You seem to only refer to your mother by her first name, not Mom or Mother. Is that your preference or was it hers? Was Witt the same?"

"I called Witt 'Papa.' Dina insisted on her first name and by the time Lani and I moved in with Grandpa, it was just how I knew her."

"Did Lani call Dina mom?"

"We don't talk about her much, but I guess sometimes. Why?"

A quick glance told him Nero was staring out at the glimpses of ocean that could be seen through the stands of trees. "It's just odd, comparatively. Most kids use Mom, Dad, whatever."

"Dina certainly wasn't most parents."

"Doesn't sound like it. Let's stop at the library first. I want to see what R. Fernsby has to say."

"Sorry, no can do. I was banned from the library when I was fourteen."

"Banned from the library," Nero repeated.

"I might have been a little wild."

"Just a little wild?" Nero teased.

Forrest shrugged. "Just a tad. Xav Stone was banned too."

"What the hell did you two do?"

"We were fourteen," Forrest started, taking the last easy curve before town, "and—"

Nero interrupted him. "As far as I know, just being fourteen isn't a reason to permanently forbid a person from entering a public building. Are you telling me you haven't been to the library in thirty years?"

He sounded outraged and Forrest couldn't help but laugh.

"Thirty years sounds about right. Remember, Xavier and me, we were acting out, and being a teenager in the small town of Cooper Springs meant the two of us got creative. Very creative."

"Keep talking."

"We snuck in one night and exchanged all the magazine innards with a bunch of skin mags we'd found at Xav's house. They'd probably been his dad's. There's no way Wanda—Xav's mom—knew they existed because she would've burned them."

"I'll bet you guys thought that was the funniest thing in the world."

"Oh yeah, we laughed so hard we couldn't breathe. Hilarious to imagine Old Steel Face—the librarian at the time was Agatha Steel—going through them and seeing what we thought were more bare naked men than she'd seen in her life."

"Fourteen-year-olds have limited imaginations."

"Especially when it came out after she passed that Agatha Steel wrote seriously steamy romance. Under a different name, of course."

"No kidding?"

"No kidding."

"And?"

"We got caught, naturally. Wanda grounded Xavier for the rest of the summer. I spent the next few months cleaning up after my grandfather's horses. I do not like horses."

"Why do I have the feeling punishment didn't stop either of you?"

Forrest felt the smile crease his cheeks and waggled his eyebrows; it felt good talking about his past with Nero. "It's like you know me already."

"Come inside with me," Nero said, "and break the library spell."

"No."

"What if they have something important to say? You might want to hear it in person."

"Oh, for fuck's sake."

"We'll be fast. Like tearing-off-a-Band-Aid fast. In and out."

"In and out is not what I think of when it's time to take off a bandage."

Nero was silent, but Forrest spotted a twitch to the corner of the lips. Forrest's cheeks warmed, along with other parts of his body. He shifted in his seat. Dammit, he'd suspected he was in trouble and now it was confirmed. He just wished he knew exactly how deep the trouble was.

"The librarian, Fernsby, said he'd be here until five. And maybe he's nicer than Old Steel Face."

"Don't tell him her nickname."

He could feel Nero staring at him. "Dude, I am sure Librarian Fernsby—who seems to take his job very seriously, from what I can tell—already knows what you called Agatha Steel back in the day. Especially since he's lived here for years." He tapped his forehead. "Librarians are observant and smart."

"Fuck, you're right. I didn't know Fernsby grew up here. Still," Forrest said, swinging a right after the town's single stop light, "let's just play innocent."

"Has that ever worked for you?" Nero teased. "Playing innocent?"

"No, it has fucking not," Forrest complained. "I feel like I deserve some slack."

There were several parking spots in front of the small library building. Forrest pulled into one and turned off the engine.

"Ready?" Nero asked him. "When we're done here, we'll go find Rufus."

"No, I am not ready. Do you really need me to come inside?" Forrest shot Nero a begging-puppy-dog glance.

"Yep," Nero said heartlessly as he opened his door and got out. "The quicker we get this part over with, the quicker you'll see my brake lights heading out of town."

"You have a point."

Forrest felt a little twinge in his chest. Did he want Nero to leave? A month ago—hell, four days ago, the answer would have been a resounding, "Yes, and don't let the door hit you on the ass on your way out." Things had changed.

With a grumble, Forrest climbed out of the truck and strode around to meet Nero on the sidewalk.

Glancing in Nero's direction, he sucked in a deep, fortifying breath. "I'm ready. Lead the way."

"Ah. I'm the fall guy, huh?"

"Absolutely."

Nero smirked at him as they headed toward the small building.

In spite of the economic downturn that Cooper Springs had suffered for decades, the library exterior was reasonably well kept up. The wood siding was in good condition, and the white paint on the windowsills wasn't peeling. A set of matching flowerpots stood on either side of the doors and currently had cheerful bright yellow daffodils blooming in them.

"Somebody's got to do it," Forrest muttered.

"What?"

"Be cheerful."

"What? Never mind. So," Nero said, leading the way up the steps to the library's front door, "whose idea was it to change out the magazines? Yours or your friend Xavier's?"

"Shhh! Don't speak of it," Forrest hissed dramatically, looking over his shoulder as if Nero might have accidentally summoned a demon.

Rolling his eyes, Nero pulled open the door and gestured for Forrest to go ahead of him. Forrest's mouth dropped open, but it was too late for him to step to the side since others had followed them up the sidewalk.

"You'll pay for this, Vik," Forrest said out of the side of his mouth as he walked past.

Nero held the door open for a mom, a young child, and a toddler before catching up to Forrest in the foyer.

"So much drama. Have you always been this dramatic? And why do I think the answer is yes?"

"I was a traumatized child," Forrest protested.

"Huh," Nero grunted. "I suspect you would have been

dramatic whether or not you'd spent the first six years of your life growing up in the woods."

Forrest admitted that Nero likely wasn't wrong, just not out loud.

The two of them approached the checkout desk. The person behind the counter was no one Forrest recognized. He did his best to appear nonchalant and harmless—nothing to see here. The mom and her two kids walked by them and headed to the children's reading area.

"Hi," Nero greeted the man with a smile. "May I speak with Mr. Fernsby?"

"I'm afraid Mr. Fernsby isn't here at the moment. His absence is causing quite a strain on our staffing, I might add." The last was said with a decided sniff.

Ah yes, one of those people who couldn't bring themselves to be sympathetic. Whatever happened was all about how it impacted them.

"That's odd." Nero frowned. "I got an email from him maybe an hour ago saying he'd be here."

"Well, I'm afraid I can't help you with that. He was supposed to be here but, as you can see, he is not."

Nero couldn't help himself. He glanced around and, unless Fernsby was hiding underneath a table or in the restroom, he really wasn't there.

"Well," said Nero when they reached Forrest's truck, "he must have changed his mind. Mr. Peacock certainly wasn't very pleasant."

"I don't think his name's Mr. Peacock," said Forrest.

"Well, that's what I'm calling him. Shall we track down Rufus?"

SIXTEEN

Nero - Saturday

"HERE WE ARE."

Forrest stopped the truck in front of a white clapboard house that looked very typical for Cooper Springs: about a thousand square feet total, shutters on either side of the windows guarding the front door, everything covered with a slightly green tinge from moss or just the sea air. There was—unsurprisingly—a seven-foot wood carving of Bigfoot in the front yard, and a live raven was currently perched on his head. The bird watched them get out of the truck, then cawed and flew off when Nero and Forrest approached the front walkway.

"That's his car," Forrest said, pointing to a car parked not quite directly in front of the home. "The black Prius."

Nero knocked and stepped back, waiting for Rufus to come to the door.

"Do you hear anything? Footsteps?" Forrest asked.

"Nothing."

"Maybe he walked over to the pub. He often does. Or he could be helping Wanda at her shop."

Nero knocked again and received the same silent result. Forrest grumbled something under his breath and drove them the four blocks to the Steam Donkey.

"Forrest... Nero." Magnus nodded as they entered the pub, one eyebrow raised. "What can I get you two?"

"You can get your mind out of the gutter," Forrest said so only Nero heard him.

"What was that?" Magnus asked.

"I said we're trying to find, ah..." he stalled out and shot Nero a panicked glance.

"Is Rufus around?" Nero asked, leaning against the bar. "We have some questions for him."

Magnus's eyebrows drew together. "I haven't seen my old man this morning. Not since the town meeting. Like you noticed, Forrest, he seemed shaken up when I caught up to him. He told me to give him some space. I figured I'd stop over at his place once Garth gets here tonight."

"We were just over there. He's not home."

"Probably at Wanda's, then."

But when they stopped by the thrift shop, Wanda hadn't seen Rufus either. "He stopped in after the town meeting about the girls but left after a few minutes. We usually talk at night, but I knew he was shocked by the news so when he didn't call, I wasn't worried. Should I be worried now?"

"He wasn't home," explained Forrest. "Or at least, he isn't answering the door. Magnus is going to go over and check on him once Garth gets in."

"To hell with waiting. I'm going over there right now. He could have fallen or something."

Something that none of them wanted to consider. In a flurry of motion, Wanda grabbed her purse and a set of keys from underneath the cash register, then headed for the door.

"Come with me. I'm not locking you two in here and I might need help."

THEY DIDN'T SAY anything while Forrest drove the truck, following Wanda the short distance back to Rufus's house. Without waiting for them, she parked and bolted out of her practical silver sedan. She jogged up the walkway to the small porch and pounded on the door loud enough to echo over the small neighborhood.

Forrest and Nero hurried up behind her and all three of them waited, staring at the front door and willing it to open. Nero didn't know about Forrest, but he was hoping they didn't find something unpleasant. Praying, actually.

Like earlier, Rufus did not come to the door. There were still no sounds from the inside. Not looking at them, Wanda fumbled with her purse, digging around in it for a moment before pulling out a keyring with a single key hanging on it.

Still not looking at them, she said in a slightly shaky voice, "We've exchanged keys. I think I'm going to ask him to marry me." Sliding the key into the lock and turning it, Wanda pushed the front door open to step inside.

They could see nothing out of the ordinary over her shoulder as they followed her, just a tidy front room with a small leather couch, a TV, and bookshelves packed two deep with books. More books were tucked in horizontally between the tops of the books and the next shelf up. Framed black-and-white photographs hung on the walls where there was space.

There was no sign of Rufus.

"I'm going to check the bedroom," Wanda said grimly.

"Let us," Forrest said, catching her arm before she could head down a short hallway. "Let me," he said more gently.

Wanda nodded, tears brimming, her lips pressed tightly together. Nero waited with her while Forrest made his way to Rufus's bedroom and pushed the door open.

"Nothing," he said. "Checking the bathroom now. Nothing there either."

"When you've looked all the logical places, I guess we need to start looking in the odd ones," Wanda said when Forrest came back out to the living room.

Instead, Wanda checked the bedroom again, the bathroom again, and the spare bedroom, which was also empty of Rufus. Nero stayed out of the way while Forrest scanned the kitchen and opened a door that clearly led to a basement or cellar.

"It's creepy down there, and the stairs are steep and narrow." Forrest flicked on a light switch, and Nero heard the stairs creak under his weight as he went down them.

"Nothing here," he called out.

Wanda came back inside through a door that led out to a patch of mossy grass and looming trees. "Nothing in the backyard, either."

"He's not here," Nero said pointlessly. Obviously, he wasn't there. But where the hell was he?

"If his car weren't here, I wouldn't be as worried as I am." Wanda looked around as if she might spot him hiding somewhere. "I don't understand where he could have gone. Why would he go somewhere without his car? Why wouldn't he tell Magnus or me anything, or at least leave a damn note?"

Neither of them had an answer.

"This just isn't like him," said Wanda. She headed back out the still open front door, expecting them to follow her. Which they did.

"Let's think about next steps," Forrest began as Wanda hunted in her purse for the key again. "First, we need to go back over to the pub and let Magnus know we can't find him. I don't know where else to look either and Nero sure doesn't because he's not from here. He also doesn't know much of anything about Rufus. It's not as if it's hiking season or anything like that since it's March..." his voice trailed off.

Forrest looked at them and then glanced at the trees behind the row of houses that made up the edge of the forest—or the edge of town, depending on how you looked at it. Following his gaze, Nero thought he knew what Forrest was thinking.

"On the other hand. Wanda, do you think he could have gone for a hike, maybe just to clear his mind? Let's check for his equipment. Do you know what he has these days?"

Wanda stared back at Forrest before turning and walking back inside to open the closet door they hadn't thought to look in. After all, why would Rufus be hiding in his front closet?

"I think some of his gear is missing," she declared after shuffling through it. "The man is an REI and Outdoor Outfitters addict, so it's difficult to tell for certain."

"What does he usually take with him when he goes out there?" Nero stared into the remarkably large closet that was, unlike the rest of the house, filled to bursting with coats, boots, hats, scarves, several bags, and plastic boxes on the upper shelves that held only Rufus knew what.

"Well, he has a hiking pack for long trips and that's here." She pointed out an orange and brown backpack tucked along one side. "But his favorite boots and hiking sticks are missing and his heavy coat too. Why wouldn't he tell me if he was going out for a ramble?"

They didn't have an answer for Wanda, but they gave each other a concerned look over her head.

"When I spoke with Rufus after the announcement, he was

very reserved," Wanda continued. "He didn't want to talk about it. I could tell he was shocked by the news that the remains found up there were those poor girls, but he seemed to almost take it personally."

"Did he say anything before he left the shop?"

Wanda frowned. "Just that he loved me."

They didn't know when he might have left. Had it been yesterday afternoon after the town meeting or earlier this morning? There was no way to tell; his house was spotless.

"That damn man, he better not have done something stupid."

Nero pretended not to notice Wanda swiping a tear from her eye.

"The house is very tidy," Nero pointed out. "Is it always like this?"

"Rufus is very proud of keeping a neat house. It makes me smile. The man is a dream, he's so tidy. I've complained that there's no way to sneak in and change anything because it's so darn clean."

Mutually, they decided to head back over to the pub. They needed to include Magnus in the Find Rufus conversation and decide what next steps should be taken. Or at least, Wanda, Magnus, and Forrest did. Nero was feeling a bit like a fifth wheel.

MAGNUS WAS CONCERNED.

"Hiking gear's missing, huh? That's a tad worrisome, but on the other hand, Dad's been tramping around in those woods longer than I've been alive. Let's give it another couple of hours. I've tried calling, but the damn man doesn't keep his cell phone on all the time since the service is so poor anyway, and it's going straight to messages. Since that's not all that unusual, I don't know that we should head straight into panic mode."

Wanda shot him a dirty look. Magnus got the message.

"Okay." He raised his hands in surrender. "I'll text Garth right now and see if he can make it in early to take over here. Then I'll go over to Dad's place and wait for him there. Wanda, do you want to wait with me or are you going to open the shop back up?"

Magnus grabbed his cellphone from next to the cash register and immediately began one-finger texting.

"I'm not about to re-open the shop, Magnus," Wanda said tartly. "No one is going to care if it's closed the rest of the day—or until we find Rufus. I'll just go slap a sign on it and tell customers to come back another time. Rufus is more important than selling used baby carriers and shell art. I'll meet you back at Rufus's place. We can wait together."

"Do you want us to wait with you?" Forrest asked.

"No," said Wanda. "You'll just make me more anxious with your pacing back and forth. You never could sit still, and I can't imagine anything has changed recently."

"Okaaay," Forrest responded. "We have some stuff we want to do back at my place anyway."

Nero had no idea what that stuff was, but he nodded agreeably anyway.

Magnus shot Forrest a look that said he knew exactly—or thought he did—what Nero and Forrest would be doing back at his house. Did he think Nero and Forrest were off to do the horizontal tango when Rufus was missing?

"Nero's looking into Ned's death. We had a few questions for Rufus since they were friends."

Magnus seemed to accept the redirect, although Nero still suspected he knew something. Did he care? Nope. Nero was more concerned about Forrest's reaction to Magnus knowing their private business; if nothing else, the man was definitely protective of his personal space.

"I'll have my landline ringer on, and my cell phone too. Please call as soon as you learn anything, and we'll head back in."

"Is there a plan if he doesn't turn up?" Nero asked. There should be a plan, and he wasn't one to shy away from hard questions. None of them wanted to think about Rufus possibly injured or worse, but if he was, he needed them to have a solid plan of action.

Magnus eyed Nero, mulling over his question. Finally, he said, "It's like three thirty in the afternoon. If he's up there, he'll be back down before dark."

Up there clearly meant the woods. What if he'd been up there since yesterday? Up there and *not* hurt? They didn't know when he'd left, only that he hadn't called Wanda the night before like he normally did.

"If he doesn't come down by dark, it'll be too late for the likes of you and me to go up after him. If we don't hear from him by this evening, I'll alert Critter and Mags, not the police. He's an adult and in fine health, so they wouldn't be able to do anything. Both because we aren't sure where he is and also because Chief Dear has limited resources. I doubt the new officers are qualified for search and rescue. But Critter and Mags, they know the trails almost as well as Pops does. It's not like he can't take care of himself, either. Aside from a lifetime of knowledge, he has every piece of hiking and survival equipment known to humankind. I'm mostly concerned because of how shaken up he seemed yesterday."

"Do you know exactly what he was shaken up about?" Nero asked. "Did he say anything?"

Magnus looked at him. "Well, son—I guess you're not quite young enough to be my son—but anyway, all I could get out of him was that he hadn't expected to learn that the remains were Morgan Blass and Sarah Turner."

Forrest nodded. "He told me that he'd always thought they'd left town for a better life than Cooper Springs had to offer, that this changed everything. That's all he would say."

SEVENTEEN

Forrest – Saturday, late afternoon

"Do you mind if we stop by the library again?" Nero asked. The truck's passenger door was still ajar, and he was only half perched on the bench seat. "I'd like to find out why Fernsby emailed me."

"Sure, but I'm not going in this time. I'm gonna sit out here and obsess about Rufus."

"Chicken," Nero said with a snort. "I don't think it will take long. I can't imagine what he has to tell me—if he's even bothered to show up."

"Seriously, I feel like I've faced down my enemy once already today. Twice is asking too much."

Nero chuckled.

"Will you still be here when I get back?"

Forrest rolled his eyes. "Yes, I promise I will be here." He tapped his fingers restlessly against the steering wheel. He wanted to take action, do something, figure out where the hell Rufus had gotten to. But there was nothing for him to do; the best course of action was not to run into the forest and see if they could find him. What if that wasn't where he'd gone?

Nero hopped back out of the truck. Forrest watched him jog down the block and disappear around the corner. What could he say? He was a gay man and Nero had an awesome ass. Not many minutes later, Nero was back and making himself comfortable in the passenger seat again.

"Fernsby never did show up, and Mr. Peacock wouldn't give me a phone number. 'For the personal safety of our staff.' I get it, but seriously, when the guy had said he wanted to meet with me?" Nero complained.

"Mr. Peacock." Forrest snorted at the made-up name. "He wouldn't give you the time of day if it wasn't already public information."

"Do you happen to know where Fernsby may live?"

"In case you hadn't noticed yet, Nero, I make it my business not to know much of anything about what happens in town. With the exception of gossip at the Donkey, and that is generally not random people's home addresses."

"So that's a no? I suppose I could ask around."

"Yep." Forrest paused for a moment, then asked, "But how about we head back to my place? I can make us something to eat."

"Sounds good to me."

Vaguely anxious about Rufus but with no idea what to do about it since they didn't have a real idea as to where he was, Forrest pulled out into the street again. He swung a quick left so they were headed back to the main drag.

"You know," he said. "I don't know that I ever did have a library card."

His comment was first met by silence.

Finally, Nero spoke. "You've never had a library card? That's, that's an abomination."

"As you know, I found plenty of things to do besides read, and Grandpa had all those books anyway. I do remember Grandpa taking me there at least once. I had a big stack of books to take home, and the librarian asked him if I would be able to read them all before they were due. Grandpa's response was to laugh and say he hoped they would keep me busy for the whole weekend, but that he doubted it."

He quickly glanced over at Nero. His passenger was staring out the window and watching the world of Cooper Springs pass by, tapping on his thigh while he did so, listening to a tune Forrest couldn't hear. Maybe worrying about Rufus—he seemed to like him.

"What else do you think was stored there?" Nero asked.

"Huh?" Forrest was confused before realizing they'd passed by the charred remains of the mansion. "Oh, I have no idea. Could've been anything, I guess. The last time anyone lived there was in the 1950s. The city was supposed to use it as a museum or other public building, but as far I'm aware, it's just sat empty. Well, obviously not entirely empty."

Forrest slowed again before turning onto the highway. They passed by Murry Evison's empty property and Forrest wondered if the crotchety old man was still in Arizona. He liked Murry; Forrest hoped to be as cantankerous as he was someday.

"Did you learn anything today?" he asked Nero. "Other than that milk cost $1.57 a gallon, the coin-op laundry had just opened, and the newly refurbished Cooper Springs Resort was reportedly expecting a banner summer of car-touring guests in 1978?"

"Ah, you were reading over my shoulder after all. I think I did. Or at least, now I have a more complete picture of what Cooper Springs was like back then. Not much about the missing girls."

"It was depressing."

If Kurt Cobain thought Aberdeen was bad, he should've come for a visit.

"There's that."

"I think town leaders were more concerned about plans for the abandoned mill, the upcoming mayoral race, and the two new shopping malls being developed in Aberdeen than about those girls." That disgusted Forrest. "The shopping mall scandal was big news, I remember. Grandpa ranted about it constantly. He was so angry about it. He, Rufus, Oliver, and Ned would sit up for hours and rant about the mayor and his cronies."

A developer had approached Cooper Springs' city leaders and they'd refused to give the company permits. In hindsight, the decision had kept Cooper Springs from turning into a smaller version of Aberdeen, but at the time, the town had been divided, especially since the residents had been in the final death throes of the timber industry. It had been dark times for the town and a lot of families had moved away to Aberdeen—which had gotten the shopping mall—Port Angeles, Olympia, and even Seattle.

"Your grandfather wanted the shopping mall?"

"Yeah, he knew Cooper Springs was headed for obscurity," Forrest said, keeping his attention on the road. "He was the last of the timber families, so it hit him hard, I think. By that, I mean, he had memories as a child of a much busier and robust Cooper Springs, but that all changed when he was still small. The rise and fall of the Cooper family fortune, as he liked to say."

The headline he didn't want to talk about was the one after Grandpa had returned with Forrest and Lani. He was forever thankful that Ernst had done his best to keep reporters away. But that hadn't stopped people from accosting Forrest on the street when he was in town or at school. Like he was some kind of freak.

Because Forrest had taught himself to read, Grandpa had

enrolled him in school soon after they'd come back to town—probably also to get a surly little boy out of his hair.

School was where Forrest learned to fight.

He shook those memories away. Grandpa had done the best he could with his feral grandchildren. Lani at least had hidden it better than Forrest. Still did. But she was just as wild inside as he was. Just as distrusting.

THEY WERE ABOUT HALFWAY BACK to Forrest's place, just where the highway curved inward before sloping downward along a serpentine hill that followed the hidden curve of the coastline, when Forrest tapped the brakes and nothing happened.

He tapped them again. They squished all the way to the floorboards.

Where there should have been resistance, there was none. They'd been fine in town—he'd slowed at the corners with no problem—but now, nothing.

"Mother fucking fucker," he growled, gripping the steering wheel. "Hold the fuck on." Lani always told him he drove too fast and today it was coming back to bite him in the ass.

"What's wrong?" Nero asked.

He was going to rip Silas Murphy a new one. Forrest had taken his truck in only a few months earlier for a tip-to-tail tune-up, and new brakes had been one of the things he'd paid a lot of money for.

"Brakes," he said with gritted teeth.

The truck was gathering speed and the forest became a blur on either side. Forrest was afraid to look anywhere but the road ahead of them as long as he could see it. They hadn't crashed yet. His fingers ached from gripping the steering wheel while he futilely pumped the brakes—as if holding tight would make the inevitable crash less painful.

"I'm sorry, *what?*" Nero's voice cracked on the last word.

"Brakes aren't working," Forrest ground out.

"Are you kidding me?"

"No, I am not fucking kidding you."

The Ford was older than Forrest, made from good old American steel, and weighed close to eight thousand pounds. They were picking up speed and when they stopped, it wouldn't be pretty and it was going to hurt.

"Downshift," Nero demanded. "Downshift now."

Why hadn't he thought of that? Probably because he was too busy trying to keep the wheel straight. And, oh yeah, panicking. Forrest took a deep breath. If he panicked, they were dead. They were lucky there were no cars within sight on the highway. For the moment.

"Hold on."

Forcing his fingers off the steering wheel, Forrest reached down and grabbed the gearshift. Quickly, he pressed in the clutch with his left foot and pushed against the stick shift, forcing the truck into third gear. The engine whined and the gears ground, protesting the shift of gears happening without a change in speed. Sweat rolled down his forehead, but Forrest couldn't risk swiping it away. Out of the corner of his eye, he saw that Nero had grabbed the grip above the door.

Fuck, fuck, fuck.

They barreled down the hill, Forrest praying to any god who would listen.

Please make it so we don't end up as unrecognizable bits being swept up off the road by emergency responders.

Lani would kill him. And then she'd revive him and kill him all over again.

The truck had slowed down but not enough. Not nearly enough.

The engine was screaming under the strain of being forced to slow down without help from the brakes, and they were about to reach a part of the road that had a notorious curve. After that, the highway flattened and straightened out again, shooting past Levi's place.

He'd steer the truck into Levi's fence. If they survived the curve, he'd pay Levi for a new one. And if all Forrest needed after today was a new transmission and not new knees, he would be happy.

"Shift down again," Nero ordered.

Gritting his teeth, Forrest forced the truck into second gear. The engine screamed even louder but slowed further. Forrest continued to uselessly stomp on the brake pedal—as if they would magically start working again.

The truck sped past several white roadside crosses, a testament to those who'd failed to navigate this tricky stretch of highway. Forrest hadn't paid much attention to them before today, but now they seemed like neon signs.

Ahead was a stand of Douglas fir trees, their trunks battered from catching vehicles that missed this last turn. There were three more of the damn crosses in quick succession. With white knuckles and aching hands, Forrest guided the truck into the S-curve, giving the trees a mental middle finger.

Not this day. Not if Forrest could help it.

They were still going too fast. Smoke billowed out from underneath the hood.

"You've got this," Nero said, his voice barely audible over the vibration of the truck barreling along the road.

How could the man sound so calm?

They made it though, and the highway ahead was straight as

an arrow. Forrest sucked in a breath and started to think they might be okay when an RV pulled out in front of them.

"Motherfucker."

The beast was going the same direction they were, probably heading up toward Forks or Port Angeles. On either side of the highway was old pasture land owned by a trust. Levi's driveway was less than a quarter mile away.

Forrest gripped the steering wheel hard enough that he thought it might crack as the truck drew closer and closer to the back end of the brown RV. He glanced at the speedometer.

"It's the fucking pedal on the right, old man," he ground out.

Nero was silent. Forrest kind of wished he'd scream.

"Pull off. Do it now."

Nero was right; there was no more time.

"Hold the fuck on."

Forrest didn't need anyone to tell him this was gonna hurt. His poor truck. He jerked the steering wheel to the right to avoid hitting the camper and the truck careened off the road, rising into the air for a millisecond before hitting the side of a drainage ditch. The shriek of shredding metal was deafening.

The hiss of disconnected hoses and smoke billowing from the engine brought Forrest back to his senses. With a groan, he opened his eyes. He hadn't realized that he'd shut them. Something dripped down his cheek and he raised a hand to swipe at it. His fingers came away red.

"Shit. Nero." Forrest twisted around to check on his passenger.

Nero stared out the shattered windshield, blood dripping down the side of his head. He was alive anyway.

"Shit, shit, shit," Forrest chanted, struggling with his seat belt.

They had to get out of the truck. Forrest had a vision of the truck catching fire and bursting into flames. Too many action movies. That didn't happen often in real life—right?

Forcing his body to move, Forrest shoulder-checked the door. It budged with a nasty creak but wouldn't open all the way. Forrest was going to have to squeeze out.

Fuck, he couldn't move.

He panicked before realizing he still hadn't unclipped his seat belt. The adrenaline gave him the strength to unhook himself. With the safety belt open, Forrest forced himself shoulder first through the too small opening, ripping some of his shirt buttons off and tearing one sleeve. Shirts could be replaced.

Almost immediately, he fell to his knees.

That hurt.

"Forrest! What the fuck? What happened? Are you okay? Of course you're not okay."

Blinking muzzily, Forrest recognized Levi Cruz's voice, but darkness closed in before he could explain.

FORREST AND NERO sat shoulder to shoulder on a damp hillock about fifty feet from what had been Forrest's pride and joy. Nero had his precious backpack sitting between his knees. Levi paced back and forth in front of them.

Even though Forrest had only passed out for a second, Levi was insisting on calling them an ambulance. Forrest was trying to convince him not to. Nero just seemed to be enjoying the argument, his gaze flicking back and forth between the two of them.

"We don't need an ambulance. Do we, Nero?"

Nero shook his head. "I'm fine, just banged up."

Levi glared at Forrest and then Nero. Pulling out his cell phone, he called the fire station and the garage while Forrest and Nero listened to his side of the conversation. And Forrest, at least, thanked fuck he was alive and relatively unhurt.

"They say they're fine. The truck is trashed, and the engine is still smoking a bit. All right, thanks." Frowning, Levi slipped the phone back into the pocket of his sweatshirt.

"Cops are busy with something. Fire's on the way. Fucking cops are always too busy. What the fuck happened?" he demanded.

Forrest knew Levi was pissed off at the world in general, not just CSPD. And nobody, not even the CSPD, blamed him.

"Dude, we're fine. We don't need the police."

Especially not Lani. Was she working today? Forrest hoped not, but he wasn't stupid enough to assume she'd stay behind her desk like the doctor wanted her to if she heard about this call.

"Don't fucking *Dude* me. You could have a concussion. You could be dead," Levi snarled.

"Not dead," Forrest muttered. "Right here. Listening to you yell at me. Us."

Levi glanced at Nero again and dismissed him.

"Oh, I'm just yelling at you. He wasn't behind the wheel."

"Why is it always my fault when the shit hits the fan?"

"Your reputation precedes you. Again, what the fuck happened?"

Forrest looked down the now empty road. The RV, oblivious to the near collision, hadn't even stopped. It was long gone, heading north.

"The brakes gave out at the top of the hill."

Or before. He wasn't sure and it didn't feel like it mattered right now.

"You could've been killed," Levi pointed out.

"Yeah, I'm gonna have a little conversation with Silas about that," Forrest said.

Levi stopped his pacing long enough to scowl at Forrest again. "Silas is a genius mechanic. Do you really think he made a mistake replacing your brakes?"

"I don't know what else it could be. They were fine this morning."

A FLATBED TOW truck arrived within a few minutes, just as it was starting to get dark. And, thank fuck, Silas was behind the wheel. The fire engine Forrest could hear in the distance was coming from the far side of town.

"Dammit," he grumbled. The last thing he wanted to do was confront the town's mechanic about shoddy work, but it had to be done. Rising to his feet, he watched the massive truck pull to a stop. Nero stood up as well.

"Just come up the drive and over," Levi yelled to Silas.

They were silent while Silas maneuvered the truck to where they were waiting. Pulling to a stop, Silas popped open the door and jumped out. Without saying anything, he strode over to take in the smoldering wreckage of Forrest's truck.

"Don't worry about us, we'll be fine," Forrest snarked. "Not dead yet."

"What happened?" Silas asked, turning to face them. He still appeared more worried about the Ford than the humans.

"Forrest says the brakes failed," Levi answered.

"They did not." Silas spun back around as if he was going to crawl under the truck and check the lines that minute.

"There is no way the brakes failed," Silas insisted, getting down on his hands and knees to peer underneath the chassis.

"At least wait to check shit until the fire department gets here and makes sure the truck isn't going to explode or something," Forrest said. The action movie images still played in his head.

Standing up again, Silas crossed his arms over his chest and frowned, clearly unhappy that his work was being called into question.

"It couldn't have been a brake failure. Absolutely not."

Silas was a quiet guy. Forrest didn't know much about him, but he did know that Silas was proud of his skills as a mechanic. He was good and he didn't fuck up. If that weren't the case, Forrest wouldn't have trusted him with his baby in the first place. Most of the work he did himself too. Apparently, he'd hired a guy once and it hadn't worked out. The guy had been gone in less than six weeks.

"Listen, Forrest, I mess up and this town will shut me down. My business would be bankrupt in months, if not weeks. No way was it mechanical error."

He and Silas stared at each other. Forrest had to admit that Silas had a point. He'd managed to keep his garage open regardless of the economics of a small town. If people complained about his work, he would be done.

"My bad," Forrest conceded. "Do you think you can figure out what happened? Maybe it was a faulty part."

"Damn right I can figure it out," Silas responded, still a tad surly. "I just need a few minutes underneath."

"Please, wait until we get the all clear," Levi said again. "I can't deal with anyone getting hurt."

"Fine," Silas agreed, sullenly glaring at the Ford.

The fire truck finally arrived and there was a flurry of activity, including one of the responders checking out both Forrest's and Nero's head wounds and shining bright lights in their eyes while they sat on the truck's bumper.

"I always recommend a trip to the ER in these situations,"

the guy informed them both. He looked familiar but Forrest didn't think they knew each other.

"I'm fine," Nero insisted. "I just have a bit of a headache."

"Ditto," added Forrest. "Not seeing double or anything."

"Ultimately, it's up to you two, but I'm still making a note on my book that I recommended you see a doctor," the EMT said as he gathered up his gear and snapped shut the lid to his first aid kit.

"Over and out," Forrest retorted. "Still not going."

"Me neither."

The responder shook his head. "Fine, get off my truck."

"Some bedside manner you have," Nero commented.

"I only play a doctor on TV," the guy said dryly.

Nero squinted at his chest, presumably reading his name tag. "T. Prosser. Nice to meet you. Thanks for the Band-Aids."

"Anytime—but not anytime again soon."

Silas was almost finished loading the truck onto the flatbed. When he was done, he hopped into the driver's seat, giving Forrest a salute and the international sign for *I'll call you* before slowly driving back to the road and turning toward town. The fire engine departed as well, leaving the three of them standing in Levi's semi-destroyed field.

"I guess I owe you a new fence."

Levi looked around at the damage and shrugged. "I don't care. It's not as if I'm planting anything."

Forrest took a longer and closer look at his nearest neighbor. The sweatshirt and worn jeans his friend wore hung loose on him, as if he'd lost weight. And now that he wasn't yelling and red in the face, Forrest realized he was pale. Not the pale of a Pacific Northwesterner who didn't get out much in the winter months, but the kind of pale that meant Levi wasn't taking care of himself properly.

"What about the cidery?" Forrest asked.

Levi shrugged again, not answering Forrest's question. This time last year, Levi had been in the midst of planning to build a cidery on his property and using his apples to make a local hard cider.

Well, crap.

If Lani were missing, Forrest would be in a similar state. He needed to be a better friend. Levi had no family, his father having died years ago. And now his much younger half-sister had been missing since before last Thanksgiving.

Speaking of sisters, a Cooper Springs PD cruiser turned into Levi's driveway and Forrest unfortunately recognized Officer Lani Cooper behind the wheel.

"Fuck," Forrest said emphatically.

EIGHTEEN

Nero – Saturday evening

"What the actual fuck, Forrest? I told you that truck was going to get you in trouble!"

Lani Cooper didn't wait for Forrest to answer. Nero saw Forrest's wince as his sister used her crutch to hobble-stomp across the turf to where Nero, Forrest, and the owner of the property they'd crashed onto, the man who'd also called 9-1-1, were standing. Even if Nero hadn't known she and Forrest were related, the red hair and the similar facial features would have made it obvious. They were both attractive, Nero had to admit, but Forrest was the sibling Nero found himself drawn to.

Why was his brain thinking about stuff like that when they'd both nearly died? Maybe it was from shock, focusing on the not-dying part.

"Believe it or not, the truck isn't sentient, Lani. It didn't try and kill me."

"Was it reckless driving? Because that's what it looks like from here. Christ, look at the gouges!"

Nero's head throbbed and so did other inexplicable parts of

his body, like his right elbow. Regardless, Nero was enjoying the exchange between the older brother and younger sister. Lani was obviously not impressed by Forrest trying to dismiss what had happened.

"Reckless driving?" Forrest repeated, his voice rising. "Are you kidding me?"

Nero was fairly sure the conversation would have continued and ramped up into serious fireworks if the as-yet-unknown-to-him guy hadn't stepped in.

"Lani, it wasn't Forrest's fault," the guy said.

She turned on him. "Are you sure about that, Levi?" Okay, one question solved. The guy's name was Levi. "Because that would be a first."

It was also amusing that Forrest didn't seem to realize he should be introducing people. But also they'd just nearly died.

"Yes, I'm sure. Forrest, do you want to explain?"

"I would've explained already if Lani would let me get a word in edgewise."

"Forrest Cooper, quit being a damn asshole." Officer Cooper's nostrils flared.

"Maybe if you didn't always jump to the wrong conclusion!"

"Conclusion?" She swept her crutch out to encompass the ravaged field and reshaped ditch. "What I see here is 'lucky again that Forrest didn't die'! How's that for a conclusion?"

"I didn't die! Jesus Christ! Why are you being so dramatic?"

Nero winced at Forrest's statement. Even he knew those were dangerous words. Lani snapped her lips shut, watching her brother with a very dangerous glint in her eyes. Her gaze flicked to Nero, who suddenly wished he had the power of invisibility.

"Furthermore, what is he doing here?" Lani pointed a crutch at Nero. Who, not being invisible, wished there was a handy rock or tree to hide behind.

For a second, Forrest appeared confused. His gaze shot

over to Nero and then his expression shifted to—Nero couldn't quite catalogue it, but Forrest's shoulders slumped in defeat.

"*He* is Nero Vik, as you full well know."

"And what is Nero Vik doing here? Exactly."

Lani wasn't backing down. Whatever was causing this reaction, Forrest was the only one who could resolve it.

Forrest hesitated, seemingly unsure how to answer her question. He glanced at Nero again.

Lani waited.

Nero opened his mouth to fill the silence, but Forrest beat him to it.

"I decided to talk to him. He came over to the house this morning."

"*Huh.* Keep talking. It isn't morning anymore."

It had to be almost five by now, Nero figured. The sun was heading toward the horizon. He pulled his phone from his pocket to confirm the time and was greeted with the text he'd ignored from Austin.

I miss you.

Nero sucked a breath through his nose. After months of separation, Austin missed him? He had a hard time believing that. It was more likely that he missed Nero paying half the utilities. He shoved the phone back where it belonged without replying.

"You were right," Forrest said with an eye roll, followed by a wince. "He's not a—"

"'Gossip monger'? Out to spread lies and take advantage of vulnerable people?"

Lai Cooper's tone was deceptively smooth. Nero suppressed a smile and decided not to be offended. He thought he understood now why Forrest was wary of him. Plus, this whole exchange was entertaining.

Forrest's cheeks reddened. Levi coughed into his hand. Lani smirked.

Forrest threw up his hands. "Fine. You were right and I was wrong. Happy now?"

"Yes." She closed the distance between them, dropped the crutch and threw her arms around her brother, hugging him tightly. "What the hell happened here?" she whispered.

"The brakes failed. But before you go after Silas, I don't think it was his fault."

"Whose then?" she asked, stepping back and using her good foot to lift the crutch so she could stick it under her arm again. "Did that jackass, Toby Prosser, take pictures?"

Now it was Forrest's turn to smirk. "Ah, yes, Toby the Tool took plenty of pictures. I should have said hi to him for you."

"No, you should not have." She narrowed her eyes at him. "You didn't, did you?"

Forrest shook his head, almost regretfully. "It didn't occur to me who he was until they'd already left. Next time. What took you so long to get here, and can you give me and Nero a ride to my place?"

"I can give you a ride," Levi interjected.

As he spoke, there was a roll of thunder followed by the crack of lightning. Almost immediately, big, fat, extra wet raindrops began to fall. Nero sighed. On top of everything, his hair was going to explode. He knew he should have worn his knit cap.

"I'll take them, Levi, but thanks for the offer."

"Yeah, sure. See ya later, then."

They all watched Levi head toward his house at the back of the property. Nero wanted to ask what was up with the dejected-looking man but decided he still didn't want to be considered a "gossip monger" at the moment.

The rain that had been threatening began to fall in earnest.

"We're going to be soaked," Lani said. "Let's go."

"This will be fun. I've never ridden in the front seat of a cop car before," Forrest said.

"Who says you're riding in front today? Vik, front or back?"

"I'm happy in the back." Picking up his backpack, Nero followed the siblings to the waiting cruiser.

"Nice to see you again, Mr. Vik. Please call me Lani," Lani said, her gaze catching his in the rearview mirror.

"Call me Nero. It's a pleasure, I'm sure," Nero responded.

"CHECK IN LATER." Nero heard Lani Cooper order her brother. "I'm on shift for another few hours, so I can't stick around here. But if you forget to call me, I'm coming back out here, and you will regret it."

"Fine, yes, I will call you. Bye, Sis." Forrest emphatically shut the passenger door and limped to where Nero was waiting. "Damn, I hurt all over."

"Me too," Nero admitted. "I think I'm going to have bruises everywhere. We were damn lucky."

"Fuck yeah." Forrest let them in the house. "I've got ibuprofen," he said.

"Yes, please and thank you."

"I'll be right back."

Forrest slowly disappeared down a hall off the living room while Nero gently lowered himself onto the couch. Probably, he should have headed back to Cabin Five, but he didn't want to yet. He and Forrest had nearly died, and Nero didn't feel like being alone with his thoughts. Didn't want to dwell on how his life of nothing much had flashed before his eyes.

"Here." Forrest was back and holding his fist out. Nero opened his hand and two ibuprofens dropped onto his palm.

"Thanks." Nero tossed them back without water.

"Ew." Forrest made a face. "How can you do that?"

"Dunno. Habit, I guess."

Forrest stood in front of Nero for a second, staring at him as if he'd just now realized the depths of his depravity.

"I promised food, didn't I?"

"You did, but with everything that's happened, I can just head back to town."

"No!" Forrest said loudly. "I mean, stay and I'll cook something. I need something to do or, as Lani says, I'll do something really stupid."

"Would it be okay if I took a shower?" Nero didn't have any clean clothes with him but he still wanted to scrub the smell of fear and near death off his skin.

Forrest looked down at his own jeans covered with grass stains and mud. "Not a bad idea. You go first. There're fresh towels under the sink. Feel free to use the shower gel or shampoo too."

Whimpering, Nero rose slowly from the couch, and he wasn't sure moving was worth the effort but the idea of the hot water hitting his aching body kept him moving toward the bathroom.

There were indeed fresh towels under the sink. Reaching into the tub surround, he turned on the water and waited for it to warm up. This was luxury compared to the tiny shower at his cabin. Stripping his clothes off and folding them on top of the toilet seat, he stepped under the spray.

It felt fucking incredible, and there was even a massage setting on the showerhead. He could've stayed in for much longer, but it probably wasn't good form to use all of your host's hot water. On the other hand, he had almost died today, so the few extra minutes were deserved.

As he rubbed lavender-scented shampoo into his hair, Nero

let the unexpected day replay in his head. Even though they'd had sex already, Nero would never have predicted that they'd spend an actual day together—and nearly die at the end of it—and to wrap it up, the man would offer to cook Nero dinner. He was a dream come true.

When he stepped out onto the bath mat a few minutes later, Nero found that Forrest had taken his grimy clothes away and replaced them with a pair of soft sweatpants, a plain white t-shirt, and a hoodie. He'd been so lost in thought that he hadn't heard the door open. The sweats were a bit long on him and the t-shirt's limits were tested by his broader chest, but the clothing was clean and it was a thoughtful gesture. The sexy, confounding man continued to surprise him.

He hung his damp towel up on a wall hook after generally wiping down the shower, not wanting to leave the bathroom a mess. No one ever said Lili Vik didn't raise a well-mannered boy. Then he opened the door and made his way back to the kitchen, where he found Forrest busy concocting something for them to eat. His stomach rumbled.

Forrest looked up from the cutting board. "Are you allergic to anything?" he asked.

"Uh, no," Nero replied.

Forrest stared at him. Or rather, they stared at each other. It was unnerving, but not in a bad way. Nero was unable to—didn't want to—break their connection. Parts that weren't banged up from a thrill ride down a hill and across a field were abruptly very aware of Forrest Cooper.

The man had changed into a clean pair of worn Levi's and a black t-shirt with *Don't Make This Ginger Snap* across the chest. Nero let his gaze fall downward to Forrest's narrow bare feet and then travel back up. The attraction he'd tamped down earlier flared, and Nero knew it showed in his expression. But he couldn't stop himself.

One scruffy red eyebrow rose upward. "Like my shirt?"

"Um," Nero said, his mouth suddenly dry. And wow, another brilliant statement on his part. Maybe he should give up podcasting altogether.

A wicked smile shaped Forrest's lips. "I'm going to take that as a yes."

"The shirt's okay," Nero finally managed. "I like the person wearing it more." He did, he admitted to himself. He liked Forrest Cooper quite a bit.

Forrest closed the distance between them so that they were only a few inches apart. Even though he hadn't showered yet, the scent of him was heady. Nero breathed deep, taking as much in as he could. As if he could memorize a smell.

"I'm about to kiss you. As you can tell, I'm not very good at asking for permission."

Nero had read about kisses that consumed a person like wildfire. Kisses that lit a person up from the inside. Kisses that were addicting. But he'd never experienced one before. From the first brush of Forrest's lips, he knew he was in trouble. This was somehow different from the other night, but maybe it was the near-death experience. Maybe it was just—Forrest Cooper.

NINETEEN

Forrest – Saturday Evening

Shutting his eyes, Forrest leaned into the kiss and wrapped his arms around Nero's strong body to keep himself from falling to the floor. Or maybe it was to keep himself from dragging Nero to his bedroom. He needed to demonstrate some self-control.

Didn't he?

Nero was strong, he'd hold them both up. Or in place.

Nero felt incredible against him. Under his fingertips. Against his skin.

Dropping one hand but keeping his mouth fused to Nero's, Forrest skimmed underneath the cotton t-shirt he'd loaned him, reveling in the feel of his bare skin, of the tangible muscle he carried and the curve of his back. Nero groaned and copied Forrest's action. Luckily for them, Nero was already leaning against the counter. Then he wrapped a leg around Forrest's calf, bringing them even closer.

"Damn, Nero," Forrest muttered.

They were both erect. Their cocks brushed against each other, sending a hot wave of need up Forrest's spine. Time fell away as they licked into each other's mouths, their tongues lunging, parrying, and thrusting as they tasted each other's desire.

Forrest hadn't experienced this level of deep attraction in years, maybe ever. He knew they should slow down, maybe even have a conversation, but he didn't want to stop. He couldn't bring himself to even pause. Then one of Nero's hands slipped between their bodies and began to caress Forrest's cock, and they thrust against each other.

"Bedroom?" he asked between desperate kisses.

"God, yes," Nero rasped before nipping Forrest's lip. "We're going to end up on the floor at this rate."

"As exciting as that sounds, I'm too old. My back will make me regret it." Forrest's back twinged in agreement, but he ignored it.

Grabbing Nero's hand, Forrest practically dragged him to his bedroom. He didn't even take time to worry about how long it'd been since he'd changed the sheets.

Once in the room, they got tangled up trying to undress each other.

"Fucking clothes." Forrest gave up and ripped off his own damn shirt and jeans.

Nero laughed as he also divested himself of unnecessary attire.

Finally, they were both naked. Forrest dived on to his bed like a kid. Nero followed suit but a bit more slowly, laying down next to Forrest.

"I knew you were trouble," Forrest grumbled, "the minute I laid eyes on you."

"I knew you were trouble before I ever saw you," Nero said.

They both laughed, making Forrest realize how glad he was that they hadn't died earlier. Rolling onto his side, he drank in the sexy body that Nero usually kept hidden underneath baggy shirts. As he looked, Nero's cock twitched.

Forrest smiled.

"That smile is dangerous," Nero observed languidly.

"Mm, probably."

Forrest lay one hand on Nero's furry chest, enjoying the crinkle of the dark hair underneath his palm before tracing a path downward across his stomach to his fully erect penis. As he watched, a bead of precome pulsed from Nero's cock, causing a similar reaction from Forrest's.

Reaching his destination, Forrest forced himself to move slowly. Using his index finger, he traced a circle around Nero's tip before moving to outline his shaft. Nero groaned again, spreading his legs and thrusting his hips upward.

"Forrest... I need more." Nero's voice was faint but raspy, as if he was barely managing to control himself.

"No condoms," Forrest said. "I need to get into Aberdeen for supplies."

Nero blinked at him, a cute frown creasing his brow.

"Just... fuck." Rolling onto his side so they faced each other again, Nero wrapped his leg over Forrest's so they were eye to eye and cock to cock. "This way."

Nero wrapped his fingers around as much of both cocks as he could while Forrest snaked his hand around the back of Nero's neck so he could plunder his lips. Nero gasped and Forrest took advantage, diving his tongue into his mouth and sucking on his tongue. Nero's body writhed against him, his hand moving wildly as he pumped them together.

Forrest tried to focus on Nero, but his balls were tight and sending warning shots up his spine. They were both leaking enough precome that Nero's hand was slippery. Fuck, it felt good.

"Fuck, Nero," Forrest gasped.

"Next time—" Nero's sentence was cut off as his back arched and come spilled out over his hand and Forrest's cock.

His own reaction was immediate. The warning shots sparked into fireworks, Forrest's balls began to empty, and it felt as if most of the oxygen in his body evaporated. Or something.

Falling back to himself, Forrest rolled onto his back to stare up at the ceiling. There was a stain in one corner where the roof had leaked years ago. He should probably fix that.

"Jesus, Nero," Forrest muttered over the pounding of his heart. "That was incredible."

When Nero didn't respond, Forrest turned to look at him. His eyes were half-open, his cheeks red from Forrest's beard. He looked properly ravaged.

"I think you broke me," he finally whispered. "I don't think I can move my legs."

"Ha, ha."

Leaning in, Forrest claimed his lips again. It was a good thing Nero Vik was only in town temporarily. Forrest could see himself getting attached.

AFTER THEY'D SHOWERED—SEPARATELY, and Nero for the second time—Forrest headed back to the kitchen to prepare the steaks he'd gotten out of the freezer. Nero offered to help but Forrest was happy having him sit at the tiny kitchen table and keep him entertained.

"Good, because I was just kidding. I don't cook."

Forrest prided himself on being a decent enough cook. Lani even liked what he put on the table. While Nero had been cleaning up the first time, Forrest had tossed the steaks in a dish with soy sauce, minced garlic, ginger, and rice vinegar. He opened the refrigerator to see what his side dish options were.

"Do you like Brussels sprouts?"

He'd gotten some freshly harvested ones from a farm up the road earlier in the week. It would be a shame not to share them.

"I don't think I've had them in years."

"Is that a no or a yes?"

"It's an 'I'll try them.'"

Nero had his phone in his hand and was scowling at the screen. Forrest wanted to ask if everything was okay but also didn't want to pry. They didn't owe each other anything.

Grabbing the bag of Brussels sprouts and a bunch of scallions, Forrest poured the sprouts out onto the cutting board, then selected a knife and began cutting off the dry ends before slicing the vegetables in half and dropping them into a large bowl. He'd slather them with olive oil and sea salt before roasting them.

He'd expected things to be slightly awkward—they had just had sex again. Maybe Nero would want to go back to his place later? There wasn't any tension that Forrest could sense, but, as Lani often pointed out, he could be an idiot.

Fine. Maybe he should ask. Maybe that was what the scowl was about.

Forrest waved the knife he was using to chop the green onions back and forth between them. "You okay with this?"

Nero looked up, a sly smile teasing his lips, making parts of Forrest twitch. "This? You mean you feeding me? Or you making me come so hard I saw stars and a comet? I'm fine with both, thanks."

An added eyebrow waggle had Forrest chuckling.

"Alright. Guess I won't worry that I was off my game."

"Nope."

Forrest still wanted to know what Nero had been frowning about but asking seemed like crossing a line. What line, he wasn't quite sure, but he wasn't going to cross it.

Then there was the very real fact that his truck was likely totaled. And Rufus Ferguson was possibly missing.

The oven beeped, so he slid the pan of spouts inside and set the timer.

"Do you think the accident, the fire, and Ned's death are related?" Nero asked abruptly.

Forrest straightened up so quickly he made himself dizzy.

"What?"

Nero spoke slowly and carefully, as if he was concerned Forrest was a bit slow on the uptake or that maybe his head injury was more serious than they thought. But really, Forrest knew he was giving him crap. "Do you think the accident just now, the fire at the mansion, and Ned's death could be related?"

"Why would they be related?"

"Well, we're snooping into what happened. Maybe we— okay, totally me—asked the wrong questions? Or maybe just me being in town telling everyone I was going to be asking questions made someone nervous?"

Huh, impressive. Nero was almost as suspicious and conspiracy theory oriented as Forrest was.

"The fire happened before Ned was killed," Forrest pointed out. "You think the librarian messed with my brakes?"

"Maybe not Fernsby, per se. But you have to admit that an awful lot has happened just in the past few days. Literally almost the second I really started to look into the cases."

Forrest had never met this Fernsby person. While he managed to piss a lot of people off, he usually knew who they were.

"I guess?" Forrest questioned.

"I don't like my thoughts any more than you do but hear me out. If we had been killed, don't you think that most people in town would've laid the blame at your feet? You've said yourself that you have a reputation. Even if it's been years since you and Xavier terrorized the town, people don't forget."

"We never lit anything or anyone on fire," he protested weakly. The lightheadedness returned and suddenly his legs felt shaky again. Forrest moved to the table and sat heavily in the chair across from Nero. "Shit. Mostly, I just keep encouraging people to think I'm kind of bonkers. It keeps them out of my hair."

"Have you talked to your sister more? Does she know about Rufus missing? I'd be surprised if she hasn't called you after her threat earlier."

Forrest groaned, wanting to pound his head against the wall. Instead, he heaved himself upright again and went in search of his phone. It lay where he'd left it on the coffee table in front of the couch after getting home.

Four missed calls. She hadn't bothered to leave a message.

"Fuck."

The last one had been while he'd been in the shower, which meant that Lani would be knocking on his door any minute.

"What?" Nero said from the doorway.

"Lani will be here any second."

The sound of gravel crunching under tires was followed by the sweep of headlights across the front of the house.

"I'm doomed. You'll protect me, right?"

Nero smiled, even though he looked as tired as Forrest felt.

"I'll do my best."

TWENTY

Nero – Saturday evening

Nero watched, as, with a heavy, put-upon sigh, Forrest wrenched the door open to reveal not only Lani Cooper but also Chief Dear. Honestly, if he didn't know Forrest was the older sibling, he would have assumed it was Lani.

"What are you doing here?" Forrest asked his sister belligerently.

Officer Cooper rolled her eyes and hobbled past her brother into the house, her crutch thumping against the floor, and Chief Dear followed behind.

"You know why I'm here, you idiot. Seriously, Forrest, I give you one instruction and you can't follow up on it. I'm checking up on you—hi, Nero—and we have some questions about what happened today."

"Oh my god, we're never going to get dinner," Forrest complained.

"You've had plenty of time to eat dinner," his sister said. "What have you been doing?"

Nero felt his cheeks heat as he pretended to be interested in his messages, but really it was just Austin texting for the third time that day. From the corner of his eye, he watched as Forrest spun around and headed back to his kitchen. Lani's intelligent gaze darted from her brother to Nero and back. She grinned.

Oh shit.

"We'll try to be quick. Now that I know neither of you are passed out from a concussion, I feel a bit better. I told you to call me and that I'd come back out here if you didn't."

"I didn't hear my phone," Forrest protested weakly.

Lani followed her brother into the kitchen, and Chief Dear was still right on her heels. Nero figured he might as well join them.

Crossing his arms over his chest, the police chief leaned back against the counter while Lani sat down at the table. Casual, but also not. Something was off about the both of them. Nero wished he could read minds, but he took the chair across from Lani instead. Forrest ignored them all and added something to the marinade.

"I'll be back in a minute." Forrest took the steaks and went out through the sliding door.

"Vik," Dear said, extending his hand. "Sorry to burst in on you two like this."

Nero forced a smile as he shook the man's hand. He wondered if Dear assumed he and Forrest were a couple. Were they? Maybe they were in the beginning stages? Did he want that? Shoving that slightly worrisome idea aside, he replied, "If you say so. What's going on? Why are you two here?"

Lani raised an eyebrow. "I did threaten Forrest with a visit if he didn't answer the phone."

"But that's not why both of you are here at this time of night," Nero insisted. "Why would the chief of police come along with you if all you were doing was checking on your brother?"

"No, you're right," replied Chief Dear. "It's not entirely a well-check visit. Vik, you've been involved in a lot of interesting things over the past few days. First, Cooper Mansion has a suspicious fire. We know you asked at the library about the archives there. You were the first person on the scene after Ned Barker was killed. And now the truck you're riding in has a suspicious accident. That's an awful lot."

"And his cabin was broken into," Forrest interjected as he came back inside through the patio door.

"When was this?" Lani demanded, glowering at Nero. "You didn't report it."

"Nothing was stolen. It was just a mess inside. It happened the night of the fire. I walked over to see what was happening and when I got back, the door was slightly open. I'm pretty sure I locked it when I left, but maybe I didn't. Maybe it was just, you know, just raccoons taking a look around." Nero's explanation sounded weak even to his own ears.

"Raccoons would have made a much bigger mess than what you described," Forrest told him.

"Squirrels. A curious wind. I don't know."

"Nothing was taken that you know of?" Dear asked.

"No, and I'm glad of that, of course. But it was weird. My laptop was inside, and a box of recording equipment. Admittedly, the laptop was kind of out of the way, leaning up against the wall underneath the table. But the recording equipment was in plain sight. Easy to take. And it's pretty high-end stuff."

"That's odd. So why didn't you report it?" Lani asked.

Nero was starting to regret his choice to wait on reporting the break-in. "Everyone in town was at the fire, including you both. I thought I'd do it later. And then, with everything else that happened, it slipped my mind. You don't think I was responsible for cutting the brake lines of Forrest's truck, do you?"

What Nero knew about cars was almost nothing.

"No, not unless you have some kind of death wish we should know about," the chief responded. "What were you two up to today?"

"We"—he glanced at Forrest, not sure how much he should say—"had some questions for Rufus Ferguson. Plus, the librarian I talked to a couple days ago sent me an email saying he might have some information I'd be interested in. Rufus wasn't around and neither was the librarian, so we ended up doing nothing anyway."

"What's up with Rufus?" Lani directed the question to her brother.

"He was shaken by the news yesterday," Forrest told them. "He even gave Magnus and Wanda the brush-off. We stopped by his house today, but he wasn't there. His car is though. Magnus is there now and is going to call if he hears from him. According to Wanda and Magnus, some of his hiking stuff is missing."

"Huh." Eyebrows very similar to Forrest's drew together in concern. "What were you really doing, Forrest?"

Lani Cooper had a well-honed bullshit meter. Nero glanced at Forrest, who shook his head ever so slightly. By unspoken agreement, neither of them were admitting to the two officers of the law that they'd decided to look into Ned Barker's murder themselves. No doubt both of them would shoot down the idea of a possible connection between Ernst Cooper's death and Ned Barker's twenty years later.

Forrest spoke. "Like Nero *told you already*, we wanted to see if Rufus could answer some questions for us, and Nero also wanted to go to the library. We started with the library, but after striking out there, we headed over to Rufus's. But he wasn't home, so we checked in at the pub. Where else would he be?"

They all nodded at that, even Nero. Where indeed would

Rufus Ferguson be if he wasn't with Wanda, at home, or at the pub?

"Magnus hasn't seen or talked to him today and neither has Wanda. Magnus tried calling, but there wasn't an answer. We went back over to Rufus's place with Wanda because she has a key. Checked all the rooms, inside and out, including the basement. We were worried that he'd fallen or something. He's definitely not there, but maybe he just went on a hike. Uh, then Nero wanted to stop at the library again to see if that Fernsby guy ever showed up, but he hadn't. You know the rest."

"And on the way home, your brakes failed. I'm impressed you're both in one piece," Dear commented.

"Gotta love an old Ford," Forrest said with a tinge of sadness to his voice.

"Murphy called us a bit ago," Lani said, looking at both of them in turn. "The brake lines were cut, easy enough to do in an old truck like yours. That thing leaks so many damn fluids, you probably would never have noticed something out of order. All Murphy had to do was take a look underneath."

Forrest looked like he wanted to protest, but the fact that someone with malicious intent had done their best to hurt or even kill them seemed to stun him.

"Forrest, quit beating around the bush. What were you and Nero Vik so urgently needing to talk to Rufus about that you actually left the house for, what, the fifth time in three days?" Lani demanded.

Nero had been wondering when Lani would get around to asking that question; it was inconvenient that she was observant. Nero directed a do-you-want-me-to-keep-talking glance at Forrest, who nodded. Lani might not question Nero as deeply as she would her brother.

Might not.

"Right. Um, so, uh, Forrest found some diaries of your

grandfather's," Nero babbled. "He was reading through them while I was doing more research on the history of Cooper Springs. I thought maybe there could be some interesting stuff in Ernst Cooper's writings." *Not exactly a lie.* "We came up with some questions that the diaries don't appear to answer. They are more day-to-day accounts," he explained.

"I was called to the school by Principal Harrison again. Worries about my ability to reach adulthood. Stuff like that," Forrest added.

Lani nodded her agreement. "It's probably a long list of Forrest's infractions, one after the other. You did like to put Grandpa through the wringer. Continue, Mr. Vik."

Nero smirked; he knew Lani was being formal because the visit had become official, but no one ever called him Mr. Vik.

"Please, call me Nero." He inhaled a deep breath and blew it back out. "Right. We decided to come into town and talk to Rufus in person. Like Forrest said, we stopped at the library first. The librarian I'd talked to before wasn't in. Which was a little odd because he'd sent an email saying he'd be there. After that, we went right over to Rufus's house and knocked. He didn't answer so we went to the pub, figuring that's where he was. Skipping forward because you've heard all this, Forrest was driving us back because I left my car here, and about halfway here, the brakes failed. Forrest did a great job of making sure we didn't die. We ended up in Forrest's neighbor's front yard and earned ourselves headaches but no concussions."

"What were you and Russel Fernsby talking about?" asked Chief Dear, his laser gaze burning through Nero. *So that's what the R stood for.* "Seems odd he'd email and then not be there. Maybe we need to check on him too." Dear pinched the bridge of his nose. Nero got the feeling Cooper Springs was maybe a harder place to keep safe than one would think. "If it were legal,

I'd put this entire community under house arrest until whatever the hell is going on sorts itself out."

"The possibility of getting access to the library's archives. As you and the entire town know by now," replied Nero, "I'm here because I'm planning a podcast about the missing girls from the 1980s whose remains were identified publicly yesterday—by you, Chief. Also, I wanted to add a bit about the history of Cooper Springs. Who all lived here at that time, who's here now, their lives, et cetera. Additionally, I'm looking for evidence that my cousin could have been brought here after he was abducted twenty-five years ago."

"Keep going," Dear encouraged.

A buzzer sounded and Forrest stepped back outside with dinner plates in his hand. Nero was so hungry that his stomach was practically inside out.

"When I learned about those remains, and the fact that they were found only a short distance from where Donny was snatched, I thought Cooper Springs could be a possibility to make headway on his disappearance. Now that I've been here for a while, I don't really think it is. Donny's abductor probably hopped on I-5 and drove north or south, which is what police thought at the time. Anyway, I discovered that the Cooper Springs newspaper wasn't saved onto microfiche. After that, I wrongly assumed there might be hard copies at the library. But no, the documents I wanted to look at were stored in the basement of Cooper Mansion. Unfortunately, I did not get access to the archive before the mansion burned," Nero concluded. "It's my hope that some handy-dandy archivist will want to salvage what's left, if there's anything, but one never knows. Oh, um, right. When I mentioned that to Rufus the night of the fire, he told me he had old copies of the Sentinel and I could come over and go through them."

Forrest returned with the steaks, setting the plates down on the kitchen counter. They smelled incredible, and Nero's mouth started to water.

"It seems too much of a coincidence that the mansion had a fire after you asked for access."

"Yeah, it does to me too." Nero shrugged. It's not like it *couldn't* have been chance.

"Our dinner's ready," Forrest grumbled. "Do I need to cut these in half?"

He so obviously wanted his sister and the chief to leave that it was almost funny.

"Dante's keeping dinner warm for me," Dear told them.

"Lani?" Forrest said.

"I want to say yes, just to irritate you that much more. But as luck would have it, I called in an order for a calzone at Pizza-Mart, so you don't have to feed me."

"I appreciate you both talking with us. We'll head out in a second," said Dear. "It's important to get what you've told us straight in my head. It feels like a lot is happening. Too much. How likely is it, Nero, that you've upset someone who, quite literally, thought they'd gotten away with murder? How would Rufus fit into that scenario? I'd like to know why he was so concerned yesterday. I know he's a national treasure, but what if he had something to do with the disappearances?"

Nero had been wondering who would bring up the possibility that Rufus Ferguson might be a perpetrator and not just a bystander.

"I don't see him as a killer, sir. Chief," offered Lani. "I know I have a personal connection but... Rufus Ferguson is not our man."

"People can hide their true selves," Dear countered, but he clearly didn't believe Rufus had anything to do with the dead girls, either. "They do it all the time."

"He was genuinely upset yesterday. He said it changed

everything, that he'd been wrong for all these years about what had happened to the girls. He's not our killer," Forrest said defiantly while plating the steaks and roasted vegetables.

If Lani and Chief Dear didn't leave soon, Nero was going to grab one of the plates and start eating in front of them. Only his mother's voice in his head kept him from being rude.

"Almost as soon as the announcement about the identity of the remains is made, a member of our community seems to have disappeared. I say *seems* because it hasn't been long enough to declare Rufus missing, and he is an adult of sound mind and body. But the fact that no one has seen or talked to him since right after the town meeting bothers me. If we don't hear something from him by morning, I'll see about sending out a Silver Alert. It could be that he had some kind of event, cardiac or a stroke, and is confused."

Dear's phone chimed, interrupting him.

"Probably Dante wondering where I am." He glanced at it. "Nope, let me take this."

Lifting his phone to his ear, the Chief stepped out of the kitchen. Lani stood up from her seat and Forrest moved to set their loaded plates down on the table. When Dear returned, his expression was grim. More grim? Grimmer. By now, Nero was so hungry that he couldn't put real words together.

"That was the county fire investigator. They found evidence that gasoline was used as an accelerant for the mansion fire."

"Dammit," Forrest muttered.

"We suspected arson right away, but it took them a little while to confirm it. The investigator wanted to be one hundred percent certain before we made an announcement."

Dear moved away again, heading to the front door.

"We'll be in touch," Lani told them, following Chief Dear. "Maybe try not to get yourselves killed between now and then. I really don't like that Rufus seems to be missing, so call if you hear anything from Magnus or Wanda." She pointed a finger Nero's direction. "You need to know that Forrest is a natural danger magnet. Both of you stay here. Stay out of trouble and call us if you think of anything else or if something else out of the ordinary happens."

"I get the message. I will call," Forrest grumbled.

The front door closed behind the officers and the house was quiet again.

"I love that she thinks she can boss me around."

"Seems like she does a pretty good job of it," Nero said before popping a crisp Brussels sprout into his mouth.

TWENTY-ONE

Forrest – Saturday Night

"Has 'stay out of trouble' ever worked for you?" Nero asked him as he set his fork down and leaned back in the chair.

They'd been quiet since Lani and Dear left, focusing on their meal and—in Forrest's case, at least—worrying about Rufus and wondering what the fuck was going on. Had Nero accidentally started something when he came to town?

"Nope," Forrest replied once he'd finished the last bite on his plate. "Lani knows that, too."

"Dinner was great, by the way. Thanks for feeding me."

"I like to cook," Forrest said. "Usually it's just me."

Forrest stared across the table at Nero. "What are we going to do until morning?" Regardless of how the day had gone and what they'd learned from Lani and Chief Dear, his guest appeared remarkably calm. And sexy. "Um, I'd rather you didn't go back to the resort until this stuff is sorted out. It doesn't feel safe. Lani said stay here and she meant you too."

Nero was watching him, a small smile on his lips. Forrest shifted in his seat. He never—and by never, he meant with a capital N as in *never*—invited men that weren't just friends to stay at his house.

"If I stay, will it be a big deal?" Nero asked. "Or can we treat it like an extended sexy sleepover?"

Forrest pretended to think about it for a moment. "I think that would work."

"Plus, you don't have a car. If I leave, you'd be stuck here."

"Honestly, I don't see the downside of being stuck here. I can go weeks without going into town if I have enough groceries. Besides, my new-to-me bus will be arriving sometime next week. I can drive to town in style."

Forrest couldn't wait to see the looks on people's faces when they saw the bus for the first time.

"Cool. I've got these." Nero collected their empty plates and carried them over to the sink.

Forrest watched because he wanted to and because he could. He liked Nero's body as well as his quirky mind. After rinsing the dishes off and sticking them in the nearly empty dishwasher, Nero turned back around.

"I think we should make a murder board," he announced. "Do you have any paper and pens? Markers if possible."

"A what?"

"A murder board. Paper. Pens. You must have heard of them?"

"Yes, but," Forrest sputtered. He'd been thinking about Nero and Nero had been thinking about murder. "Okay, I might have some paper in my office. Let me check."

He did in fact have a partially used ream of eleven-by-seventeen paper and some black and red Sharpies. He had no idea why. Grabbing them, he took the collection back out to the kitchen.

"Will this do?"

"Yep," Nero said, choosing several sheets of paper and laying them out on the kitchen table.

"Okay, let's get started."

FORREST'S BODY ached from the crash and he was beginning to rub sleep out of his eyes by the time Nero stepped back and declared the board finished. Several sheets of wadded-up paper had been tossed to the floor after some false starts, and one pen had run dry.

"The only incident I can't really connect is Lizzy Harlow's death. She's older than the other victims and wasn't found in the woods. That doesn't mean that she isn't connected though. It may just mean that we haven't found the link."

Lizzy was just a name with no lines heading from it.

"Ned was male and in his seventies," Forrest pointed out just to be contrary.

"Yes. But you know as well as I do that there's a connection, even if it's not obvious right now. We don't have enough pieces of the puzzle." He turned to look at Forrest. "And I'm afraid that Rufus does."

Nero had drawn boxes along the left side with all the names they could think of, living and dead. Rufus's name was there, as well as Ernst Cooper's and even Forrest's and Lani's. About the only name not listed was Nero's.

While Nero had been working on the board, Forrest had flipped through his grandpa's journals again. Again, nothing stood out. These were just the notes of an apple farmer who owned a couple of horses.

He wondered what had brought together such different-seeming men as Ernst Cooper, Rufus Ferguson, Oliver Cox, and Ned Barker. He remembered listening to them talk out on the patio, their deep male voices a soothing rhythm as he tried to sleep or when he woke up from a nightmare.

"Something bad happened before Lani and I came to live with him, I think—not to Grandpa, I mean at the camp. Do you think that Grandpa, Ned, and Rufus all know what it was? Grandpa died twenty years ago, so why would someone kill Ned now? Is Oliver Cox safe?"

Forrest didn't want to hash over his recurring nightmare. It was just images and sounds, nothing specific. But he was beginning to believe that he'd witnessed something horrific and his brain was doing its best to hide it from him, only to then ambush him in his sleep.

Nero sat down, biting his lip while he thought.

"I think it's vital we talk to Rufus." He tapped the papers. "If we think this is all connected—which we do—then he may be the only key we have left. Yes, Oliver Cox may know something, and he may not be safe if he's on his way back now, but based on Rufus's response to the bones, I think we need to go with that first." Nero started going through each step outlined on his papers. "The heavy rains and storms in the past few months were responsible for the remains being found, we know that. When the news broke, it spread far. So far, in fact, that I decided to come here and didn't keep my reason a secret."

"True."

"But I didn't really get around to asking questions until this week. And then an arson fire destroyed possible information, a murder removed one of the last living friends of your grandfather, who had also died in a similar manner, identities of the remains were revealed, and now Rufus is missing."

"We need to find Rufus."

"There's nothing we can do tonight, and besides, where would we look?"

"Where you found Ned is very close to the trail that leads to

Crook's Trail. I don't know exactly where the homestead was, but I'm pretty sure it was that direction."

Nero released a huge sigh. "You believe Rufus went up there alone?"

"Since some of his gear is missing? Yes, I do."

"You said before that your worst fear is that Dina might still be alive and living up there. Do you think she'd be alone?"

"I think all of this could be me making wild conclusions. I wish we knew more."

"Hand me my laptop. Maybe I can find something more." Nero snapped his fingers. "Wait, do you think Magnus would let me look at the copies of the Sentinel that Rufus saved?"

"Only one way to find out." Forrest picked his cell phone up and sent a quick text to Magnus.

TWENTY-TWO

Nero – Very Early Sunday Morning

THE SUN HADN'T RISEN, and Rufus's porch light was still on. It was Magnus who opened the door before they could knock.

"You want to look through my old man's stack of newspapers? I've been trying to get him to recycle the damn things for years."

"I'm glad you didn't," Nero said. "It's possible they hold a clue as to why he's missing. Thanks for letting us come over."

"Not like I was sleeping. Too worried. Make yourself at home."

Forrest led the way inside. It wasn't as tidy as it had been earlier. A blanket was draped over the easy chair and a book sat open-faced on the end table next to it.

Nero set his backpack down on the coffee table and peeled off his jacket. "Where is his collection?"

"Last I knew, in the basement."

"Why does everyone around here store important documents in their basements? For fuck's sake, it floods all the damn time."

Not waiting for an answer, Nero headed for the kitchen and the door to the basement.

"It's a good thing we aren't in a horror movie," he called out as he flicked up the light switch and carefully made his way down the creaky wooden stairs.

The basement was exactly what he expected: the same size as the main floor, slightly musty and damp-smelling, but clean enough. Rufus's tidiness extended down there as well. Nero perused the metal shelves that held everything from two-person and four-person tents to gardening equipment—the quintessential Pacific Northwest weed whacker and several different rakes—to what looked like a homemade log-home play set. Nero wondered if it had been Magnus's as a child.

Eventually, he found the old newspapers.

"Holy moly."

Rufus hadn't been kidding when he said he'd saved them all. Nero estimated there had to be somewhere around two thousand. Rufus stored them in deep plastic containers with lids, but some of them must've gotten damp at some point; he could see old water damage through some of the clear boxes. It was impossible to keep things dry all the time in this environment.

The best part was that Rufus had marked each box with dates by year.

"Yessss," Nero whispered as he scanned for the dates they wanted.

They were easy to find only because the paper had ceased printing in the early 1990s. Dragging the correct box off the shelf, Nero carried it back up the stairs. Magnus and Forrest were still in the living room. They'd been talking but abruptly stopped as he entered the room.

Magnus looked pissed. Forrest looked guilty.

Nero wondered what they'd been talking about—him, probably—but he decided that, whatever it was, it wasn't something he needed to worry about.

"Found the right year. I hope anyway. This box appears to cover the issues published from 1978 to 1980. We may want to look in one of the earlier or later ones, but I thought we'd start here."

Forrest removed the lid and started to pick up the top paper.

"Oh, do I need gloves or anything?"

"No," Nero assured him. "Latex gloves are more harmful to old documents than the oils in human skin. And these aren't all that old anyway, plus they have some water damage already."

"What are you looking for?" Magnus asked, taking a few papers for himself.

"Any article that might mention who else decided to play pioneer with Dina and Witt Cooper."

"I have the idea this is the start of a very long day after an already long one yesterday. How about I make us a pot of coffee?" Magnus set the stack of papers down and ambled into Rufus's kitchen.

"Thanks, Magnus," said Nero, his focus already on the documents in front of him.

It took about an hour before Nero found any mention of the pioneers. He was seriously missing the modern search-and-find function; they had to scan every single page of every edition.

Similar to the article he'd found online in the Globe, this one said that the handfasted couple, Dina Paulson and Witt Cooper, were planning to live life as Mother Nature intended. As of the date of the article, they were expected to leave any day. The title of the article was "An Experiment in Human Ingenuity: Can we return to times of old?"

What utter horse shit.

"What does that even mean, as Mother Nature intended?"

Nero demanded. "Sure, back before penicillin was discovered and the smallpox vaccine. I can't hardly wait."

Forrest came around to sit next to him and read the article.

"As far as I remember, it also meant cold and damp."

Magnus rattled the edition he was reading through. "Here's another one. It looks like Robert was doing a human-interest series on the group." He cleared his throat. "'Hometown pioneers, Witt Cooper and Dina Paulsen, will be joined by Dale and Jane Lockwood from Timber, Oregon, and Karl and Brenda Fossen, who recently relocated from Hayden Lake, Idaho.' Christ, they make it sound like they were on a season of *Survivor*."

"Anything else?" Forrest asked.

"Hmm, let me see here. Blah, blah, just what they can grow and produce on their own. The heathier, natural, human way of life. In touch with Mother Earth. They sound out of touch more than anything. Oh, and here Dale mentions the Iron Man of the Hoh."

"Who?"

"John Huelsdonk, a real person. One of those one in a million people who defy any kind of bell curve. He was born in Europe, I think, and his family moved to the Midwest, but he ended up out here as a young man. Iron Man John. I haven't thought about him in years. He was incredible. He and his wife built a homestead in the Hoh rainforest and lived there for decades. I read that Dora Huelsdonk spent sixteen years out there and had four children before leaving the farm and traveling to Seattle for the Alaska-Yukon-Pacific Exposition in 1909. She hated it and went back home."

"Magnus, this is scintillating information, but what's your point?"

Magnus scowled at Forrest's interruption. "Well, I just mean the Huelsdonks built a real farm out there, with chickens and cattle. Even grew vegetables. Iron Man John was a huge man. Even as an old man, he was strong enough to carry a fifty-pound bag of flour with one hand. He carried most of their supplies in himself and earned extra money packing for timber companies in his spare time. He firmly believed that the forest belonged to those who knew how to live in it. When the government started changing rules, he protested. I'm just thinking that these folks may have been influenced by his story, thinking they could best The Deep. But I don't think many people can. And a group of six seems like a recipe for disaster."

"Do either of you know Rufus's Wi-Fi password?" Nero interjected. He was fairly sure they would get sidetracked for hours if Magnus kept on about Iron Man John.

Magnus rattled off the password, very boring compared to Forrest's, and Nero logged on.

"What are you looking for?" Forrest asked.

"Are these modern pioneers still alive? Was this the last time any of them were seen? We already know there's been no sign of Dina or Witt."

Quickly, he typed the names of Witt and Dina's homesteader pals into the search bar. Unsurprisingly, there were no results. Nero didn't know what the women's birth names might have been. Alive, dead? They had no idea.

"Huh," said Forrest. "Here's an article about Kaylee Fernsby's disappearance."

"What does it say?"

"It's a photograph with her stats and a number to call. Not much else. It says here that she'd last been seen the week before. They took their time, didn't they?" He set the edition down and looked through the stack. "Ah, here." He plucked another out and waved it at Nero. "Front page news now. 'Local Girl Found Dead.'"

"She was found outside of Zenith, right?"

Geographically, Zenith was the next closest town, if you could call it that, connected to Cooper Springs by an incredibly twisty road that doubled the distance between the population centers.

"Yeah, it says here she was found by someone walking their dog."

"It's always the dog walker," Nero muttered under his breath.

"This is a waste of our time," Magnus said, tossing the stack of papers to one side. "For whatever reasons, Pops must have been convinced there could be someone living up there. If he thought the bones were Dina's or Witt's all this time and wasn't bothered with that outcome—sorry, Forrest—he may now believe that one or both of them are alive and responsible for the girls' deaths."

"Or maybe he wants to prove to himself that there's no one up there," Nero offered.

"Magnus, you know better than anyone that just because Rufus didn't take a tent doesn't mean he's in trouble out there. He knows those woods better than anyone," Forrest reminded him.

"I can know it and not have to like it," Magnus said, standing so, presumably, he could pace around and continue to drive both Forrest and Nero to distraction. "I can't go up after him. Someone has to stay here."

"We don't all need to go. I'll do it," said Forrest, his mouth set in a grim line.

Nero tossed the pen he'd been fiddling with down onto the table where it landed with a clack.

"No single person is disappearing into those woods. I've seen the movie and read the book already. One by one, would-be rescuers will be picked off by an unseen monster until we are all doomed. There has to be a better plan."

"Fine," said Forrest. "You and I will go up together. Magnus will stay back and if we don't get back in a reasonable amount of time, he'll contact Chief Dear, Critter, and Mags."

"WHY DID I AGREE TO THIS?" Nero muttered as a droplet of rain dripped down the bridge of his nose.

He knew why though. He'd agreed because he was worried about Rufus Ferguson and the very real concern that there likely was a dangerous human or humans living in the forest.

They'd stayed at Rufus's house pouring over his maps of the area for hours and had headed out just as the sky was beginning to lighten. After barely getting any sleep, Nero was a tad cranky. Nero liked his sleep. Magnus agreed to open the Donkey rather than stay in Rufus's house. Nero had argued that people might come to the pub with tips, and if Rufus returned and discovered they'd all disappeared, who knew what he might do. Magnus had left a note on Rufus's coffee table before they locked up.

"He'd think we were idiots," Magnus grumbled.

Nero had come up with the idea they should post on the town's Facebook page asking if there had been other sightings of the "creepy man" before the day Ned had been killed, and anyone who may have seen something was to contact Magnus.

"What am I doing with this information? The crackpots are going to seep out of the woodwork."

"This is why you're perfect for this," Nero had said. "You know everyone, Magnus. You'll know who is likely to be telling the truth and who might be embellishing or flat-out lying to get attention. Maybe no one saw anyone unusual, but I keep going back to that one comment I saw. So keep track of responses. Oh, and maybe reach out to them and see if we can get a more complete description."

"And if the two of you aren't back by dark?" Magnus had asked. "This scheme has horror movie written all over it."

"Do you have a better idea?" Forrest demanded.

Magnus had admitted that no, he did not.

THEY'D LEFT Rufus's house before five a.m. and headed over to the trailhead. First light was around seven, but Forrest had wanted to get going sooner. He'd warned Nero that the hike was difficult and had made him look up the Staircase Trail on the other side of the mountain range so he'd have an idea of how hard it truly was.

Nero was determined not to let Rufus down. If he had hiked up this way after he'd last been seen, he'd been in the woods for too long.

"I feel a bit like the person who can't swim that jumps in the river to try and save a friend," Nero commented now. "Rufus is way more competent than we are."

"At least Magnus knows the route we're taking once we get up past Crook's Trail."

Forrest had texted his sister but not until the last minute.

"Lani's going to be pissed," Nero said, frowning.

"She couldn't come anyway. Her leg isn't fully healed."

Nero snorted. "You know that isn't why she's going to be furious."

"I know," Forrest admitted. "I'll apologize to her when we get back. I don't want to wait around and have to explain everything to her and Chief Dear. Time is of the essence and she and Dear will need to do everything by the book. We just need to find Rufus."

So, here Nero was, huffing and puffing his way up a wooded trail in the cold and rain. *After* surviving a car accident yesterday. The upside of the hike—if there was one—was that Forrest was in front so Nero got the pleasure of watching his strong form move ahead of him. Forrest may not like hiking into the woods but, to Nero at least, he seemed to know what he was doing.

"If I'm guessing right, we're close to where Nick and Martin found the bones in January," Forrest said, breaking into his thoughts.

Nero sped up a bit. He was interested in seeing the recovery site. But, he reminded himself, this foray into the woods was not about his podcast, this was about Rufus Ferguson, who, as far as they knew and hoped, was very much alive. Nero's thighs were already complaining about the burn as they slogged through several hairpin turns that were inexorably guiding them farther and farther up the mountain.

He was focusing on Forrest's shoulders again, trying to distract himself from his body's reminders that he did not do this sort of thing very often, when he imagined he'd heard something out of place. Something that didn't belong.

Daylight was doing its best to creep in through the soggy, moss-covered branches. There'd been a few bird calls but for the most part, the uphill slog had seemed remarkably silent. Almost as if flora and fauna were holding their breaths.

A bank of Oregon grape and wild rhododendron on the left side of the trail rustled, and the drops of rain that had managed to cling to the leaves fell with a splatter to the ground. Nero spun to face it, not sure what he was expecting to see. Maybe a Sasquatch? A guy could always hope.

"Vik," Rufus hissed quietly. It was Rufus's voice anyway.

Nero stopped walking and peered into the bushes for a moment before the face of Rufus Ferguson resolved into something that made sense to his brain. The older man was peering out from a seven-foot shrub. Forrest was still moving up the trail ahead of Nero.

"Rufus?" Nero whispered back. "We're looking for you," he said stupidly.

"Well, I'm right fucking here, aren't I? And you two idiots are walking right into danger. Get Forrest back here. Pretend you've just seen the largest banana slug in existence or even better, pretend you tripped and hurt yourself or something. Just do it now."

The expression on Rufus's face told Nero this was not the time for questions.

"Forrest," Nero called out. "I need a hand. I think I twisted my ankle."

He sat down on a fallen log and rubbed his leg to give proof to the lie.

About sixty feet ahead of where Nero waited, Forrest stopped walking and turned around to head back down the path.

"What happened?" he asked when he was closer.

Nero rubbed his thighs—they did hurt—and nodded in the direction of the man-height rhododendron.

"What?"

"Look closely and don't make loud noises. But also pretend like you're checking on me. Mostly because I'd like that."

Forrest did as Nero directed, kneeling and running his hand along Nero's thigh and shin without saying anything innuendo-ish—which went to show how anxious he was—while looking toward the bushes.

"Don't say anything. I'm fine," Rufus said. "You two need to get back down this mountain and into town. Just pretend like Vik can't make it any further. Do not ask why, just do it. Now."

Nero had never heard Rufus use a tone like that before and

based on Forrest's expression, Nero guessed that he hadn't either.

Nodding, Forrest said, "Damn, Nero, you did a number on yourself. We're going to have to head back."

"I don't know what happened. I tripped and next thing I knew..." Nero stared down at his leg ruefully.

"Don't go overboard with the drama," Rufus said quietly. "Just get the hell off the mountain. I'll meet you at the pub. One hour. Do. Not. Argue."

"Let's get back to town," Forrest said, offering Nero a hand. "There's no point in making your injury worse. Can you put any weight on it at all?"

Nero let Forrest help him to his feet. "A little, but I won't be running any marathons for a while." As if he *ever* ran marathons.

TWENTY-THREE

Forrest - Sunday

ONCE HE AND Nero reached the trailhead, they stopped pretending Nero was injured and broke into a jog. They'd been silent until then, only the sound of Nero's occasional fake groans breaking the quiet. The groans would've been funny if Forrest hadn't been so freaked out. The lack of waking bird chirps was disturbing. The forest creatures knew something was out there.

Rufus had warned them. He'd been hiding from someone, and Forrest had an idea he knew who it was.

"Fucking fuck a duck," Forrest hissed as they kept up the pace through the still quiet streets of Cooper Springs. He resisted mentioning his parents out loud, as if uttering their names would raise ghosts like the famous scene in *The Mummy*. The entire city would be contaminated with zombie-inducing spore, and he and Nero would be the only ones left.

No one appeared to be out and about yet. Rain and mist didn't keep Cooper Springs citizens inside their homes, but unless you were a fisherman or coffee stand owner, there was no reason to be outside this early in the morning.

"I guess we'll find out in less than half an hour. I wouldn't be surprised if Rufus beat us back down," Nero said with a calm Forrest did not feel.

"Right, that."

They were half a block away. He picked up the pace, knowing Nero would be close behind.

As he had just a few days earlier, after his most recent nightmare, Forrest hammered on the door of the Steam Donkey. They didn't have to wait long. Magnus opened the door almost immediately; he must have been downstairs waiting for them.

"Where's Pops?" he demanded looking past Forrest and Nero for Rufus.

"He said he'd meet us here in an hour. That was"—Nero looked at his watch—"about forty-five minutes ago."

"Alright, alright. Get inside already." Magnus shooed them past him, then shut and locked the door.

"Coffee?"

"Yeah," said Forrest, "and not the crap you serve the hoi polloi either. I need high-test good stuff."

"I second that," said Nero.

"He didn't tell you anything?" Magnus asked, walking behind the bar and toward the kitchen.

"No time to chat. He was lurking under some bushes and didn't want us sticking around."

He didn't know about Nero, but Forrest was covered with a gross mix of sweaty, sticky fear that was making him clammy underneath his clothing. He unzipped his coat and hung it on the back of a chair, then chose to sit at a table instead of the bar. As shaky as he was, he was afraid he'd fall off a barstool. Nero took off his coat too and sat down next to him.

They settled in, not speaking, just staring across the table at each other. Adrenaline whooshed through Forrest's veins, making him feel lightheaded. Over the ringing in his ears, he heard Magnus clattering around in the kitchen as if this was a perfectly normal morning—the clink of him getting down ceramic mugs, the hiss of his personal-sized espresso machine. The soothing sounds that helped Forrest calm himself.

"Here," Magnus said a few minutes later, plunking down three Americanos on the table. Then he sat down with them. "Tell me everything."

Nero wrapped his hands around the mug, hunkering over it protectively—a coffee gargoyle. Forrest laughed but it sounded odd even to his ears.

"There's not much to tell," Forrest said. "I didn't see him at first. He stopped Nero and told him to fake an injury or something. Right, Nero?" Nero nodded, lifting his coffee to sip the hot beverage. The man was braver than Forrest, who was going to wait just a bit longer for it to cool down. "He said he'd meet us here in an hour."

A scuffle and bang alerted them to someone's presence at the back of the building. Hopefully, it was Rufus and not whoever he was hiding from. Magnus was just rising to his feet when a grimy but very much alive Rufus emerged from the hallway.

"Pops, where've you been?" Magnus demanded, striding across the room and wrapping the older man in a hug. "You can't just disappear without telling me."

"We don't have time for this," Rufus said, thumping his son on the shoulder and then making Magnus release him. He crossed to the table where Forrest and Nero sat.

"There's no way to sugarcoat this, son. Dina Paulson's still alive, and she's got a lackey doing very nasty work for her. Sounded like his name's Dale."

"There was a Dale Lockwood and his wife, Jane, who were

part of the original homesteading group that Dina and Witt Cooper were in," said Nero.

Peeling off his parka, Rufus hung it across one of the railings between the bar and the seating area.

"I need some of that coffee while we figure out what we're going to do. And something to eat too. I hate those protein bars I took with me."

Magnus handed his dad the espresso he'd made for himself but didn't move toward the kitchen. "Keep talking," he said, crossing his arms over his chest, maybe to hide the fact that his hands were shaking.

Accepting the mug, Rufus sat down heavily at the table. He was obviously tired and probably wanted a shower or warm bath to go along with something decent to eat. All three of them looked at the old man and waited. Forrest hated how much Rufus seemed to have aged since Ned's murder and the announcement about the teens.

"This likely doesn't come as a big surprise to any of you, but both of them are off the rails. I know it's not PC or whatever, but it's the truth. Dina Paulson is pure evil and Lockwood—I don't know about him, but he's in her thrall at the very least. Any shred of humanity he had is gone because of Dina, who never had any in the first place. That's the only way to put it." He looked at Forrest with sadness. "I'm sorry, son."

Forrest shrugged. "I think I've always known that about Dina." He tapped the side of his head. "My nightmares. I guess I'm glad to know they were memories and not a figment of a child's imagination. But then again, maybe not."

"I hiked up to where I estimated the original encampment was located," Rufus said. "It took me longer than I thought it would, even with no pack or anything. I didn't get there until almost nightfall. Most of the few structures they had set up have rotted away. Our weather isn't kind to untreated wood buildings —such as they were. If I hadn't had an idea what I was looking for, I might have missed it."

He grimaced, catching Forrest's eye again.

"Once this is over, I imagine that the chief is going to bring in forensic types. I'm sure there're more remains up there. Likely your dad is one of them." Rufus leaned back and dug around in the front pocket of his hiking pants, finally pulling out a lump of metal. "I found this. It's what's left of a Swiss Army fisherman knife Ernst gave Witt. Kid carried it everywhere."

Forrest stared at the red plastic and stainless steel. "Did they try to burn it?"

"Looks like. Anyway, when it was light enough yesterday morning, I started hunting around, thinking they'd moved the camp because there were things missing, not just abandoned and left behind. And I was right. It took me more than a few hours, but I finally tracked them to an area closer to town but still well concealed. I wouldn't have found them if I hadn't been carefully searching."

"Damn," said Magnus.

"I got as close as I could without being spotted, close enough to hear them clearly. Both of them are paranoid and delusional, talking about spirits, sacrifice, potions. Dina spent a good hour or so ripping Dale up and down about killing Ned."

"So, we know he did it," Nero said.

"Can't say if it will be admissible in court but..." Rufus shrugged. "From what I gathered, the creeper, Dale, was after someone else, but Ned got in his way. A teenaged girl."

All four of them were quiet while that sunk in. Forrest knew in his heart that Ned, if his spirit was still around, would be glad it'd been him rather than another girl. The thought didn't really make Forrest feel any better though.

"I never saw Dina with my own eyes, but I sure heard her. It's a hornet's nest of two up there. At one point, she ranted a bit about how it wasn't enough. Dale kept saying it was too dangerous right now, but she insisted there was no time. I never did hear what 'it' was, but I can make a damn good guess. Made me sick to my stomach for a bit if you want to know the truth."

Rufus stopped, staring around the table at the rest of them. They were all quiet again for a minute, mulling over all the possibilities of what 'it' could be. Forrest was pretty sure they all got to the same idea.

More murder.

Magnus spoke up. "I forgot to tell you, three other folks who live near the trailhead and cut through to the high school posted on the page that they'd recently seen someone skulking in the area before Ned was killed."

"Ned was an accident and Dina wants her puppet to finish the job she sent him to do in the first place," said Rufus.

"What happened, exactly? Why were you hiding in the bushes?" Magnus asked.

"It was the oddest thing." Rufus began raising a hand to forestall argument. "I know you aren't believers like I am, so just hear me out. I wanted to hear as much of what they were saying as I could. I was quiet, but Dale's extremely paranoid. He kept circling the compound, such as it is, starting at every sound real or imagined. Where I was hidden, I couldn't just sneak away without him possibly spotting or hearing me. So I waited until nightfall again. I'd finally managed to ease away, maybe one hundred yards or so, and was starting to head for where I knew the trail lay when I saw him."

"Lockwood?" Nero asked.

Forrest figured that wouldn't be Rufus's answer.

"No, the Sasquatch. I was about to step out on the trail

when he appeared about fifty feet away, looking right at me. He raised his arm and pointed upward, gesturing for me to head that way instead of down. I didn't hesitate. About four minutes later, Lockhart was right where I'd been. If I'd stayed on course, he would've seen me. And I fear mine would've been the next body you found. I managed to turn the tables on Dale and followed him to another blind he must hide in. He stayed there but rose early and began making his way toward town this morning."

"Did he see us coming up?" Asked Forrest.

Rufus snorted. "Of course he did. You two were louder than a herd of damn elephants. On the positive, it may have slowed him down a bit."

"He's on the hunt, isn't he?" Magnus said.

"He is."

"How are we going to stop him?" Forrest asked.

"I had a lot of time to think about this since Friday."

"Yeah? What's your idea?"

Magnus was eyeing his dad with a mix of affection and exasperation. Forrest was fairly sure that once this was over Rufus would be on the receiving end of a lecture.

"I think we need to set up Forrest or Lani as a lure. Lani would be best. Dina seems to be obsessed with, er, needing female blood for a sacrifice." Rufus shuddered.

"What the fucking hell." Forrest wasn't letting Lani put herself in danger. She already did that every day of the week. "No way. Lani is still recovering from being shot."

"As if telling Lani she can't do something has ever worked," Magnus remarked.

"Right now, *today*," Rufus said, "is our best shot at getting this guy. As Nero says, he's on the hunt. Dina is desperate—why, I don't rightly know, but if we don't stop him, another innocent will die."

"SO," Lani said as she stared around at them. They were all seated in Rufus's living room, where they were pawing through Rufus's old newspapers for any hints that could help them. Lani, Wanda Stone, and Chief Dear had joined them, and Dear had declared the house a makeshift command center. "My role is to play the helpless woman while the brawny men use me as bait and then rescue me from a psychopath who has possibly been killing women since I was a girl, all on the orders of our mother. Have I summed it up right?"

Lani wore casual clothing—jeans, sneakers, and a thick, black hoodie with CSBFS in block letters and the silhouette of a walking Sasquatch making the international sign for peace. She'd been at home and probably bored. Again. It wasn't as easy for her to circumvent doctors' orders when things were quiet in town. When Forrest had called her, his sister had answered on the first ring. Personally, he thought she sounded a little too excited about acting as bait for a killer.

"When you put it like that," Magnus sputtered.

"Nah, I get it." She shrugged carelessly. "But I'm older than his usual target."

"I'm no expert on the psychology of serial killers," Dear said. "But it sounds like Dale is acting on Dina Paulson's orders, not that he has a type. I wish we knew who he'd been after when he ended up killing Ned. I'd like to make sure they are safe."

"Probably one of the teens who cuts through town heading for PizzaMart or something, maybe someone who lives around Yew street? Wanda lives close by there," Rufus said, "and Romy would cut through if she was heading over to walk the dogs."

Wanda's gasp was immediately followed by a growled, "Over my dead body."

Forrest blanched at the thought of Vincent Barone's

daughter being targeted. Or anyone's kid, for that matter. He didn't want Lani out there, but she was the logical choice. Their only choice. He might remember her as a toddler with her face pressed into his neck, but these days she was a trained police officer with a few tricks up her sleeve.

"We need to get a move on," Rufus snapped, rising from his seat on the couch. "He's close. I can feel it in my bones."

"Alright." Lani fluffed her shoulder-length red hair before pulling up her hood. "I don't think I look eighteen, but I could probably pass for late twenties."

"You look a lot like Dina did back then," Nero said from behind one of the newspapers.

Forrest peered over Nero's shoulder. He'd opened the Sentinel to the page with the article about the group. A picture of all six of the pioneers was set under the fold. Dina and Witt stood side by side in the middle, with Dale and Jane on one side and the third couple on the other. The resemblance to Dina and Witt was plain as day.

"You want me to pretend I lost my dog, or what?" asked Lani.

"Maybe a cat," suggested Rufus. "A dog might frighten him off."

"Plus, it gives a good reason for you to be out there for a long time. We all know cats don't come when you call," said Dear. "We'll do our best to hang back but use the signal if you're in immediate danger. We know nothing about this guy."

Lani had tucked a walkie-talkie in the pocket of her hoodie. If something happened where no one could see her, she would press the panic button.

"We do know Dale tried to enlist in 1976 but was given a 4F," Nero said. "Who knows, maybe he had bad teeth? He was probably very bitter about being rejected. Jane and Dale married in 1977, no kids that I've been able to find. It looks like

Jane might still have relatives in Timber, but I didn't find any Lockwoods when I searched. What we do know is that he's dangerous."

"We need to get moving," Rufus said, heading abruptly toward the door. "Now."

TWENTY-FOUR

Nero - Sunday

AFTER A HEATED DISCUSSION about how best to keep eyes on Lani without being spotted, they'd relocated to the house of one of Wanda's friends. Currently, the Perrys were snowbirding in Arizona, so the house was vacant and she had keys. The Perrys had a much better view of the street that ran past the park than either Rufus's or Wanda's homes. Chief Dear had also called in his two newest patrol officers and had them parked down the street and out of sight.

"Mags, Critter, Rufus, and I are heading up to retrieve Dina Paulson," Dear said glaring at each one of them in turn. "Forrest, Nero, Wanda, your jobs are to stay here and stay out of danger. Burgess and Quincy are in place. They may be new, but I wouldn't have brought them on if I didn't think they could do their job."

Nero felt a little sorry for Chief Dear. The likelihood of the plan not going... as planned was high and he had a bunch of freethinkers to deal with. When Dear's stern gaze landed on him though, Nero nodded.

"Vik, why do I feel like you might be the only one who follows instructions today?" Dear grumbled.

As soon as everyone had settled down, Lani headed out, a single crutch firmly tucked under one armpit. Dear's plan was for her to walk all the way to the cut, through it, and back again, and then repeat. Hopefully, Lockwood would take the bait.

"He's frantic," Chief Dear had said. "He's down here and he's desperate. Based on what Rufus has told us, I don't think you're going to have to wait long."

There was nothing for Nero, Forrest, and Magnus to do now but wait, along with Wanda, while Lani Cooper put herself in the path of danger. Rufus, Dear, Critter, and Mags had already left to hike up to the encampment.

Nero could tell Forrest loathed every second of sitting around. Nero would too, if it had been his sister out there. He hated it for Forrest, but Dina Paulson and Dale Lockwood—if that's who it was—needed to be stopped. He may not have known Forrest Cooper for long, but he knew Forrest would do anything for his sister, even step into the path of a killer. But Lani was the only one who could do it.

Chief Dear's plan was to take Dina Paulson into custody while Dale Lockwood wasn't around. Since Rufus had been adamant that she seemed physically ill, Dear figured they could subdue her with nonviolent measures without Lockwood around to protect her.

"I fucking hate this," Forrest said for the twentieth time after completing his twenty-fifth circuit from the living room to the kitchen and back again.

Wanda ignored him. She sat curled up on the couch, her gaze not moving from the residential street where Lani hobbled back and forth calling for her non-existent cat. Nero didn't know who Wanda was more focused on remaining unhurt, Rufus or Lani—but it was probably close to a tie.

"I don't like this, but I want the bastard caught. I want to know that Romy and all the other kids are safe. I want Ned's killer brought to justice." She'd glared at Rufus before he'd departed. "Don't do anything stupid. You may know more about the back country that the rest of these kids put together, but you're not as young as you used to be. And no damn heroics. You either," she'd said to Lani.

Nero noticed that neither Rufus nor Lani made any promises. He was pretty sure Wanda noticed too.

"You're going to wear a hole in the carpet," Nero told Forrest from where he sat next to Wanda on the couch.

Forrest stopped at the front door. "I'm taking a walk."

"Forrest," Nero warned—as if he could sway Forrest Cooper when he was determined to do something. For crying out loud, four days ago Forrest hadn't been speaking to him.

"I'll offer to help find her fake cat maybe, I don't know, but I can't just wait here and do nothing."

It had been less than an hour since the others had left to find Dina and the weather had decided to dial it up to eleven. What had been light rain was now a downpour. Occasionally, they could hear Lani calling for the imaginary cat, but nothing else. With luck, no residents were going to rush out and help her in this rain.

Rufus and his team were probably only just getting started. What if this Dale guy decided not to come down here after all? What if he had decided on another direction after Rufus had left? Nero didn't like thinking about all the ways this half-assed scheme could go wrong.

Rufus was certain Lockwood was headed to Cooper Springs and that he would be drawn to Lani Cooper if only because she looked like Dina. Nero wanted to agree with him but who could tell what Lani looked like in this weather? There was so much that could go wrong.

"Wait." Wanda got up onto her knees and all but pressed her nose to the glass. Nero copied her movements. "Do you see that? Is that someone?"

Magnus and Forrest rushed to the window, nearly bowling each other over in the process.

"Where?" Forrest demanded.

Wanda pointed to the right. "There."

Like spectators at a tennis match, all four of them looked the direction she was pointing.

Lani had moved into the shrubbery—pretending that her imaginary cat might be hunkered down, Nero supposed. Beyond her, a shadowy figure neared her location. If he hadn't been looking closely, Nero might have missed him. Lockwood seemed a bit like a woodland creature himself, wearing animal fur and buckskin pants and skirting the darkest edges of the forest. Flitting from one deep shadow to the next.

Things happened so quickly that later, when Nero was asked about it, he had to close his eyes and visualize it all like some sort of old-timey stop-motion film.

Lani paused, then called out again as if she had no idea he was lurking ten feet away. She had to know; Nero's entire body clenched with anticipation.

Lockwood sprang and Lani whirled. There was a glint of metal that wasn't Lani's crutch and Nero realized that the Deep Dweller held a knife in his grip.

Raising her crutch and spinning on one foot, Lani wielded it like a baton. The crutch caught Lockwood directly in the side of his head but, unfortunately, it didn't slow him down much. Shaking his head, he sprang again, showing the agility of a much younger man.

"Motherfucker."

Jerking the door open, Forrest ran to the aid of his sister. The other three raced after him but stayed back from the action. Nero was pretty sure that Lani was holding her own, and he reminded himself the other two officers were close by.

"Where did she learn that?" Nero asked as Lani and her crutch spun and twirled, crashing into her attacker and knocking him off-balance.

"Capoeira," Wanda whispered. "It's a Brazilian martial art. Lani never did go for the normal self-defense stuff."

Lani's moves were impressive, and Nero made a mental note to look up capoeira when this was over. Just as he had that thought, Lockwood managed to get a grip on Lani's weapon. With a powerful yank, he jerked it out of her grasp. Then he pulled his arm back and a meaty fist landed on the side of her head. Lani slumped sideways.

"No!" Wanda hissed, her body jerking.

Nero couldn't breathe. Dropping the crutch to the ground, the attacker grabbed Lani's arm and began trying to drag her toward the hiking path while she kicked out at him.

With a shout of anger and fear, Forrest flew into the fray.

"What does that boy think he's doing?" Wanda demanded.

A rhetorical question, because obviously he was trying to protect his sister. Forrest literally couldn't stand by and watch Lani be assaulted.

Forrest tried to jump onto the attacker's back from behind, but they were too close to the same size and Lockwood was too strong. After all those years of surviving in the woods, Dale Lockwood could give the Iron Man of the Hoh a run for his money. He shook Forrest off like he was just a fly. Careening backward, Forrest landed hard on his back, releasing a pained groan. Lockwood's hold on Lani had loosened though; she rolled away and rose to her feet in a partial crouch, her hands out ready for combat.

"Where's the knife?" Wanda hissed. "God dammit, Forrest Cooper, if you get yourself killed, I will never forgive you."

The older woman started forward again. Magnus grabbed her arm in a firm grip.

"No," Nero added. At less than one hundred feet away, they were close enough to the battle.

Seriously, if Wanda got hurt while Nero was on watch, he'd never forgive himself and Rufus would probably run him out of town.

She shook Magnus's hold off with a huffy, "fine."

As they watched, unable to do anything, Lani jerked the crutch back out of Lockwood's grip. Nero hissed when she lost her balance and stumbled. Forrest still lay on the ground.

"Get up, dammit," Nero said. "Get up already."

Nero was about to break his own rule when he saw Lockwood glancing between the brother and sister, probably trying to decide which one to go for next—Lani, without her weaponized crutch, or Forrest, trying to get up from the ground but kicking out with his feet to keep Lockwood away.

Lockwood's lips were moving; was he saying something to the siblings? They were too far away for Nero to make out the words. The huge mountain man darted toward Forrest again. The knife in his raised hand glinted, a ray of sunlight that had finally made its way over the forest canopy falling on to the blade.

"Stop where you are! Drop your weapon and put your hands up," a voice boomed.

Lockwood froze but only for a millisecond, long enough to look from the edge of the forest scrub and spot who was yelling. Something about his expression told Nero what the man was about to do.

The woodsman had no intention of stopping, putting his hands up, or letting the patrol officer arrest him. Knife clearly still raised, Lockwood charged out of the woods and into the street, heading directly for the young officer whose service weapon was raised and aimed directly at him.

The single gunshot echoed loudly across the quiet neighborhood. At only twenty or so feet away, it was an easy shot.

Nero thought he saw Lockwood smile in the millisecond before he crumpled to the pavement.

"Holy crap," Nero said as he bolted into action, followed by Wanda and Magnus, needing to see if Forrest and Lani were okay.

In the few seconds it took for them to get to him, Forrest had pulled himself into a sitting position, but he was awkwardly holding his forearm. Grabbing the crutch—but not using it—Lani also limped to her brother's side.

"You idiot! I told you to stay away."

"Just a flesh wound," Forrest replied meekly. "You don't look so good yourself."

Nero had to admit that Lani did look a bit rough. A trickle of blood rolled down her cheek where Lockwood had punched her, and she was favoring her previously injured leg.

Bending down, Lani whacked her brother's uninjured shoulder with a thwack. "Don't try to be funny, either. You could've been killed, dammit."

"You could've too," Forrest returned hotly, then groaned as he got to his feet.

"Yes, but it's literally my job! Did he get you anywhere else?" Lani demanded.

"No, just my arm. You should probably check on them."

Forrest nodded toward the two officers and the prone man sprawled in the middle of the street. From where he stood, Nero could see a small pool of blood. It didn't seem to be getting any larger.

"Right," Lani agreed as she stuck her crutch under one arm and bumped over to Dale Lockwood's final stand.

If it hadn't been Cooper Springs, Forrest, Nero, Magnus and Wanda would've been ordered to stay away but as it was, they trailed after Lani, stopping a respectful fifteen feet away.

The second of the two uniformed officers was on his knees beside Lockwood's body while the first hadn't moved and looked to be breathing heavily. Officer number two had pulled on a pair of gloves and appeared to be checking for a pulse. Lani stopped at his side, but the officer shook his head at her and stood back up.

"Can't say I'm super shook up," Lani said grimly, "but the paperwork is going to be a nightmare. Officer Burgess, thank you for the backup. We all appreciate it."

Burgess visibly swallowed. "Just doing my job, ma'am."

TWENTY-FIVE

Forrest – Sunday afternoon

THE SLASH on Forrest's arm was deep enough for stitches. Lani paced around the exam room, alternating between muttering about her idiot brother during one round and stopping to wrap her arms around him and squeeze all the oxygen out of his lungs on the next.

"I'm fine," Forrest repeated himself for the fourth or fifth time. "It's just a few stitches. I wasn't shot." He raised his eyebrows meaningfully. "Now you know how I feel when you're out doing your job."

"I know, I know. I do. I just—"

She stopped her rant to pull her phone out of her pocket and glance at the screen. "Chief's back. Dina's here. Shall we?"

"Are you sure I can come along?" He didn't really want to. Never seeing Dina Paulson again was fine with him, but he'd never make Lani go on her own. She might act tough, but he was still her protector.

"Yeah. Forrest, Dear says she's very ill. If we want to talk to her, best to do it now. Either they are going to give her something for the pain soon or they already did. Either way, we only have a small window of time."

Forrest took a deep breath. "Lead the way, Pine Cone."

FORREST STARED down at the wizened form that was left of Dina Paulson. Whereas Dale Lockwood seemed to have become bigger and stronger living in The Deep, Dina had withered away to almost nothing. She barely resembled the pictures he'd seen of her when she'd been a young woman. Now he knew what it was like to face one's own nightmare. It was freeing in a way, but also not.

He wished Nero could be in the room with them, which, considering his opinion of Nero at the beginning of the week, was beyond ironic. Nero would've had an interesting take on what Dina had to say. Unfortunately, doctors were only allowing Forrest and Lani because they were family and Chief Dear was there in a professional capacity.

"Ten minutes," the nurse informed them.

Ten minutes was about nine minutes too long, Forrest thought grimly. But he nodded his agreement. He could always leave the room, he didn't have to stay.

While they'd waited for the ambulance to arrive and carry Forrest off to the hospital in Aberdeen, Lani had called the county coroner to come and collect Lockwood's body. She'd also connected with the county sheriff's office. "We cover for each other on occasion," she'd explained to Nero. They were going to put up crime scene tape, take Burgess's weapon into evidence, and take down his statement.

In the meantime, Chief Dear and Mags had carried Dina down the mountain in a litter. She was tiny and too ill to walk on her own but apparently, she'd had enough energy to rant and rave until they'd reached a place from where they could call for assistance. Rufus was now leading Critter to the original encampment site, but the two men planned to be back before nightfall. Magnus and Wanda were impatiently waiting back at the pub.

Now, Forrest stood next to Lani and stared into a pair of faded blue eyes filled with a depth of malevolence he could not begin to fathom. Dina was partially propped up in the bed, her body almost buried under the sheets and blankets. Regardless of her age and the illness ravaging her body, Forrest barely managed to stop himself from grabbing Lani and taking a step back from the hospital bed. Ill or not, their mother still exuded pure evil.

"So, my children are alive," Dina whispered, glancing back and forth between them.

Forrest shuddered at the words. When he got home later, he was wrapping his arm in a plastic bag and taking as hot a shower as he could stand.

"I thought the forest took you long ago. It kept asking for you. It should have had you like it wanted. Witt"—she sneered speaking his name—"kept getting in the way, saving you. You made me sick, you made me like this." Dina slowly moved her skeletal hand to point at Lani and then Forrest.

"I knew you were behind this when the grass bracelet showed up at... at the home of someone special to me," Forrest said. "You had Lockwood leave it at the cabin as a warning, didn't you?"

Nero had been in grave danger and hadn't even known it. Forrest clenched his fists and winced when the slice in his arm protested.

"Dale followed him. He was worried that whoever had found the man's body might have seen him. It was a curse of sorts. Didn't work." The last two words were spoken with venomous fury.

There was no response to a madness like Dina's. Forrest could only shake his head. This person may have given birth to them, but she had never been a parent. And now, undiagnosed mental illness and decades in The Deep had robbed her of any sort of humanity she may have once had.

"I feel sorry for you," Forrest said. And started slightly when he realized that he meant what he'd said. "Lani and I, we've done pretty well for ourselves, we've succeeded in spite of you. Grandpa Cooper took care of us, gave us a home. Lani's a kickass police officer and I have a farm. You allowed yourself to marinate in loathing and hate." He paused a moment before asking his next question. "Why did you kill those girls?"

Forrest knew Dina had killed the girls, even if she hadn't done it with her own hands. They all knew.

"I didn't kill them. They were meant to die. The forest wanted it that way. Dale brought them to the forest and me, and their sacrifice gave us many happy years."

Forrest stomach turned and he looked over at Dear. Dear nodded, holding up a handheld voice recorder. He also showed Forrest a handwritten note.

Ask about Blair Cruz.

"And recent... sacrifices? Were there any of those?" Forrest asked. "A girl went missing a few months ago."

"I am ill. There's only one way to cure an illness such as this. But I needed more. She wasn't enough."

Forrest's stomach sank. Investigators would likely find Blair's remains somewhere around the newer campsite. Levi was going to be devastated. And even though it had been Lockwood who'd killed her, Forrest felt he was somehow responsible too.

"What about Witt? Why?"

"Witt didn't believe," she said, sneering at them. "He couldn't do what had to be done—not like Dale did. Witt didn't understand the need. He had to go."

The door to the room opened. "Your ten minutes are up," the nurse informed them.

"That's fine. She has nothing to say that we want to hear." He stepped away from the bed, what do you say to a murderer he wondered? Forrest turned back. "Hell is too good a place for you."

A raspy, mocking laughter followed the three of them out of the hospital room. Forrest shivered.

"We should let the fire department burn the house down." Forrest said. "It needs to go."

"Yes," Lani replied.

NERO WAS WAITING in the small sitting area at the end of the hall. He stood up as they approached. It was too soon, but Forrest knew he didn't want Nero to leave town. If he did leave, he wanted Nero to come back.

"I'm ready to go home," Forrest said. "Can I grab a ride?"

A small smiled played across Nero's lips. "I'd be happy to take you home. Do you mind if I stop and pick up some fresh clothes?"

"If you insist," Forrest replied, grabbing Nero's hand and practically dragging him down the hall.

"See you later!" Lani's voice floated after them.

"Shouldn't we make sure she gets home okay?" Nero asked as they headed toward the exit.

Forrest smirked. "Nah, she's got a ride waiting. Toby Prosser's hanging around, the EMT who responded to the truck accident."

"Toby the Tool?" Nero said slowly.

"The one and only. He's turned out to be good guy. Unfortunately, he pissed her off in high school and she still hasn't forgotten. I think she's about ready to. She wasn't nearly as mean to him as usual."

"That sounds suspiciously familiar."

"Trust me. Compared to Lani, I'm the easygoing one."

TWENTY-SIX

Nero – Monday Morning

WHEN HE OPENED his eyes the next morning, Nero was surprised to realize he'd slept relatively well. Things hadn't even been awkward when they'd gotten back to Forrest's the night before, probably because both of them had been too tired to get weird about things. Forrest had showered and they'd both stripped down boxers and t-shirts and fallen into Forrest's bed.

If the rhythmic sound of Forrest's breathing was any indication, he wouldn't wake up for a little while, so any potential weirdness would be held at bay for a bit longer.

Slipping out from under the covers, Nero padded silently to the kitchen. He'd spotted Forrest's coffee stash on his first visit. Without too much clanking and banging, he got the coffee machine going. Another peek into the bedroom told him Forrest slept on. Nero hopped in the shower while the coffee brewed.

When he got out again, feeling much cleaner and his hair not yet doing its regularly scheduled Robert Plant impression, Nero checked in the bedroom again only to find it empty.

Forrest was seated at the kitchen table, hunkered down around a massive cup of fresh coffee. Nero chuckled; he looked somewhat like a dragon.

"I see you found the coffee."

"If you promise to make coffee every day, I might ask you to marry me."

"That's a big ask. Every day?"

Nero was just going to avoid the part that sounded like he low-key wanted Nero to stick around.

"How you feeling this morning?"

"Arm's sore."

"What about the rest of you?" Nero asked while he poured himself a mug of the dark brew.

"Meh. I mean, yeah, fine but weird. I thought maybe I'd have a nightmare last night after everything, but nope."

"That's good, I think."

"Your phone keeps buzzing," Forrest said, nodding to where the offending device sat on the counter. "Sorry, I looked," he said, not sounding very sorry. "I thought maybe it was your mom."

"It's Austin the Ex, isn't it?"

"Mm-hmm." Forrest used his good arm to raise his mug to his lips and then took a long sip.

"Well, fuck."

With a sigh, Nero set his coffee down and picked up his cell phone. He didn't bother to read the texts, he just pressed the green Call icon and waited for Austin to pick up.

"Nero?" He sounded out of breath, like he'd had to run to answer in time.

"Yes, Austin. Who did you think would be calling from this number?"

"Well, I—you haven't answered before." Austin breathed in sharply. "I miss you, Nero."

Oh boy. This was going to be hard. Giving Forrest a chin nod, Nero took his phone and went back into the living room. Nero didn't need the privacy, but he weirdly felt that Austin might.

"Look, Austin, before this conversation goes on much longer, I don't plan on moving back. I've met someone here in Cooper Springs."

There was a moment of silence before Austin responded. "Already? That was fast, replacing me so soon."

Austin sounded bitter now. Nero wasn't sure he deserved it, all things considered and seeing as it had been six weeks since they'd even spoken, but he decided that maybe he should just be the bigger person and let Austin have his feelings. Austin was his past, and hopefully Forrest Cooper was his future.

"Maybe it is? I can't say, it just feels right. I apologize for not realizing sooner that we weren't right together. In fact, I think you probably knew it first, but we both ignored it. You don't like what I do and I'm not stopping just because you want me to."

"So that's it, you're cutting me loose?"

"Austin," Nero said, exasperated, "we cut each other loose, and probably did so a long time before I actually left. Now it's time for us to say goodbye. I wish you the best."

There was a long pause before Austin finally spoke. He sounded resigned.

"Goodbye, Nero," he said before clicking off.

Nero tucked the phone into his back pocket and stepped back into the kitchen. Forrest was still hunched over his steaming mug of coffee. From the gleam in his eyes, he'd listened to Nero's side of the conversation but was trying—and failing—to act cool about it. Pretending not to notice, Nero lifted his mug to his lips and took a long sip.

Forrest shot him an exasperated glance. "Well?"

"Sheesh, I haven't even had my own cup of coffee yet."

"So now it's really Austin the Ex?"

Nero didn't even mind that Forrest had been listening in. "Oh, we've been ex-ed for a while. I do wonder if he thought I'd eventually come back. Maybe he figured he could bluff me."

"Huh. Well, that's good. I mean, it's good that you're really and truly ex-ed. Are you planning on staying in town?"

"If a certain sexy redhead is okay with me sticking around? He may have had some issues with me, but it's looking like things have changed in the past few days." Cripes, it had been fast. Nero shrugged.

"I *already said* I might ask you to marry me if you make me coffee every morning."

"You did," Nero acknowledged. "Every day is quite a commitment though. I'm not sure if I'm up for that quite yet. I am willing to put it on the back burner though."

"We'll start slow." Forrest waggled his eyebrows suggestively. "Slow is good." He shifted around and patted his parted thighs.

Nero moved to stand in the vee of Forrest's lap. "Probably should take care we don't bump your arm."

"I'm pretty sure we can think of something that won't bother it."

TWENTY-SEVEN

Nero – The Following Thursday

NERO SLOWED to a stop so he could fully appreciate the façade of the Cooper Springs police station. Andre Dear had agreed to speak with him today—on his day off—and Nero's list of questions was long and tucked inside his backpack.

The station, designed in the 1950s, was hardly bigger than the library. Nero suspected it had been remodeled again in the seventies so that the building now looked like the bastard child of Walter Gropius and Frank Gehry.

Unfortunate.

Inside, Nick Waugh sat behind a metal desk that also looked like it came from the 1950s. He didn't smile, but he also didn't tell Nero to take a hike. About par for Nick.

"I have an appointment with Chief Dear," Nero told him.

Nick pressed a button somewhere before saying, "Chief, your visitor has arrived. Have a seat," Nick said to Nero.

The only chair was a spindly looking thing not meant for the likes of Nero.

"I'll stand, thanks."

"Suit yourself."

Nick returned his attention to the computer screen, leaving Nero to his own thoughts. Quickly, he ran through what he wanted to ask Chief Dear. Nero hoped there might be some new news about what had happened in the forest. Or about Elizabeth Harlow.

"Nero, good to see you safe and sound," Dear said as he approached Nero, holding his hand out. "Especially after last weekend. How's Forrest?"

"As if Lani hasn't kept you updated. He's healing fine though. Thanks for agreeing to meet with me, Chief."

"It's my pleasure. Come back this way. Also, you can call me Andre when I'm not on the clock."

Following Dear down a long hallway, Nero wondered if the chief was ever not on the clock. He also noted the plaques on the closed doors they passed, one of which read Evidence Room. He hoped he got the chance to see what was inside. That was why he was here, after all—to dig into the unsolved cases of Cooper Springs.

Dear's office was at the end of the hall and near an exit door. It was about a five on the scale of tidy to messy. Nero had definitely seen worse. Secretly, he didn't trust people whose offices were Martha Stewart levels of tidy.

"Have a seat. Let me clear off that chair for you."

Dear moved a stack of files and found a spot for them on the corner of his desk.

"Thanks for meeting with me," Nero said, setting his backpack down on the floor as he sat.

"You're the talk of the town right now," Dear said. "I feel like I'm talking to a celebrity."

Nero snorted. "I think maybe celebrity is a bit over the top."

Although to be honest, he appreciated Andre's acceptance of his interference. All he'd done was find a body.

"Nah, you coming here ultimately ended up with us solving four separate murder cases."

Dear stepped behind his desk and sat down, scooting forward to lean his elbows on the surface.

Nero unzipped the top of his pack and retrieved his tablet so he could take notes. He may have figured out a fifth murder too, but he didn't want to get Dear's hopes up.

"It wasn't all me. Rufus figured it out before anyone."

Dear frowned. "He did, but it would've been better if he'd come to us before charging up into the wilderness alone."

"I think he didn't want to believe it himself until he confirmed Dina Paulson was still alive and living up there. He didn't want it to be possible."

"He's lucky to be alive. You all are."

"I suppose that's true." Nero didn't feel like he'd been in danger—more that he'd been a catalyst that had been a long time coming.

"Anyway, you said you had some questions about the Kaylee Fernsby case?"

"I do. Do you mind if I take notes?"

They rehashed the disappearance of Kaylee Fernsby and subsequent discovery of her body.

"There's just so little in the file. Why?" Nero asked.

"Sloppy work all around," Dear agreed.

"Were the clothes she was wearing when she was recovered tested for semen or anything else? There's no indication in the report I read."

"Likely not," Dear said. "The budget probably wouldn't have covered it and DNA evidence was just coming into use back then anyway."

"If the clothing is still in evidence, would you be willing to send it to a lab?"

"That's been a long time." Andre ran a hand through his silver hair before crossing his arms. "Most likely anything left is degraded."

"It doesn't hurt to try."

Andre spread his hands. "I have the same problem as my incompetent predecessor. No money. Especially not for a cold case."

"What if I knew a lab that would do it as a charity?"

Andre's eyebrows drew together. "I've heard about labs that do this work, but isn't there a waiting list?"

"There is, but I have an in. A close friend of mine, Lindsay Horton, runs a lab and is invested in these cases. We've worked together before. She works out of San Francisco, so getting her the sample would be fairly easy. At least we wouldn't have to drive it across country like the last time she and I did this."

"I'm not going to say no, but before I say yes, why this case? Why Cooper Springs? There are thousands of cold cases, Janes, Johns and Jays. Missing persons from across the United States."

"Like I said before, I no longer think Donny was brought here. But I've been here for a while now, and I feel tied to the town. I want to know what happened to Kaylee, the third lost girl of Cooper Springs. Initially, I thought they were connected, but that doesn't appear to be the case. Her family deserves closure just as much as Morgan's and Sarah's did."

Andre nodded, biting his lip.

"My gut is telling me that this is our chance to find out who killed Kaylee. Will we actually find any DNA that leads to an arrest? Maybe not. It's been a long time. But it would be good to have closure."

Nero moved to the next item on his list. "And what about Ms. Harlow's death? Has she been tied to Dina at all?"

Dear sat back, recrossing his arms over his chest. His eyes were narrowed and his gaze intense. Nero shifted in his seat, glad he wasn't being interrogated.

"At the moment, there is nothing to link the Harlow case with Morgan Blass and Sarah Turner. They were decades apart. But the fact that Ms. Harlow lived in Zenith and we now know that Dale Lockwood used that trail on occasion certainly raises questions. Questions we may never know the answers to."

A bland answer if there ever was one.

"She was killed around the same time Blair Cruz disappeared, correct? And Blair's remains haven't been found yet. What if Ms. Harlow saw something she shouldn't have? What if she saw Lockwood in Zenith or even abducting Blair?" Nero theorized.

"It's possible, even probable. But we don't have any proof. And with Lockwood dead and Dina Paulson heavily medicated and dying herself, I don't know if we ever will recover Ms. Cruz's remains. The story will have to be put together by the forensic team sometime in the future."

"If there's anything I can do to help," Nero offered.

Lips pressed into a thin line, Dear rose to his feet. He pulled a heavy set of keys out of the top drawer. "I want to show you the evidence room. Leave your bag here, it will be secure."

The police chief moved around his desk and headed into the hallway, Nero right on his heels. Dear stopped at the evidence room door and, after flipping through the keys, inserted one into the door's lock. The lock protested but turned. Dear pushed the door open and motioned Nero inside.

"This is the glory of our evidence room. The West Coast Forensics team looked around in here, but they didn't find anything pertaining to the remains that were found. They collected DNA from Morgan's mother and Sarah's brother and used those samples to compare to the remaining DNA, but they didn't have time to organize the rest of this and see if there were clues to the other cold cases."

Nero peered over his shoulder. Wooden shelves were stacked with aging cardboard boxes. Some sat on top of other boxes, and some were crumpled and sagging.

"I'm trying to get a grant to bring an expert in to get this into some semblance of order. I don't know if it ever was set up correctly." Dear sighed.

"How far back does it go? How many years?"

Dear shook his head, staring at the shelves. "All the way to 1925, when Cooper Springs set up its own police force."

Nero sympathized. He'd been in evidence rooms in small, underfunded police stations before, and the state of this one wasn't surprising.

"If you can find what you're looking for, I'm willing to have it sent to your lab."

"Are you serious?"

"As a heart attack. Nick can help you."

"Are you certain about that? I think he'd rather have me gone." Nick Waugh had warmed up a bit to Nero, but not enough to spend hours with him in a small room.

"I'm sure. I'll have a chat with him. He'll come around. Nick's a good person."

Nero's gaze took in the piles of boxes, overwhelmed by the remnants of the lives they held within them.

"It's a shame," Dear said, echoing his thoughts. "I'm not a superstitious guy, but this room is full of ghosts."

EPILOGUE

Late Summer

Forrest sipped at his lemonade, the ice chinking musically against the sides of the tumbler, as he relaxed on the patio he'd had installed outside his Greyhound bus. Nero was ensconced in what had once been Forrest's office, claiming he'd be "Done in a minute." Experience told Forrest it could be a minute, an hour, or longer, and he was okay with that.

Nero was putting the finishing touches on a new podcast. Part two of the one about Cooper Springs. The results of the DNA testing on Kaylee Fernsby's clothing had come back over a month ago and, even after Dina Paulson and Dale Lockwood, the results had shocked the citizens of Cooper Springs again.

When Chief Dear and Lani Cooper had arrived at his home to question him, Fernsby had almost immediately confessed to the decades-old crime. Russel Fernsby had been arrested for the rape and subsequent murder of his cousin and hauled off to jail where he was currently awaiting trial. He'd also confessed to setting fire to Cooper Mansion in an attempt to get rid of anything that might have linked him with her death, ransacking

Cabin Five to see what Nero may have figured out, and, in a last-ditch effort to stop Nero, cutting the brake lines of Forrest's beloved truck.

The town had been shocked by the revelation that the mild-mannered librarian who'd lived in Cooper Springs all his life had been Kaylee's killer. After that first confession, Fernsby had clammed up, so whether Kaylee Fernsby had been his only victim was still unknown.

Forrest looked around, taking in Purple Phaze in all its calming lavender glory. He was perfectly fine with trading workspaces with Nero. He'd already moved his office out to the bus itself. The big, glorious bus that he loved *almost* as much as he loved Nero Vik.

Weird.

Loving someone who was (thankfully) not Lani or Ernst was the weirdest thing he'd ever done, the biggest leap of faith he'd ever made. But it was a good weird. The best weird. Forrest was as happy and content as he'd ever been in his life. Even if Magnus and Rufus claimed to take the credit for getting them together.

Fine.

Let them crow about it all they wanted. Forrest was happy.

He still preferred to stay home most of the time, and Nero's plan was to travel for whatever he needed to do. *Grave Secrets* was doing better and better, and Nero was always going to need to be at ground zero to get the flavor of a scene, interview those close to the case, and offer to transport evidence to Lindsay when needed. Forrest would go with him occasionally but when he didn't, he'd be here when Nero got home.

Forrest had faith that Nero would always come home.

A bonus was that Forrest had a better view of the lavender fields from his bus office than from inside the house. As planned, the Greyhound was set up to double as a gift shop during the summer months, a place where visitors could sip an espresso or glass of lemonade and peruse through lavender-themed tchotchkes.

While Forrest wasn't one for banking on the future—too many things could go wrong, thus making sure the future never happened—he was as close to sure as he could be that Nero was sticking around. Forever.

There were no plans for Nero to pack up his butt-ugly Explorer and leave town with his worldly goods. He'd moved his precious recording equipment into the office and that was that. Purple Phaze Farm was Nero Vik's home base.

Forrest liked the sound of home coming from Nero's lips.

And now that Dina and Dale Lockwood were gone, Forrest's nightmares had largely ceased. He'd had only one since Lockwood had tried to kill Lani. Was that because the ghosts were dead or because Nero Vik slept next to him every night? Likely a little bit of both, but Forrest wasn't complaining.

Forrest ran a hand along the arm of where he sat, enjoying the handmade outdoor furniture Liam had brought by earlier in the week, especially the long cedar bench with its wide seat. It felt a bit like a throne.

"These are just taking up space in my yard. They belong here," Liam had claimed. Silas had helped unload them from Liam's truck—silent as usual—and they'd driven off, refusing any payment.

Shutting his eyes, Forrest tilted his head back, better to enjoy the warmth of the sun on his skin. Seconds later, a flap of wings had him opening his eyes again.

A glossy black raven perched on the back of one of the intricately carved chairs.

"What are you doing here? You're going to put claw prints on those," he complained.

The bird didn't answer, just gave Forrest a beady eyeball.

"Polly want a peanut?"

Was that a look of disgust? Forrest suspected it was.

"You're right. I'm sorry, that was terrible. Polly does not suit you at all. What about Midnight? No?"

"Did I just hear you admit you were wrong and I missed it? Who are you talking to?" Nero claimed the spot next to Forrest, snaking a leg over Forrest's longer one and dropping a kiss on his cheek.

Forrest pointed his chin toward the bird. "Talking to the bird."

"My attention was on you, didn't see the bird."

"It's not just any bird, and we're discussing names. I suggested Polly and have been scorned."

"Of course you were. What about Yáahl? That's the Haida word for raven."

"How do you know that?"

"I know lots of interesting things, it's part of my charm. Raven is a god, of course. A trickster, one of the creators of the universe. Oh, also a shapeshifter. Yáahl can take human form and, this is the coolest, bore a son called the Rainbow Crow because his feathers shimmered with all the colors of a rainbow."

Forrest shifted closer to Nero and slung his arm over his shoulders. Always being close to him was good. It fed something in Forrest that he hadn't known was hungry.

"Yáahl it is, then. Wouldn't it be funny if our raven really was Yáahl?"

"Did I ever tell you that I found Ned because a raven flew into the side of my car? If that hadn't happened, I might not have seen him."

"Did I remember to tell you I think I'm in love with you?"

The raven disappeared around the side of the bus, its shiny

feathers catching the day's sunlight. It was probably hunting for bugs.

Nero grinned and bumped Forrest's chest with his shoulder. "Once or twice. I think you've even sung it although we don't need to repeat that experience. Feel free to tell me again though."

"I love you, Nero Vik."

Forrest knew it was nerdy and ridiculous, but he loved saying those words. Who'd have predicted he'd be such a sap when it came to love.

"I love you, Forrest Cooper."

And he loved hearing the words too. Grandpa Ernst had cared enough to take them into his home, but he'd never been demonstrative. Lani usually punched him in the shoulder first and then told him she loved him. Nero just said the words randomly and meant them.

"That's pretty damn cool."

They sat there for a few minutes not speaking. Forrest listened to the familiar sounds of his world: the ocean thundering against the shores in the distance, bees humming in the lavender, an eagle or hawk whistling high over their heads hunting mice or something else to fill its belly.

"What's Yáahl got there?" Nero asked, pulling Forrest out of his reverie.

Forrest looked around for the bird and spotted it hopping their direction with something glittery in its beak. The bird was fearless; Forrest had learned that over the past few weeks that it had been hanging around. It came right up to them, cocked its head, and dropped a piece of colorful mylar ribbon at his feet.

Action completed, it fluttered off to perch on the back of the chair across from them. Forrest swore it was silently castigating him to hurry the fuck up.

"What is it?" Nero asked.

"Ribbon." Forrest picked it up to show Nero. He wrapped it around his index finger and flashed it at Nero.

"I think I'm being courted."

"He's mine, bird," Nero said, staring across at the raven.

"Yours, huh?" Forrest said with a lazy grin.

"Yep. Mine," Nero confirmed.

"Have you decided about the job with the high school?"

The school district had offered Nero a part-time position teaching journalism. The offer was likely fueled by the success of *Grave Secrets* and the fact that Nero was a semi-celebrity around town after Fernsby was arrested and charged.

"I'm going to accept, but you knew that."

"I didn't know for certain, but I hoped."

"You're sure about this?" Nero waved between them. "About us?"

Forrest smiled, something he'd been doing more of since the year began.

"I'm sure."

Twisting around on the bench, Forrest gripped Nero's chin and proceeded to plant a a sloppy smack on Nero's sexy lips.

"Mm," said Nero between breaths. "I like this kind of celebration."

The kiss turned to something more passionate, and soon enough they heard the rustle of wings as Yáahl fluttered away with a raspy and possibly disgusted caw.

"I told you, bird, he's mine."

NEXT UP IN the Elle-verse is In the Nick of Time, which is part of the Subparhero series world. It's a departure from my quirky small-town work but so much fun, and amazing nonetheless. And yes, one or too dead bodies. So, not *too* much of a departure.

Have you always thought you were special?

Perennially unemployed loner Nick Sedgewick applies to an online job opening with that exact phrase and expects nothing to come of it. It was likely a no-so-funny prank after all.

If Doug 'Long Shot' Swanson wanted a new work partner he'd hire one himself. He's perfectly happy on his own and if he plays his cards right he might retire sooner rather than later. And he certainly wouldn't hire an irritating spicy-candy-eating slacker who'd probably miss his own funeral.

WHAT HAPPENS with Wanda and Rufus...? Join my newsletter the highway to Elle and find out! This is a newsletter exclusive short story.

WHILE I HAVE plans for more Cooper Springs and Reclaimed Hearts, even a cover—I cannot reveal them at the moment! I know, it's the worst.

THE VERY BEST way to stay *in the know* is to subscribe to my newsletter. If you haven't already, download a free copy of a Rufus prequel story here and join the fun!

MORE FROM ELLE

If you enjoyed *Code Violation*, I would greatly appreciate if you would let your friends know so they can meet Nero, Forrest, and the rest of the Cooper Springs crew.

If you leave a review for Code Violation or any of my books, on the site from which you purchased the book, Goodreads, Bookbub, or your own blog, I would love to read it! Email me the link at elle@ellekeaton.com

Keep up-to-date with new releases and sales, *The Highway to Elle* hits your in-box approximately every two weeks, sometimes more sometimes less. I include deals, freebies and new releases as well as a sort of rambling running commentary on what *this* author's life is like. I'd love to have you aboard! I also have a reader group called the Highway to Elle, come say hi!

ABOUT ELLE

Writing inclusive romance featuring complex characters and a unique sense of place is my happy place. The characters start out broken, and maybe they're still a tad banged up by the end, but they find the other half of their hearts and ALWAYS get their happily ever after.

In 2017 I pressed the publish button for the first time and never looked back—making this the longest period of time I've stuck with a job--in my entire life. Currently, there are over thirty-five Elle Keaton books available for you to read or listen to.

I love cats and dogs. Star Wars and Star Trek. Pineapple on pizza, and have a cribbage habit my husband encourages. Connecting with readers is very important to me. If you are so inclined, join my newsletter, The Highway to Elle, and keep up to date with everything Elle related.

Including, but not limited to, 'where are my glasses?', and 'why are there cats?'. I can also be found on Facebook, Instagram and occasionally TikTok.

AFTERWORD

This is a work of fiction, created without use of AI technology. Any names, characters, places or incidents are products of the author's imagination and used in a fictitious manner. Any resemblance to actual people, places, or events is purely coincidental or fictional.

The author, Elle Keaton, supports the right of humans to control their artistic works. No part of this book has been created using AI-generated images or narrative, as known by the author. The primary style sources used in the writing of this book are the online versions of the Merriam-Webster Dictionary and The Chicago Manual of Style. Due to their inherent limitations for fiction-writing and the author's personal style choices, there are instances where other style guide rules have been consistently applied. Region-based idioms, age- or era-appropriate slang, UK spelling and style rules, and other deviations based on specific dialects may inform some of these choices. Should you have questions, please contact the author at: dirtydogpress@gmail.com

Copyright © 2024 by Elle Keaton

All rights reserved.

No part of this book may be reproduced in any form or by any electronic or mechanical means, including information storage and retrieval systems, without written permission from the author, except for the use of brief quotations in a book review.

Cover design T. E. Black

Edited by The Elusive SB

Cover photo: Christopher John Photography

Model: Victor Rahl

ACKNOWLEDGMENTS

This author is proof that it takes a village to get a book out in to the world. I couldn't do this without the support of the amazing people who are willing to work with me, specifically The Elusive SB and NolaKim. Also MrE who puts up with my rants and raves, and very dark humor when it feels like the world is falling apart.

Thank you also to the DNA genealogists and scientists who have made such stride in identifying Does.

Books I read specifically for Code Violation were:

Lay Them to Rest, *on the road with the Cold Case Investigators who identify the nameless,* by Laura Norton. Very readable I highly recommend this book, Norton helped me understand quite a lot about new techniques without making it boring.

I Know Who You Are, *how an Amateur DNA sleuth unmasked the Golden State Killer and changed crime fighting forever,* by Barbara Rae-Venter. This was an incredible account of the search for the GSK and how Barbara got to the place where she was able to search for him. I literally could not put this book down.

The Forever Witness, *how DNA and Genealogy saved a cold case double murder,* by Edward Humes. An intense look at how a murder was solved, good reading.

The Last Wilderness, *a history of the Olympic Peninsula,* by

Murray Morgan. If you like history told in the vernacular I highly recommend Morgan's book, amazing.

Thank you,

Elle

Printed in Great Britain
by Amazon